Praise for Court Stevens

"*Last Girl Breathing* is a breakneck thriller set along the slow, snaking rivers of the South, a sweet-talking, hard-hitting, heart-wrenching whodunnit that keeps a reader guessing until its very last breath."

—Sharon Cameron, *New York Times* bestselling author of *Bluebird* and *The Light in Hidden Places*

"Stevens' sentence-level writing sizzles, effectively conveying both Nyla's heart and the Kentucky setting."

—*Kirkus* for *We Were Kings*

"Easily consumable with a fast-paced plot, this is a quick and enticing read for fans of murder mysteries and family dramas. Stevens delivers a cunning tale that will appeal to existing fans and could attract some new readers. A solid addition to any YA collection."

—*School Library Journal* for *We Were Kings*

"Stevens deftly weaves multiple threads, including diamonds, meth, national politics, and human trafficking, into a riveting narrative of betrayed friendships and fraught family ties. Pairing old-fashioned amateur sleuthing with a decidedly on-trend, online true crime investigation, this taut mystery unspools with a chillingly calibrated pace, and the violent, stunning payoff is sure to surprise even the most genre-familiar reader . . . Readers looking for their next addictive page-turner can mine this well-crafted whodunit for every worthy twist."

—*Bulletin of the Center for Children's Books* for *We Were Kings*

"*We Were Kings* is the best kind of mystery novel—intelligent and bursting with heart. As Nyla untangled her family's secrets, the twists left me breathless."

—Brittany Cavallaro, *New York Times* bestselling author

"Bingeable. Atmospheric. A book that grabs hold and doesn't let go. As a lifelong fan of suspense novels, I found *We Were Kings* brilliantly fresh while also saturated with a classic feel. A Nancy Drew for modern audiences."

—Caroline George, author of *The Summer We Forgot*

"The final reveal is surprising and chilling."

—*Kirkus* for *The June Boys*

"Stevens takes a good swing at resolving lost faith and trust while trying to rebuild the strengths and bonds of family and friends."

—*Publishers Weekly* for *The June Boys*

"Tense and haunting, *The June Boys* is not only a terrifying story of the missing, but a heartbreaking, hopeful journey through the darkness. Beautifully written and sharply plotted, this is a story that lingers long after you turn the final page."

—Megan Miranda, *New York Times* bestselling author of *All the Missing Girls* and *The Last House Guest*

"Masterfully plotted with stunning twists and turns. Hang on tight, *The June Boys* is a fantastically crafted suspense that keeps you guessing until the last page!"

—Ruta Sepetys, international bestselling author

"*The June Boys* by Court Stevens is a gripping suspense that hooked me from the first sentence. Fabulous characterization and a layered plot with tension that escalated with every page. Highly recommended!"

—Colleen Coble, *USA TODAY* bestselling author of
One Little Lie and the Lavender Tides series

"I just finished *The June Boys*, and I loved it. The feeling of the intensity of friendship at that age, the tension of the chase to find Welder, all the twists to get to who it was—I was hooked and couldn't stop reading. I wanted to cry with Aulus every time I read his letters and felt that Thea was that friend everyone needs. Though flawed, she is devoted to her friends with a ferocity that I loved."

—Catherine Bock, book buyer for Parnassus Books

LAST GIRL BREATHING

Also by Court Stevens

We Were Kings

The June Boys

Four Three Two One

Dress Codes for Small Towns

The Lies About Truth

The Blue-Haired Boy

Faking Normal

LAST GIRL BREATHING

A NOVEL

COURT STEVENS

THOMAS NELSON
Since 1798

Last Girl Breathing

Copyright © 2023 Courtney Stevens

Published in Nashville, Tennessee, by Thomas Nelson. Thomas Nelson is a registered trademark of HarperCollins Christian Publishing, Inc.

Thomas Nelson titles may be purchased in bulk for educational, business, fundraising, or sales promotional use. For information, please email SpecialMarkets@ThomasNelson.com.

Publisher's Note: This novel is a work of fiction. Names, characters, places, and incidents are either products of the author's imagination or used fictitiously. All characters are fictional, and any similarity to people living or dead is purely coincidental.

ISBN 978-0-8407-0710-9 (HC)
ISBN 978-0-8407-0724-6 (epub)
ISBN 978-0-8407-0738-3 (audio download)

Library of Congress Cataloging-in-Publication Data
[CIP TO COME]

Printed in the United States of America
23 24 25 26 27 LBC 5 4 3 2 1

For Ms. Ann Pfisterer
At your table, I learned to persevere with joy

For the Morgans
I pray he comes home.

Romans 5:3–5

A Note from the Author

I am from a small river town that's not far from the Kentucky Dam. Western Kentucky shaped my childhood and therefore, my creative life returns again and again to small towns and misbehaving waterways. I never steal the exact setting for my novels, but pieces from the entire region morph into a newly created location with familiar sounding restaurants and features. You'll see plenty of Western Kentucky in the fictional town of Grand Junction.

I also have to stop here and issue a trigger warning to some of my dearest friends from home. I had a full draft of this novel written prior to a river accident that took the life of my childhood friend's son. It was never my intention for *Last Girl Breathing* to reflect the direct loss of a beautiful son from my hometown; this story was in my heart long before. For those of you who live with Tyler's loss daily, I love you and I pray that if you end up with this book in your hands that it heals and helps the same way you have healed and helped so many during your grief.

Part One

It is an easy lie that has wormed its way into my mind: I am the center that must hold.

—KATE BOWLER

Chapter One

The bulk of Mom's messages come through in a span of thirty-eight minutes.

> Martin's not answering his phone.
> If you're near school, check for his truck.
> I'm texting Coach.
> Martin didn't show up at pregame.
> Tell me if y'all are together.
> Something must be wrong. He would never miss
>   pregame today.
> Lucy, call me. Please.
> His game bag is on the bed and his jersey's hanging

where I left it yesterday. Is there ANY reason he'd
    be late to Regionals?
I'm headed to the football stadium. If he texts, tell
    him to go straight there. I have his stuff with me.
His truck isn't here.
If you skipped school to shoot without telling me, I
    swear I'll cancel your flight to the Walther Cup.
Lucy, I'm really scared.

Martin is my seventeen-year-old stepbrother. We got
him when Mom acquired her second husband, Robert
Carlin. If Mom hadn't been in love with Robert, she'd
likely have married him for Martin alone, and I would
have seconded the decision.

Martin currently lives in a scrawny six-foot-three
body that contains a heart the size of an ocean. He's
easy. With easy emotions and easy logic and easy friends
and easy hobbies. Easy. Easy. Easy. And when he isn't
easy, he's earnest, charming, and determined. Sweet in
a way that worries you someone might bulldoze him. I
basically love him so much it hurts.

I type out a quick text to Martin. Where are you? My
fingers hover over the letters on my phone and I consider
how to finish the message. Should I mention what happened earlier or stick to the topic at hand? I decide to
finish with, Mom's freaking out. Text me back ASAP.

The message doesn't deliver. Must be the signal on his
end since I'm on Wi-Fi.

I wait to answer Mom. I am not heartless, far from it, but better to answer with facts than admit I haven't heard from Martin in several hours. My family role—de-escalating my worrywart mother—requires an extraordinary amount of patience. In her world, every plane might crash, all boats sink, and cars break down next to cults and murderers. I should be more like her, but for some reason our biggest tragedies hit her one way and me another. Her brain says, *Martin's in a ditch*, and mine says, *He's probably stuck behind a tractor on a road with no signal.* Because ninety-nine percent of the time, the worst hasn't happened.

What are the odds we're having another one percent crisis?

Within the hour the universe will respond: one hundred percent.

Chapter Two

The shooting range behind Parson's Landing is my second home. I'm walking between the range and the restaurant, strategizing a response to Mom's next wave of worried texts, thinking about everything Martin said this afternoon, when Parson sticks his head out the back door and waves. "Neil's here," he calls.

Words that once made me happy now cause me stress.

"Did you finish strong?" he asks.

I lift my rifle and equipment bag, throw on an air of conceit, and say, "You know it," to my coach, then point at my truck. "Let me drop my stuff. I'll be inside in a minute." I need to gain my composure. Why is Neil home?

I pitch my gear into the back seat, send off a preliminary Take a deep breath text to Mom, and attempt to follow my own advice. One deep breath and then one foot in front of the other across the parking lot.

Neil's supposed to be in West Virginia. Not Grand Junction. It's just like him to show up *today*. I should drive to the football stadium and wait on Martin with my mom. Neil would understand. He's witnessed more than one of Mom's panic episodes. Instead, I arrive back inside and accept a fist bump from my coach as his wordless and semi-unenthusiastic encouragement for a long practice today.

We step into the bustling kitchen and the aroma is threefold: onions, barbecue, and bacon. *Heaven will smell like this*, I think. I say to Parson, "The Walther Cup is three weeks away. What's he doing here?"

Neil, like me, is a Three-Position Air Rifler. The Walther is a major tournament. Even though he's already made the Olympic team, I can't believe his university coach doesn't have him on the range this weekend.

"You'll have to ask him," Parson says with a coy wink, eating up this reunion. My coach is of the opinion that I shoot better when I'm not distracted, and I've been quite distracted since Neil and I broke up.

"Parse, don't start," I say, weaving around the delivery boxes on the floor.

"Hey, speaking of people being in unexpected places, why were you on the range today instead of at school? You weren't supposed to be here until four."

I shrug. My day was a doozy long before Mom melted down and my ex came home for the weekend. Knowing he won't get an answer, Parson leads me through the swinging door and out into the crowded room. I don't recognize any of the diners. They must be out-of-towners because everyone from Grand Junction is headed to the football game.

Neil's slumped in a booth in the corner, his right hand in his lap, his left sliding a saltshaker back and forth across the knotted pine. My phone buzzes against my thigh, begging me to answer Mom. I weave in and around the tables, reaching him before he notices. His eyes are locked on the saltshaker. I clear my throat. He lifts his chin, and the expression in his eyes is so sad I almost throw my arms around him. Instead, I say, "You didn't mention you were coming in this weekend."

"Oh, I promised Astrid," he says, attempting a weak smile, his jaw locked.

I want to ask what's wrong or if maybe he's in pain, but since I might be the cause of the injury, I keep my mouth shut.

Eight hours is a long way to come for a marching band solo, but he's always been a great big brother. He'll need a shower before the game. Phew. I can smell the dirt and sweat from here. There's mud ground into the skin of his forearms and water lines on his pants from where he's been wading through the marsh. When I look closer, dried crimson lines the creases of his hands and hides under his nail beds.

"You look like a hobo," I tease. "I mean, you should maybe Clorox the blood off your coveralls before you head to the game. Or at least wash your hands."

He almost grins and then looks up for the first time. "You could do with a shower too, Michaels. How long have you been on the range today? Fifteen hours?"

Neil's use of my last name makes us smile. We both glance toward the bar, where my coach and Neil's former coach stands, pouring himself a drink. We watch a vibrant tension fill his handsome face. Probably there because of us. Or more specifically, me. He needs me at my best, and I'm far from it. He catches Neil and me watching him and gives me an encouraging nod. A nod that means something between a coach and athlete. *Do what you need to do here so you can do what you have to do on the range.* I translate the particulars: *Get back with Neil or get over him.*

Parson's not much on feelings.

He's a man in need of results. If results require feelings, he'll muster them. Otherwise, he wants performance. My ability to understand this makes us a great team. And it's how he managed to build this restaurant when he was so young. To this day, Parson's Landing is the only establishment in the country where you can order two bacon-wrapped quail grilled to perfection or deep-fried water moccasin tenders in a velouté sauce. A fancy magazine wrote an article recently titled "Parson's Landing: Where Camouflage Meets Culture." Around here people say *bougie rednecks* with pride. On the range when I miss, Parson yells, "Luce, focus. I want you on the cover of *Magnolia Magazine* with the headline 'Farmhouse Olympian Strikes Gold.'"

"He hasn't changed a bit," Neil says.

"He misses coaching you."

Neil starts to say something and then stops.

"Well," I say, turning back to the booth, thinking Mom is going to kill me if I don't answer her soon.

"Well," Neil repeats.

There's a long pause. Long enough I have to think of what to do with my hands. "Astrid's going to be great tonight," I say, trying to find a natural way to exit.

"She always is."

Astrid's the best drum majorette and soloist in years, maybe ever. Neil's an Olympic gold hopeful, but his little sister is on her way to Carnegie Hall with a short stopover at Harvard or Yale.

"Okay, well, I'll see you at the game." I start my retreat.

"Yeah, totally," Neil says, but he's grinding his teeth and staring at a stuffed bobcat mounted to the wall above my head.

I'm almost out the door when I turn and ask, "So did you get one today?" I point up at another mounted creature, a fifteen-point deer with dark, hollow eyes.

Neil gestures to the blood splatter on the fabric at his knees. "You could say that," he says with little to no enthusiasm.

I'd lay good odds there's a dead deer splayed across his truck bed and its rack is not big enough to satisfy him. They never are. I should ask him if he wants to practice in the morning. That would make Parson happy. I don't. I take my phone from my pocket and think, *Maybe I'll ask him at the game and maybe I won't.*

MOM: CALL ME NOW.

I'm tapping her name, knowing I can't avoid her any longer, when the phone rings in my hand. It's her, calling again. I think, *Martin, I'm gonna kill you,* and start apologizing before she has a chance to get a word out. "Hey, Mom. Sorry. I was on the range. What can I do to help?"

She's silent.

Raising my blood pressure is a feat. I train day in and day out to control my breathing and heart rate under enormous pressure on the range. I am exceptionally steady. This, her silence, devours me. The first hollowish heartbeat thuds in my chest.

"Mom?" My voice shakes.

"There's blood, Luce. Lots of blood."

"What?" I ask, holding the phone closer to my ear, unsure of what I heard.

"Someone found Martin's Hummer and there's blood everywhere."

Chapter Three

I try not to think about what Martin told me earlier today.

I try not to think about someone hurting him, but the thought explodes like grease popping off a hot skillet. Maybe this is how Mom feels all the time.

Joanny Michaels Carlin—my mother—is a tiny woman with hair so golden people whisper the word *bleach* when she passes. She manages the mess with two braids that fall below her shoulders and a ball cap that never quite contains the flyaway yellow wisps. She wears two-decades-old cowboy boots that her father, my PoppaJack, bought for her high school graduation and a daily version of the same uniform: jeans and a T-shirt in summer; jeans and a sweatshirt in fall. Right now I can bet a hundred dollars that she's in the parking lot of the school, looking like a lost child in the shadow of the football stadium. She'll have dropped into a squat, her arms cradling her head and her face buried in the neckline of a GJHS hoodie.

Add a few inches, delete a few fine lines and freckles, straighten my spine, and that's also a picture of me. Our differences start under the skin. I am the taskmaster of hard things. That's because if you make the mistake of keeping your cool during personal tragedies, people expect you to continue the trend forever. They use big words and phrases like "strong" and "older than your years," and then they lean on you until you're sure you'll fall over or die trying to stay up.

I will not let my brain run away on a fear marathon.

Martin could have a bad nosebleed and Mom would say he was in critical condition. I need to see *lots of blood* rather than take the word of a woman terrified something awful will happen to her children. Her fear, it's founded; it has receipts. My little brother, Clay, died. And since then, Mom became a fatalistic thinker and I became someone who quoted the unlikely odds of terrible things repeating themselves in the same family. I whisper, "This brother will not die," and then Martin's voice echoes through my head, *"If I'm right about what happened on the day Clay died, none of us are safe."* That sounded so exaggerated at the time. Now I tell myself not to panic.

I take a blue whale breath, as a former therapist encouraged me to do, imagining I'm filling the biggest lungs possible and then letting the air go. "Mom, who is saying this? And where's Martin's truck?"

"LaRue," she says, answering the second question instead of the first. "Trailhead number three."

"Okay," I say calmly. At least that's nearby. "He's not Clay, okay?"

"Baby," she says, and I know where her head is, the precise shape of her fear.

Per Wikipedia, LaRue is three things:

- A corporately owned eighty-mile, state-run recreational area that butts up to a bend in the Tennessee River at the westernmost edge of Kentucky. Known for exceptional fishing, hunting, boating, ATVing, and bird-watching.
- Home to Grand Hydro Electric, the wildly successful hydroelectric energy project of Presidential Medal of Freedom recipient and *Time*'s Man of the Year Robert Carlin. Previously owned by Carlin's father-in-law, Jack Rickard.
- The infamous site of the LaRue Dam, predecessor of the Grand Hydro Dam, which broke during catastrophic flooding on the Tennessee River and killed fourteen Boy Scouts from Troop 1404 (and my little brother, Clay Michaels). *See also: LaRue Dam Break.*

On the other end of the phone, Mom fails to suppress a worried sob.

"Hey." I embody the calm I do not feel and coax more information from her. "Who found his truck? Tell me where you heard about the blood?"

"Owl's radio," she cries.

I pull my mouth away from the phone and cuss. Owl Uri is the Cleary County sheriff and coroner—two positions that often double up in smaller Kentucky counties like ours—and one of Mom's oldest friends. He's a dad-like creature for me and an old boyfriend for her. I'm not surprised she went straight to him when she couldn't locate Martin. I once arrived home fifteen minutes after curfew to find three officers in our living room and Owl wrapping a wet towel around Mom's neck.

If he's worried about Martin, I should be too.

"Mom, what's Owl saying?"

"I don't know. He's on his way to the trailhead in LaRue."

"And Robert?" I ask. "Does he know there's a—" What should I call the current predicament that won't exaggerate the danger? "Does Robert know Martin's running late to the game?"

Breathy gaps fill Mom's answer. "The Spector Group meeting's today. He said he'd be online until closing time in California and that he thought he'd be late to the game."

"Interrupt him."

"I tried. He didn't answer."

I check my watch. Robert might be on the call for another hour. Spector is a pharmaceutical company trying to court Grand Hydro for some hush-hush thing. We've barely seen Robert this week.

I reverse the truck and almost rear-end Parson's dumpster with my tailgate. That makes me pull forward, put the truck in Park, and focus on the conversation while I have a signal. "Listen, stay at the stadium. I'm at Parson's and can be at trailhead three in six or seven minutes. Martin could have run out of gas, or it might not even be his truck."

The latter suggestion is a stretch. Martin drives a matte-gray Hummer with custom yellow trim, making it highly unlikely the truck has been misidentified, but it's no time to add vinegar to the situation. Because my hands are sweating profusely, I shift Mom to speakerphone and put the phone in my lap. The moment I do, my phone glides into the seat belt crevice and thunks into the bowels of no-man's-land.

"Lucy!" Mom shouts through the phone speakers. "Are you okay?"

I yell toward the floormats, "Talk loud. I dropped my phone."

Unlike my stepbrother, I drive a beat-up Nissan Frontier that I bought with my own money, and it doesn't have Generation Z luxuries like CarPlay or even air-conditioning. My iPhone speakers aren't quite up to factory standards either.

Mom's muted yelling continues. "You didn't, like, get Martin into anything, did you? I heard you two fighting this morning."

"We weren't fighting."

How much did she hear?

"Luce, you spend a lot of time with guns—"

Whoa. "Air guns—" I say angrily and she cuts me off.

"—accidents happen when weapons are involved."

"Stop," I say.

I am sharp, too sharp. But under normal circumstances, she doesn't accuse me of making Martin late for Regionals because of an invented air rifle incident. When it comes to competitive shooting, she's my biggest supporter.

Digging under the seat requires an act of contortion from my wrist, but I drag up my phone from the crumbs and hair ties. "Buy some popcorn," I say, more in control. "I'll ring you when I know something."

Mom lowers her voice. "Please don't go out there, baby. What if there's a murderer on the loose?"

I want to pipe back, *A murderer? In LaRue?* Instead, I say, "Hey, it's probably deer blood or a paintball. I'm fine. Martin's fine." I am not at all sure he is fine.

"You're probably right," she admits. "I love you so much."

"I love you too."

We hang up.

My message to Martin still doesn't show as delivered.

I think, *You will not worry. The worst things that can happen have already happened.* I lost a brother in a freak flood and an environmental tragedy. Unless God is unfairly targeting me, losing another brother doesn't strike me as statistically likely.

But what if for once my mother is right?

There could be a murderer in LaRue.

And according to Martin, there is.

That Weekend

Dad said the weather forecast was bunk and promised we'd lucked into a last perfect weekend of the fall. Two fifteen-passenger vans' worth of Boy Scouts clearly hoped the same. LaRue was our playground for the next three days. I loved LaRue.

Our crew was spoiled, having had four weekends in a row at PoppaJack's campground, everyone's schedules aligning perfectly for the most beautiful season of the year. Fall smelled so dang good I wanted to eat it with a spoon and a s'more. We wouldn't get another chance like this until next year.

Or at least that was what the adults, with their adult

schedules, threatened. Parson would be away at college. Deuce, a star first baseman for Grand Junction High, would have fall ball. Neil had swimming and soccer tournaments. Astrid had violin competitions. Blah, blah, blah. The kids were not always the busy ones, but the parents sure liked to make us feel that way.

Instead of the tent and portable shower Mom assigned me to carry, I slung Clay on my back. The little poop bag gave me a wet willy, so I scooped up a snail and set it on his arm. He sent the snail airborne and it landed with a splash in Parson's coffee cup. To Clay's delight, Parson dropped the cup, feigned anger, and heaved the squirming, squealing mass of limbs into the air. While Clay kicked, Parson lifted Clay's shirt and blew the biggest raspberry he could manage onto Clay's tummy before returning him to my back.

The rain didn't come that night. It came the next.

Chapter Four

Night had come while I was inside Parson's.

The Friday evening crowd spills across the restaurant's front porch into the lamplit yard. Patrons stop what they're doing when the first siren cuts the country air. Their faces scrunch with worry and curiosity. They look toward town and then swivel toward LaRue, like they're watching a tennis match. Another shrill of the siren and everyone registers the sound is approaching us. Most people return to their cornhole games; a few check their phones for a notification.

I consider going inside to get Parson or Neil but decide I don't have time if I want to follow the ambulance, and that seems like the most logical decision given what Mom said about the blood on the Hummer.

The siren closes in. Red and blue flashes break the early evening light. Headlights appear. The EMS vehicle stops across the intersection from Parson's, at the entrance to LaRue, before easing onto the covered bridge over Vespers Creek. That bridge is the gateway to a different civilization, one of dirt and gravel, a zoo without a fence, the place where technology hasn't stretched yet. Out here, the wilds are overgrown, the kudzu's thicker than the beard of a mountain man, and the Tennessee River will rise up and lick your boots if you don't watch it closely.

I cross onto the bridge too, keeping the taillights of the ambulance in sight. Adrenaline whips through my bloodstream. I'm glad I'm familiar with the road. I usually take the highway from school to shooting practice at Parson's; it's much faster. But most evenings I drive home through LaRue on the access road. I love this land. The visual. The way it smells. The song it sings. I always open my windows when I cross the creek and listen to the wooden boards squeak under my tires. I'm glad the little triangle of my life—home, Parson's range, and school— has two points anchored to the place where I last held Clay's warm little hand.

The deep blue bomb of evening sky mushrooms over the treetops. You can't drive LaRue like you own it; the land and its many waters have the upper hand. I pass the first two trailheads, Old Camp and Indian Mounds. No vehicles are coming or going or parked in the pull-offs. I make the last curve to trailhead three and grip the wheel of the truck, my knuckles turning white. Flashing lights cut the darkness into red and white strobes. Multiple EMS and police vehicles are parked along the side of the road leading up to the Spillway trailhead. Once upon a time, that trail was the gravel road that led to the old LaRue Dam. It's overgrown now. You could get a four-wheeler down it, but you wouldn't want to risk anything wider.

I coast into the space behind the vehicles and kill the engine. Gravel dust and diesel exhaust sink into my lungs when I exit the truck. I cough and an EMS worker turns sharply and scowls.

"You don't want to be here." He hoists a navy bag from the back bay. His partner nudges him and whispers. He recognizes me. A third of the police force attended the ribbon cutting of Grand Hydro Stadium last spring; another third remember me from the dam break; the final third know me as "that shooting girl going to the Olympics." It's an unusual reputation to navigate. One of my reputations helps me out. The second EMS guy waves me forward.

Martin parked crookedly. The passenger side panel of the Hummer is fully exposed by the headlights of the ambulance. There's a long red smear of blood from front to back. Wet? Dry? I can't tell from here. The ground below it looks like red placemats laid on the dirt. Pools of blood.

You can't look at either without thinking someone is definitely dead.

Chapter Five

Or.

Or some*thing* could be dead.

Find your logic, Luce. There's no body. Martin's not lying in all that blood. Nothing is. Around here deer season stocks a freezer and empties the clips. Drains of local car washes run red and brown from September to November. LaRue's a hunting sanctuary, a mecca for outdoorsmen visiting from around the world. This is bow season, not as popular as modern gun, but any number of Grand Junction locals and plenty of out-of-town huntsmen start their days here.

This isn't a preschool.

Things bleed out here.

I am not a hunter. I am accuracy without authority. No matter what I do, I cannot make myself shoot moving things. I tried once—under the tutelage of my PoppaJack— but I cried so hard he swore he'd never take me again. Meanwhile, Neil, an unusually staunch environmentalist on many fronts, toggles with ease between a paper target and a creature he knows mothers or fathers their young. "I never waste anything," he says as a defense. And he doesn't. When his family doesn't need the meat, he pays to process it for a local food pantry. I don't judge him, except maybe a little, but I can't admit that in a place like Grand Junction. Everyone hunts. Everyone has a taxidermist saved in Favorite Contacts. There are people who'd go hungry if they didn't. But since I have an endless supply of Doritos, I stick to prepackaged goods that never had heartbeats.

Martin's views are closer to mine. He turns down hunting opportunities with teammates all the time. But he was out here today, earlier, and he wasn't scared of morality choices; he was scared of my stepdad and what he might have done.

The two EMS guys from the ambulance run toward an older man, their captain, I presume. I look around for Owl. There's a crowd of men and women in navy polos and police uniforms gathered near the hood of the Hummer, but he's not with them.

I do spot Parson's Auntie Wilma. "Auntie!" I yell, and

she shields her eyes from the headlights, then waves for me to join her. Auntie raised Parson and she likes to say she raised me, and if she's feeling particularly spunky, she'll claim she raised most everyone in Grand Junction under the age of seventy. She's fifty, so it's obviously a triumph she managed this. Right now she's leaning against the police cruiser parked next to Martin's Hummer in her leopard print workout clothes, trying to look like she belongs here. Owl will let her stay, but she's going to freeze without a coat.

Did Martin have a coat on?

I picture him in our garage this morning, leaning on the drink fridge door, sucking two Yoo-hoos, one right after the other. He hadn't been wearing his jacket then and he hadn't been wearing it later in the day. Just his gameday jersey. He'll freeze out here if we don't find him soon.

An officer rolling yellow crime scene tape interrupts my thoughts. "Step away, ma'am. Ma'am, please, step away." His perimeter includes the cruiser.

Auntie Wilma and I scoot into the roughage near a barbed wire fence. Wilma tucks her hands into her armpits and shivers. "Girl, it is colder than T's on a bull."

I laugh at both the G rating and the misuse of the phrase, which draws a look of disdain from the serious-faced officer nearby. "Auntie," I correct affectionately, "the saying is *useless* as, uh, T's on a bull, not cold."

"Don't you laugh at me. So whose T's is it colder than?" she asks, swatting wildly in my direction.

"Witches'."

"All the same," Wilma says, hands thrown in the air. "Am I right, Lu-Lu?"

"You're always right," I say obediently, which makes her laugh, and then I laugh, and then I realize she's staged the whole conversation so I won't think about the blood on Martin's Hummer. She's good like that.

Auntie and Parson aren't just my coach and surrogate family. They represent one-fourth of our longtime camping partner families. The dearest friends my mother and I possess.

The weekend of the dam break, all four families were together, camping in LaRue. It's a true miracle any of us survived. I shake away a memory of Clay and Parson, flying snails and buckets of rain.

The county sheriff sedans are all lookalikes, but our friend Deuce—also of the camping menagerie—never leaves home without his GJHS baseball cap. I spot the beat-up thing lying on the cruiser's dash before we're shooed away.

"Deuce's sedan?" I ask Wilma, hoping Deuce will read us in when we see him.

Wilma runs a hand through her short-cropped gray hair. "It is." Nothing's ever lost on Auntie.

Behind us, someone cranks generators and hooks up floodlights. Bugs zip toward the lights at alarming speeds. With the floodlights come the pop-up tents and a sense of organization and operation. The speed at which they work spins fresh dread in my gut. I don't know what I expected, but it wasn't this. Surely this is a mistake and Martin will walk out of the woods any minute and say, "Sorry, guys. Got lost. Can someone give me a ride to the stadium?" and then I'll be back at the football game wondering why Neil is home, laughing at Wilma's ultra-Southern voice spitting out mixed colloquialisms, and hoping I haven't screwed up one of the best relationships in my life. (Assuming I'm sure which of the two relationships is in fact the best of my life.)

Parson jogs up the road and joins us. "You should have yelled at me to ride with you," he says. "And, Auntie, how'd you get here so fast?" he asks, even though Wilma, runner-up in Grand Junction's recent mayoral race, keeps a police radio in her purse. She brings up the forty-five-hundred-dollar purchase nearly every time we're with her.

"Joanny called." Wilma's eyes grow wild with sympathy. She bounces from side to side in her Skechers. "And there's all this blood, but we're staying calm. Yes indeedy, we are staying calm."

Wilma sat next to Mom at Clay's funeral and stood beside her when she married Robert Carlin. The women are thick as thieves and as different as can be. Mom kiboshed group camping post–dam break, but that didn't keep our four families from sticking like glue. Mom, Wilma, Owl, and Molly (Neil's mom) went from kindergarten to graduation together in Cleary County; they were so close, you couldn't fit the Holy Spirit between them when they got going.

With the exception of Neil and me taking a break, the second generation, the forever kids' table to our parents, are equally close. In order of age, we are Parson, Deuce, Neil, Me, Astrid (and Clay).

"Is that blood in the dirt?" Parson asks, staring slack-jawed at the Hummer. "Because that's a lot of blood."

"Parson," Wilma snaps and jabs her head at me sympathetically.

I step forward, not wanting to hear her explain to my coach how he might be being a tad insensitive, and try to get the attention of a nearby officer. "Hey, what do we know?"

I'm ignored.

That's all Wilma needs to go to work. She tugs up the waistline of those leopard tights, sticks out her chest, and says, "There's Owl now. I'll find out the workin' theory." She leaves Parson and me at a clip, those Skechers moving faster than they have in years, and heads straight toward Owl. He's smothered in young officers and emergency professionals. No wonder I didn't spot him earlier. Auntie busts right into the middle of their circle with a big "Y'all."

In Wilma's absence, Parson and I stare at each other and then away. In my peripheral view, he lifts his shoulders and tugs his apron subconsciously over his stomach. There are finger-smeared barbecue stains across the front pocket. Since the magazine article, Parson's more self-conscious about the way people see him. He doesn't mind shoving me in front of an Olympic crowd, but put him out here in an apron with condiment stains and he's lost. His discomfort morphs into action as he removes the Landing apron and pitches it onto the hood of Deuce's sedan. He's sweating, even in the cold. Usually he smells of catfish batter and hickory smoke, and there isn't enough Downy in the world to rinse it out. Tonight he needs a shower. Stat.

"We'll get through this, Luce," he promises. Like this is another tournament he needs to coach me through.

"I'm okay," I say, because he appreciates levelheadedness. "How long do you think it'll take to figure out if this is like a *thing thing* or a misunderstanding?" I'm trying to stay hopeful. The blood makes it nearly impossible. "Do you think they'll have us, like, look for him?"

"No idea," he says. "I hoped to make it out to the game to watch Astrid. Auntie said we needed to be all hands on deck"—he raises his arms like he can't imagine how a band halftime show might require his presence— "but . . ." He points back to the Hummer. "Who knows."

Wilma returns to us and squeezes my hand. "Lu-Lu, they don't know if that's blood, but they think so. Martin's not answering his phone or in yelling distance. The search and rescue team for this area is coming. According to state law, they have to lead the search parties and they'll decide if volunteers are allowed to help. Owl thinks they will, given the potential acreage that needs to be searched."

Blood. Search and rescue. Are we already to that point?

Right on cue, a megaphone pierces the air with a staticky *pop*. Owl Uri's deep voice says, "Listen up. A formal check-in process will begin soon. Afterward, you'll be assigned to a team and given an area to search by a SARs personnel. Search and rescue are part of emergency management—Kentucky Task Force 1—and are trained on missing person cases and protocol in the state of Kentucky. They will be following the Incident Command System and it's imperative that no one goes off book. It's dark out here, folks, and it's going to get darker by the minute, but we're going to find Martin."

"Let's get in line," Parson says, dragging me toward the tent.

Owl catches my eye, and his expression is grim. He says nothing about Martin and issues a singular warning when I add my name to the volunteer list. "Your mom will kill me if you aren't careful."

"I'll be careful," I promise.

Parson and I end up in a group led by a SARs woman with short brown hair and a gap between her front teeth. She has a deep country accent and I miss her name—Jenny or Cindy, maybe. She issues basic instructions: fan out in lines and stay within hollerin' distance.

We walk forty minutes before someone yells, "I've got a shoe."

Chapter Six

Owl pulls me out of my search team and back to the operations tent.

The gray sneaker is the same brand and series of HOKAs that Martin wears most days. The two of us gather under the tent and stare at the bagged evidence like it might start moving. The police chief crosses his forearms over his chest and takes a long, sad breath when I confirm, "Yeah, that's his."

My gosh, the smell of his feet is in the air.

Owl says, "Okay, kiddo, what do you make of this?"

My knees bob and my body twitches with energy. "Martin wouldn't miss the game, and I can't think of any good reason he'd remove his shoe."

The shoe frightens me as much as the blood. I think back to everything Martin said this afternoon. What can I share? What should I keep to myself? I haven't been this wound up in years. Owl's heavy arm falls around my shoulders. "Hey, hey. It's okay."

"I'm fine."

I don't convince either of us.

Owl's a big guy and he reminds me of a hawk, like one day he might take flight with his big old arms and chest, his skinny legs dragged into the air. He raises his chin and lifts his eyes skyward to offer a one-sentence prayer before patting the tailgate of the nearest truck. We both need a breath. We sit side by side, boots swinging. The cold metal bites through the fabric of my jeans. I check my phone because that's what I do when my hands are idle and my brain hurts. Nothing. The text I sent Martin is still undelivered.

He's out here somewhere. Somewhere there's no signal.

Owl sighs heavily, falling deep into his own thoughts before emerging with commentary that's probably not meant for me. "There's blood on the Hummer and pooled on the dirt, but there's no trail. Not of blood or extra tires. Which doesn't make sense. Then we find a shoe?"

"What's your theory?" I ask.

"Best guess? Hunting accident with a cover-up. If I were a betting man, I'd say someone shot someone and moved the body on foot." He turns, looking every bit like a bird twisting one part of his body without moving the rest. "Okay. Help me out. Why was Martin in LaRue today? I need a timeline, and I need one badly."

Martin didn't want me talking to anyone about his theories or the evidence he thought he had on Robert. The implications are too large. For our family and the town. Probably even for the ten states who get their power from Grand Hydro. I focus my facial muscles into something akin to deep reflection. Then I give Owl a truth. "We're out here all the time."

"We?"

I look away from Owl. "Not like that," I say.

Owl shifts closer, not quite a hug, but the lean of one. "He's not a blood relation. And if you ask me, Neil might need some competition to get his act together."

I laugh and it comes out like an unconvincing snort. Then I'm out of my head and into my heart. That's dangerous territory. I cut back to the problem instead. "Owl, this blood, the one shoe . . . How scared are you?"

"Scared," he admits. "What time did you two leave for school this morning?"

"Same as usual. Seven ten."

"And he went?"

"Yeah, we parked next to each other and walked in door two. Gym entrance."

"And did you see him again at school?"

"No," I say truthfully. "Our schedules don't match up. Not even for lunch."

"Hmm. Does he have a girlfriend?"

"No!" I answer too fast.

Owl lifts his eyebrows into his hairline and moves on. "Well, you gotta figure that the penalty for skipping school might have resulted in a suspension from tonight's game. And a kid like Martin wouldn't have risked that for something low stakes. I've got an officer checking the school cameras, but until we hear for sure, we'll say whatever happened out here occurred after school let out and before the first call came through dispatch about blood on a Hummer in LaRue. We're likely working with a three-hour window. We know, if he's alive, he's on foot because we've got his car."

I shake my head. How far could someone go after they lost that much blood? "Who made the initial call?" I ask instead, wishing our school camera didn't exist.

"Tracking that down. Wasn't a local number. Earlier Joanny made a point of saying Martin did a project on Indian Mounds for school. She thought we should search heavily in that direction."

"That was a US History project. He turned it in." He'd waited for the grade to show up on Infinite Campus like it was a lotto number. "Mom say anything else?"

"Only that she couldn't get ahold of Robert." Owl doesn't hide that this is precisely the behavior he expects from my stepdad. "But I reached him by phone right before the team found the shoe."

"How'd that go?"

Based on Owl's grimace, the exchange matched most

of their other exchanges. Under his breath, he adds, "I wish I liked him as much as everyone else in this town." Then he smacks the top of my boot playfully. "Don't tell your mom I said that."

"Never," I promise.

I understand the sentiment.

Robert changed Grand Junction radically. There's minimal gray area among the locals on whether they like or hate the changes, on whether they bow to or cuss the big-time executive in our small-town world. I'd never tell Robert, but I miss the farmland turned housing developments, the old drive-in Mom and I sneaked into after the movies started—they'd demoed that to build a new elementary school. I even miss being able to laugh and tell city folk that Grand Junction doesn't have a traffic light. We have nine now, and we suggest you leave fifteen minutes early to get places. People like the money in their banks, but progress isn't on everyone's Christmas list. For Owl, progress meant he could hire Deuce, and it meant more crime.

"Robert doesn't like me much," Owl needlessly confesses.

"He thinks you love Mom."

"Well, he thinks right. Just not how he imagines."

My stepdad's a strange combination of selfless and selfish. One minute he drops everything to install a security system for the daughter-in-law of a contract worker at Grand Hydro; the next, he will make everyone stay at the table and play Monopoly until he wins. Like a child. He gives. He takes. And you're never quite sure which action is coming next. But again, he's great to my mom, so what do you do?

This afternoon Martin had plenty to say about his dad and none of it was about his need to win Monopoly. In fact, some of it was scary. That weighs on me now. I don't know what Martin would want me to do if our roles were reversed.

Owl says, "Can't say I blame Robert tonight. His son's missing. If this were Deuce, well, I'd . . ." The chief stops and places a fatherly hand on my knee. "Well, you know what it's like to lose someone out here, so I don't need to explain it to you."

"I haven't seen Deuce yet," I say.

"Me either, but I'm sure he's searching."

Owl might have said more, but a large vehicle with high headlights weaves a tight path around the parked cars on the access road and stops directly in front of the operations tent. The Grand Junction football coaching staff exits the school bus first and beelines to Owl. "You need searchers? I got the team with me and the boys are ready to do whatever you say," the head coach says.

Owl isn't about to turn down help; he leaves me to register the new volunteers. Word trickles around that the Kentucky High School Athletic Association postponed the regional final until the next day, so Coach loaded everyone up and drove straight to LaRue. As I rejoin my SAR team in the woods, Martin's teammates yell hopeful things like, "Martin Carlin, get your skinny butt out here!"

More than one thought spins a dizzy circle in my head.

One, at what point do I tell Owl more? Soon. I think it has to be soon. I can't let Martin be missing for much longer without telling Owl about Martin's crazy theory and how it might be why we're out here. Two, Owl said there aren't other physical clues. Or at least I assume that's what he meant by saying there's no trail. Does "no tire tracks" mean Martin couldn't have gotten in a car with someone? Or did he mean no ATV tracks into LaRue? I wish I knew we were searching in the right place.

Surely if he is at an area hospital, Owl would know. Maybe someone else got hurt and he had to take them somewhere. But he would answer his phone if that were the case, and who gave him a ride? My extrapolations sound like Mom, but I'm not the only one jumping to conclusions.

A nearby searcher's voice floats through the trees. "I hope the police set up roadblocks."

A woman replies, "If someone took him, he's long gone."

Then another voice: "Maybe someone's not happy with Mr. Robert Grand Hydro Carlin."

Another: "I'll bet you a box of Miller Lite this is a ransom."

Another: "Nah. Hunting accident."

Headlamps cast my way and catch my profile. One brave soul calls out, "What do you think, Lucy?"

When I don't answer, they shut up. Not long ago, Robert and Mom discussed the potential of added security if the upcoming deal with the Spector Group went the way Robert anticipated. He even floated security details for each of us. I laughed and chalked it up to Robert's self-inflation. I shouldn't have laughed so hard.

Within the hour, an officer radios that 487 registered volunteers are in LaRue. You don't have to listen too hard to hear that people followed the bus from the stadium and some came from Parson's after they had dinner. Others drove out to LaRue as social media blew up. A news crew from Paducah has a live feed rolling on Facebook to see if anyone in the community has information on the whereabouts of Martin Carlin.

Hours later, an air horn blows—the signal to return to the operations tent. I don't wait on my team or Parson; I run ahead, praying the entire way.

Owl begins a message he will repeat multiple times as the other search and rescue teams arrive.

"Officer Deuce Uri is now presumed to be in trouble and/or missing as well."

Chapter Seven

Deuce missing?

That news hits me like a tractor. No way. He's a police officer.

A low hum from the aging speaker system accompanies Owl's voice. "As of now, we have confirmed the blood on the Hummer is human, and we believe Officer Uri arrived at the scene before the 911 call, identified the Hummer as Martin Carlin's, and proceeded into the woods on foot. Officer Uri's radio is in his car, along with his personal phone, and our last radio contact with Officer Uri occurred at 14:34. He was known to be in the area on his lunch break, which might explain why he didn't have communication devices on his person. Please report any contact with Officer Uri and Martin Carlin immediately."

In the chaos of first responders, no one realized the rookie patrolman wasn't on the scene; he was part of it.

A barrage of questions follows the announcement.

"How large is the expected search area?"

"Have area hospitals been contacted?"

"Is Deuce in uniform?"

"Has anything other than a shoe been identified as belonging to Martin or Deuce?"

"With the amount of blood present at the scene, do you suspect foul play?"

Owl gives a matter-of-fact reply that avoids each and every one. "We can anticipate very little at this point. I urge all searchers to use extreme caution. It's dark. The land is rocky. Please wear proper cold-weather gear as the temperature drops. I've placed a statewide emergency management request. By morning, we should have a search and rescue dog as well as a mounted team. We've updated the Kentucky State Police, who are en route, and Air Evac has agreed to search the area by helicopter at daylight if we haven't located them by then."

"Will you issue an Amber Alert?" someone in the crowd yells.

To this, Owl says, "Not yet. We don't have enough information to do so at this time."

Another voice pipes up: "Do we think Martin and Deuce are out there together somewhere?"

"I hope so."

If you know Owl, you catch the slight crack in his composure with that last answer. The hurt ages him. His posture's slumped instead of ramrod straight; his crow's-feet wrinkles are canyon deep. Deuce is a fourth-generation cop and Owl's only kid. Smart and strong, with a logical head on his shoulders. All of which doesn't add up to him leaving his radio or phone in the cruiser. Not even on his lunch break.

My police procedural knowledge is from television shows and the occasional true-crime podcast. Cleary County's reaction to this potential missing person's case might be your basic small-town crisis treatment or what happens when a football player doesn't show up for the biggest game of his career, or, and I suspect this is the truth, what happens when LaRue is once again ground zero of a disaster.

The post–dam break era of Grand Junction forged a new town. The physical property damage gutted the visual of LaRue, but it was nothing compared to the emotional damage of fifteen missing kids. That's an asteroid strike of trauma. Weeks stretched into months. Searchers came, after work and before, walking riverbanks, picking through moss and briars, dredging the water until there was everything left to find and absolutely no hope of finding it. Most of the bodies were recovered. Some weren't.

Clay wasn't.

We had a funeral. We even had a graveside service.

Mom buried Ribbit, Clay's beloved stuffed frog, all while swearing to Ribbit she'd dig him up the minute Clay came home. You can know someone is dead without seeing them dead, but it's harder.

If we don't find Martin and Deuce, I don't know what I'll do. I can't picture myself walking around these woods for the rest of my life, but I might have to. If I don't, what kind of person am I?

Someone's shaking me.

"Luce. Luce."

I look up and see Parson. He's not crying; he never cries. He's blank. "I don't . . ." He tries to say something and nothing comes out.

He has to be thinking about the six of us. Himself. Deuce. Neil. Me. Astrid. Clay. How we are back at LaRue with trouble in our pockets. Sometimes the six of us are frozen in time. Like we exist in amber brooches. Standing with Parson, even though I'm eighteen and he's twenty-eight, time rewinds: I am nine again. Parson's nineteen. Deuce, seventeen.

When you're nine, you fall in love with people all the time. It's so easy. It happens when they give you ice cream and when they put a worm on your fishing hook and when they agree to play catch with you and when they buy you a Dr Pepper at the store and when they lift you to the top of the Christmas tree to hang an ornament and when they put their stinky ball cap on your head and make you smell the brim. Your heart is like a toenail; it grows and grows, and no one notices it's too big until it's coming through your shoes. That's how I loved those guys. I loved them and I wanted to be them, and I wanted them to love me the way I loved them. I remember my mom telling me I couldn't go shirtless like Deuce and I screamed, "I hate you." That's nine-year-old love.

Here's the worst secret of all: parts of me are still nine years old.

I think those parts are showing tonight. In me and in Parson.

I want to be done losing people, and there's no one on the planet who can promise me I am.

Chapter Eight

"Have you seen Neil since earlier?"

It's Parson asking. He's out of his blank emotional state and standing on tiptoe surveying the crowd.

"I haven't." I squint against the harsh raised flood-lights and check all the little circles of searchers for him. "Maybe he hasn't heard?"

"If he's alive, he's heard." Parson stops talking the minute he realizes what he's said. "He's fine, obviously. We were with him when this happened. I was thinking . . . the fact that he isn't here looks bad. Since you're, like, his ex, and Martin's, like, your flex."

"Martin's not my flex, whatever that means," I say.

Parson's face says, *We both know that isn't true.*

"I'm saying, get a text through to him. Make sure he knows. I'm gonna attempt to call Auntie and tell her about Deuce. I sent her to the restaurant." He holds his phone above his head as he walks toward the area other searchers claim has signal. One or two bars is the best he'll find.

I tried Mom earlier. The call dropped twice before she answered. "Nothing yet," I said first, followed by, "There are so many people out here looking. We'll find him."

She didn't say, *I told you I was right to worry.* She only asked if I was warm enough. *Uh, no,* on the warmth. My skin is so cold I can't feel either set of cheeks. I check my phone now. There are texts from her and my battery is down.

MOM: Watching on Facebook. I'm losing my mind.
    Hug Owl from me.
MOM: Tell Robert to call me when he can.
MOM: I love you. I'm sorry I'm not there.
MOM: I wish I were as strong as you.
MOM: I'm so scared.

I'm not feeling strong.

I send a text to Neil that sounds moronic because if he hasn't heard about the search, none of it will make sense and then another to Mom: No news. Still searching. Stay calm. Love you.

I haven't seen more than a glimpse of Robert, and I'm grateful. We passed each other in the woods and exchanged weak hellos. For him: the sight of me, his sort-of kid, had to have reminded him of Martin. For me: the sight of him scared me. I can't wrap my head around him hurting Martin, not like this, but it's on the edge of my mind, for sure. The timing can't be coincidental.

During Owl's announcements, the space around Robert fills with loyal employees. Worried men and women in Grand Hydro puffer jackets, offering him hot chocolate and flasks of bourbon. I don't know if they're genuinely empathic or pledging their allegiance. Almost as if in their minds, Martin is a lost treasure and when they find him, their fearless king will offer raises and carry them up the corporate ladder in a red velvet armchair.

Parson and I meet up again and join another group headed toward Indian Mounds, and we end up two miles into LaRue. My voice cracks from yelling. I am dehydrated and stumbling on the terrain. My vision shifts from blurry surroundings to sharp details, like my contacts are rolling on and off my eyes.

"This fog sucks," says Parson sometime after midnight. He's walking like a mummy, with his arms outstretched. I can see him only because we're feet apart.

A radio crackles. "All search teams should report to the operations tent ASAP."

There's a long drawl to the words and they're completely vacant of enthusiasm.

"That's not good," Parson says.

Maybe the guys have been found and have hypothermia. Maybe they're already in an ambulance on their way to the hospital. Maybe another hunter picked them up without realizing we were looking for them.

Exhausted and freezing, I put one foot in front of the other and follow Parson and the two other searchers on our team. As we cross the field, the volunteers—flashlights raised, headlamps blinking—look like a field of fireflies in the mist.

Clay had trouble pronouncing his *g*'s, so *glowbug*, his word for fireflies, came out *lowbu*. "Thank goodness they didn't name you Gas or Grunt," Deuce used to tease. That made Clay scream, "I'm not a 'ass or a 'runt!" My little brother was the only one of us who wouldn't be punished for cussing, and Deuce loved to make the adults do a *we shouldn't be laughing at this* squirm.

"Lowbu," I whisper to the crowd in the same squeaky voice Clay used when he chased insects with a mason jar. My heart aches with gratitude for this tiny memory, for my community, for all the people who show up to help.

It takes forty long, wet, painstaking minutes to find the access road in the fog. We almost make it to the lower valley, to Duck Pond marsh, with the bottoms and river beyond, when Owl calls for all searchers to crowd in around the operations tent. We run toward the sound of his voice and join the throng of fearful people. They smell damp, and I'm sure I do too.

Owl leaps atop a generator and calls, "Attention. Attention." The sound system cuts out. One of his men shouts that the last search and rescue group is here, all volunteers accounted for, and Owl lifts the microphone again. "Ladies and gentlemen, we're stopping the search until daylight due to the fog."

There are varying responses. Some understand and agree; others call this a mistake. Robert's voice is crass and loud. "You're giving up on our boys!"

Owl moves the microphone away from his mouth and speaks directly to Robert. "Robert." He uses the name like a warning. Something in it says, *My son is out there too,* and Robert deflates into his jacket's collar.

Owl speaks again to everyone. "Emergency management believes it is no longer safe to search due to our escalating weather situation. Please check Cleary County Sheriff's Department social media accounts for updates. We'll be using those to communicate additional volunteer needs at dawn. Hopefully we won't need you because we'll have located Martin and Deuce. Until then, be careful going home in the fog, get some sleep, and thank you." The final two words ring across the night.

The weather system rolled in off the Tennessee and into the creeks when our backs were turned. Heavy clouds hang above the squad cars and hover over the oaks. That mist will be opaque in the next ten minutes, and not only will searching be impossible, but someone might fall in the river or down a ravine.

Owl has done the right thing, even I know that, but there's no doubt he's upset. The crowd disperses toward their cars and along the access road. Robert rushes Owl before he's able to climb off the generator. I slip closer to the two men and listen. "I'll have someone here tomorrow who knows what they're doing," my stepdad says. "I'm going back out. I don't care what you say."

Owl smiles sadly. "Whatever you think is best," he says. "I've never been able to tell you what to do, have I?"

That means something to Robert and he softens. "I'm sorry," he says and runs his hand through his thinning hair until it sticks up straight and wild. "I'm crazy right now."

"Me too," Owl says, and the two fathers sigh.

Chapter Nine

Parson lets me walk to the truck alone since it's within sight of the tent. He plans to stick around and study Owl's map of LaRue. I don't argue. I want to be off my feet.

I arrive at the Nissan and find Neil sacked out in the passenger seat. All of Grand Junction is searching LaRue and Neil's snoring? Seriously? Deuce is practically family and Martin is his ex-girlfriend's brother and he knows what it's like to be trapped out here. Who sleeps through this? I am angry and cold and don't feel like hiding it when I open the truck.

I get in and slam the door. "Where have you been?"

Neil's eyelids flutter. His pupils grow huge in the overhead light. "It's a long story," he says groggily.

I untie the laces of my shoes and throw them over my shoulder onto the floorboard. "Martin and Deuce are missing, and your response to missing the search party is 'It's a long story'?"

I expect him to defend himself; instead, he raises his right hand and shows off a white plaster cast running from knuckles to elbow. "I lost a fight to that deer in the back of my truck and ended up in the ER. Broken in several places." His face twists in pain.

"Broken in several places," I repeat, leaning closer to examine the swelling in his fingers. Twice their usual size. I can't hold in my gasp. "Neil! I'm—" *Sorry? Worried? Shocked?* The word choice feels delicate given why we're in my truck in the middle of the night in LaRue, but the implications are bad. Maybe not equally bad, but bad all the same.

His scholarship. The Olympics. They could be on the line.

"When? How?" I sputter, thinking about the look of pain etched across his features at the Landing earlier this evening.

"I don't want to talk about it."

"But how does a dead deer do all that damage?"

"It happened. Nothing I can do about it now," he says, almost coldly. "Anyway, my folks are with your mom. Or they were when I left them. They didn't want me to drive on pain meds, but news broke about Deuce, and I told them I was coming whether they liked it or not. They took my keys, so I ran here." He lifts his sodden sneakers up from the floormat. "I don't recommend running four miles on pain meds," he adds with a sad but satisfied grin. "See? A long story."

There's nothing to do but swallow my attitude. "Neil, I'm so sorry. Are you okay? Do you want me to drive you home?"

"No. I was fine until I hit a wall about an hour ago. I tried to text about sleeping in your truck, but it wouldn't go through."

"I can't believe your hand—" I'm stuck in that thought wave.

He raises his cast as if to say, *Nothing I can do about it now,* or maybe, *That's not the biggest problem of the moment,* before reaching across the console and saying, "Is there any news on Deuce or Martin?"

I shake my head.

"You've been out here the whole time?" he asks.

I nod.

"That's a long time in the cold, Luce." He slides off his jacket, working the fabric slowly over the cast, then tucks it gently around my shoulders and waist.

"You'll be cold now," I argue.

"I'm a hunter. I'm good at cold." He reaches across the seats and console and touches the end of my nose with his index finger. As promised, his touch is warm. That finger, a fire. "You, though, are going to lose that nose to frostbite."

I put on a nasal voice. "Then I would sound very funny, huh?"

"Yes, and I would have to tell all the Olympians and Parisians that you aren't trying to be Voldemort."

We let ourselves sigh-laugh and lean in close. Not close enough to kiss, but close enough the heat of his breath touches my cheek. I say, "Thanks for—"

"—breaking into your truck to tell you a long story," he says coyly. "Anytime."

There are words in my head—kind words and maybe even cruel words too. But I don't trust either. I'm tired and cold and sad and in no condition to tell love from loneliness. Neil hurt me, and part of me wants to ignore the hurt and lean into how it feels when his hand is next to mine. Part of me feels like an alarm is trilling in my brain.

How do you know the difference between a hurt that's normal and a hurt that's a warning signal? Especially when it's coming from someone you've known all your life. You're a frog in a slow-boiling pot with a hurt like that.

"Yeah?" he prods.

I settle on something true and far less complicated. "I'm glad you're home."

A deep breath from him sends a cloud of heat to my nose. "You've only missed me for my Tic Tacs."

"Truth," I say, knowing it will make him laugh, and it does.

Our Tic Tac obsession is one of those ritualistic things that you only understand if you're a competitive athlete. You have three and a half orange Tic Tacs before the best competition of your life and you keep having three and a half orange Tic Tacs for the rest of it. Neil has always been in charge of our Tic Tac supply.

"I have missed you, Luce."

I put up a hand to stop whatever might come after that.

His fist tightens and then releases. Even though he's clearly angry and probably feeling rejected, he pivots. "I can't believe this. Deuce wouldn't get lost. Not out here."

"No, he wouldn't."

We grow into our quiet. Neil works an empty Styrofoam cup with the stub of his thumbnail before crushing it in his palm. I stare into the darkness, wondering if we should drive to my house or stay out here. It's below forty and I only have an eighth of a tank of gas, so I can't risk turning on the truck's heat like other searchers refuging in their cars. If we go home, our parents are there. That's a whole second round of emotions. I'd rather sleep here, close but not too close to Neil. I tug out my phone and find one bar of service that lets me send a message to Mom and Robert.

ME: Napping in the truck until daylight. I'll text as
soon as there's news. Love you.

Mom answers immediately. Are you alone? I don't want you alone. Come home.

ME: Neil's here. Owl's nearby. I'm safe.

Neil reads over my shoulder and knows me well enough to understand I'm just as worried about her as she is about me. He says, "My folks were planning to stay with her tonight. She'll be fine. You can't rescue everyone all the time, Luce."

"I know that."

He keeps himself from saying, *Do you?* with words, but not with his body language. I grimace and he apologizes. "Sorry. Last thing you need right now. So, you seen Deuce lately?"

"Not for any quality time. We overlap at Parson's, but you know how that is. We don't talk when we're shooting. Last Saturday Martin and I ran into him at Greg's Supermarket when we were picking up a pizza. I asked how working for his dad was treating him and he claimed it was kicking his butt, but Owl told Mom the training is a piece of cake for him."

"Getting pizza, huh," Neil says in a way that lets me know he's thinking about how much time I spend with Martin.

"Deuce asked about you."

Neil shifts sideways onto his hip, being careful to baby his arm. "Oh yeah?"

"Yeah. Wanted to know if we patched things up." I told Neil not to go there, and I end up being the one who can't avoid the topic.

Neil exhales. "So he knows . . ."—I feel him selecting a phrase—"our current status?"

"Uh, yeah."

This is Grand Junction. The town knew we were on the outs the minute I walked out of my room crying to Mom. She told Wilma and Wilma told Parson and the waitress at the lodge overheard and mentioned me as a "prayer request" to a friend at church and then the news was on Facebook.

"What'd you say?" Neil asks.

"That he'd have to ask you, but that you told me you'd be at the Walther Cup."

"I will be," he says.

The upcoming competition is one of my last shots to make the USA Olympic team in Three-Position Air Rifle. Neil's already on the team. Or he was. The broken arm might force him out.

At fourteen, Parson put a Bleiker Challenger smallbore rifle in my arms and said, "Your turn to give it a whirl, Lucy." The year before, he'd lured Neil into joining a traveling air rifle team and started coaching him privately as he launched the shooting range business behind the lodge. In a place like Grand Junction, everyone needs a side hustle. Turned out Neil is an exceptional marksman.

And so am I.

Of my first fifteen rounds with the Bleiker, all but one hit within the inner circles. We tried again at twenty meters, ten meters farther than the competition standard.

That's like hitting a fingernail from forty-five feet. Same result. An optometrist would later tell me my eyes were born to shoot.

I'm the one percent of the world with no dominant eye.

That day changed my life and it set Parson, Neil, and me on an interwoven path of training, traveling, and competing. Within a year, I landed in the top twenty-five female competitors in the world, thanks to a competition in Tucson, Arizona. From there, I set my sights on the Paris Olympics. The trouble is, the Covid-19 pandemic kept me from traveling out of the country during subsequent World Cup and Olympic qualifiers. Neil's college team at the University of West Virginia went to more competitions than I could. Six months ago, he competed well enough to secure his place on the US team.

"You feeling ready to compete?" Neil asks.

"I don't *feel* ready for anything currently."

"Yeah, me either." He raps his fingernails against the cast.

I change the subject to something safer. "What about you? When's the last time you saw Deuce?"

Neil reclines the seat and stretches both arms toward the ceiling. He picks at a loose piece of foam around the overhead light and says, "You know. The day Parson had us working on the grain bin bar for the lodge's outdoor patio."

I know the day.

It's the day we broke up.

Chapter Ten

On that day, the sky was an amazing shade of pink, Parson was over the moon with his new grain bin bar, and Neil and I were on our way back to return the rented skid steer. I'd been chewing on words all day and I didn't think I could stomach them anymore.

"Listen, don't get mad," I began, even though those are words that ensure someone is about to get mad. "I asked Robert to get me a ticket to Rio. I should qualify for the Olympics at the Walther Cup, but if I don't, that ticket to Rio's competition is my backup plan."

"Luce." The judgment in Neil's voice cut a path right through my chest.

"You already made the team," I argued. "Don't ask me to apologize for going after my dream."

"Your dream is in your hand. You won't need Rio, and you certainly don't need Robert."

"Too late. He already bought it," I said.

Neil glared long enough and hard enough that he lost control of the skid steer and barreled into the rental building's overhead door. He swore up one side and down the other and cut the engine. To which I said, "You always want me to ask for help, and now when I do, you go crazy. How is that fair?"

He growled. Probably at the skid steer, but at the time it felt personal.

"I'm not the crazy one here." He ground his fist into his thigh.

"You make me feel so shallow when you get this way. Like I'm a terrible person for letting someone pay for my airline ticket."

"Not *someone*. Robert," he argued.

"He's my stepdad. Get over it."

Neil bent over the steering controls and exhaled long and deep exasperation. "I'm not sure what's more ironic. That your mom married a dam builder after a dam broke our lives or that I'm with someone who doesn't see the irony in that at all."

"What do you want me to do, Neil?"

"I want you to care enough to take a stand."

"About dams?"

His face contorts in disappointment. "About how men like Robert disrespect creation and get away with it. Clay would be alive if men like Robert didn't exist."

"Wow. Just wow," I said. "Talk about crazy."

I knew asking my stepdad to book the flight to Rio in December would cost me something with Neil. I had dreaded telling him and put it off until I knew I couldn't any longer. He hated Robert, and he harbored a special anger for any involvement Robert had in my shooting career. That started when Robert surprised me with a Walther LG400 Alutec Competition rifle and Neil demanded I return the gun.

"It was a gift," I had yelled. "Get over it."

"You don't get over principles, Lucy. You either have them or you don't."

"It's an air rifle, not a black-market kidney."

"But how does he have the money to pay for your fancy new rifle, Luce? Grand Hydro. I can't believe you'll hold that weapon in your hands after what the dam took from us."

"A terrible storm took Clay *from me* and Robert didn't make it rain."

"You don't understand," he said, like I had committed a deep betrayal.

I understood; I didn't agree.

The weekend Clay died, we all started becoming something else. Slowly at first—we were kids—and then all at once.

I, a rescuer. Deuce, a protector. Parson, a coach. Astrid, an artist. Neil, a passionate, hot-headed environmentalist, who by the time he was fifteen could articulate (to anyone who listened) how the removal of dams from all major rivers was a basic environmental necessity.

When you're first in love, you don't care if people change. They still fit you. But then little changes add up, and it's like weight gain; one day you go to put on your size fours and discover you're a six. That's shocking when it happens because you're sure you had on those same jeans the day before.

I love Neil.

So I wiggled and contorted and prayed and held on for dear life.

We agreed I'd keep the rifle, for the sake of my Olympic career, if I didn't accept anything else beyond daily essentials from Robert. And I hadn't. Robert was so busy with Grand Hydro and all his moving and shaking that we had very few interactions. But then Covid hit and two things happened: my family became a family who ate meals together and played board games, and I felt the Olympics sliding away. I needed that airline ticket, Robert had the money to get me there, and we finally had a semi-real relationship. Politics aside, Robert is very good to my mother. Martin's words rang in my head: "*You don't need anyone's permission to be yourself.*"

I found myself sliding off the skid steer seat, glaring at Neil and the damaged overhead door, thinking I could not contort myself any further for someone who wouldn't also contort for me.

"Where am I supposed to go with this?" I gestured to the space between us, not truly understanding the gravity of my own question until it was out of my mouth. "I mean, how are we ever going to work out if you hate my family and, like . . . should I even have to be asking that question now? I'm eighteen, not thirty. And if we're not going to work out and we're sure about that now, what are we even doing?"

"What are you saying?" Neil asked.

"I'm saying . . . I guess I'm saying . . . Mom married Robert; he's in my life. Please get on board and stop holding him against me."

"And if I can't?"

"I don't know. I don't want to make any more stupid deals where I can't have something because it's coming from Robert. I don't have it in me. On literally everything else in the world, you're amazing, and I love you so much, but I don't have the energy to argue about something that won't ever change."

"We're done," he said.

"Arguing?" I asked.

"No. Just done."

We might have changed our minds, might have walked back the emotion, but the next day broke something in Neil. At our practices, two hundred miles apart—his in West Virginia, mine at Parson's—neither of us hit the bull's-eye for the first time since we started shooting.

He mailed me seven boxes of orange Tic Tacs with a note that said, *Goodbye and good luck*.

That was that.

Chapter Eleven

Neil and I don't talk more about Deuce. We spend the next ten minutes in silence. The armrest digs into my back when I turn away from him, but I do it anyway. There are only a few hours to rest before daylight. The dizziness of sleep sinks through my skull and I push away every terrible fear I have for Deuce and Martin. I am almost to the blackness when Neil says, "Luce, I need to tell you something."

My automatic fear is that he wants to talk about our relationship and I'm out of emotional bandwidth. "Huh?" I say, trying not to fully engage.

"I was out here—in LaRue—with Martin earlier."

"So? You were hunting. Like you said already."

"Can you look at me?" he asks.

I peek over my shoulder. Neil's frozen and focused, the way he behaves during competitions. Except tears are rolling down his cheeks. "Hey," I say gently and turn toward him.

His voice comes out in a stutter. "Whatever . . . happens, with Martin, and Deuce, even if it's bad, I need you . . . to believe that I didn't have anything to do with it." He massages his temple so hard I hear his hair follicles scraping against his scalp.

I tug his hand away so he won't rub the skin raw. "Why wouldn't I believe you?"

"Because we've been fighting, and now they're missing, and you know how I feel about Robert. I . . ."

"Neil, please." I sigh. "Let's try to sleep. We'll find them in the morning, when the fog is gone."

"So you believe me?"

I nod confidently. I do. Why wouldn't I?

Neil lays his cheek in my palm, and I feel the curve of his smile as he says, "Thank you."

Then, as he's falling asleep, he says, "Love you, Lucy," and I answer, "Love you, Neil," because we do, even when we don't, because we always have and always will, because I'm a size six, but I can be a size four for a few minutes.

Chapter Twelve

Neil's dad, Danny, raps on the window of my Nissan at 5:42 a.m. The sky's dark, the air bitter. At some point in the night, I shoved Neil's Carhartt jacket under me to cut the cold seeping through the leather seat into my bum.

Mr. Danny's presence brings two thoughts: one, *They found Martin and Deuce*, and two, *I hope he brought coffee.*

I crack the door, trying to keep any warm air left inside, and say, "Hey, Mr. Danny."

Neil stretches his feet onto the dash. "Hey, Dad."

Danny opens the door wider and leans over me into the back seat. "Astrid with you?" he asks, as if his daughter is curled up next to my shooting jacket on the rear bench.

"No," I say, wishing he would back up or get in the cab. He's wearing a GJHS hoodie and a salt-and-pepper beard shadow that suggests he hasn't been home since yesterday either. His deep gray eyes, like his son's, mirror exhaustion.

"Have you seen her?" Danny asks his son.

"No. She didn't even know I was driving in for the weekend. I was surprising her at the game." When Neil adds, "Dad, are you saying Astrid didn't come home last night?" I wake up all at once.

"Hop in the back, Mr. Danny," I say, and he obliges, scooting toward the middle of the truck.

"About an hour ago, Wendy, Astrid's bandmate, came to the house, freaking out." He breathes gruffly through his nose and sounds like a tiger. "Evidently Astrid re-cruited Wendy to text your mom and me from her phone yesterday, saying that Astrid was staying in the library between school and the game and couldn't text because she'd left her bag in a classroom. Wendy thought the lie was so Astrid could hook up with someone." Mr. Danny blushes slightly and Neil says, "Uh-huh." Danny con-tinues, "We didn't notice at first because we were at the ER—"

"With me," Neil says, nodding.

"Yeah, and then later, once we knew the boys were missing, we texted Wendy and she texted back saying that

Astrid was searching LaRue with the team to buy Astrid more time for whatever Wendy thought Astrid was doing. But then Astrid never answered Wendy's texts either. And Wendy knew she had her phone with her."

Not wanting to jump to conclusions, I say, "She might have been out here. There were seven hundred volunteers by the end of the night. We didn't see her, but that doesn't mean she wasn't here. There's no signal."

Danny bites the skin around his index fingernail. "Right? Except, before I found you two, I checked the volunteer sign-up and she's not on the list."

Owl was adamant we register as volunteers. He assigned a rookie officer to the task. I showed my ID more than once to prove I'd already logged my official attendance. If she's not on the list, she likely wasn't out here.

"Dad, are you saying you haven't heard from or seen Astrid since yesterday?"

"I'm saying I haven't talked to anyone who has."

Chapter Thirteen

Martin. Deuce. Astrid.

Missing.

Are they all missing for the same reason? Missing in conjunction with each other? Occam's razor would argue yes. And these three share a unique connection through our families.

I don't know whether it's better or worse to think they're together.

"Listen," I say. "They can't all be gone. Poof. Disappeared. There's got to be a reasonable explanation for the whole thing."

"Yeah, Dad. Lucy's right."

Danny's eyes lift heavenward; a prayer forms on his lips.

"Did you tell Owl?" I ask. "When you were at the tent looking at the volunteer list?"

Danny shakes his head.

"Let's do that," Neil says. "Then he can get on the radio and see if anyone has seen Astrid and we can clear this up."

Early morning dew soaks our shoes and pant legs, and they hadn't exactly dried out from the night before. Mr. Danny, Neil, and I walk beside the line of emergency vehicles. Before we reach the operations tent, I gather my hair into a messy ponytail and dig the sleep crust out of my eyes. Lights gleam from beneath the closed flaps. I lay money Owl's there and he hasn't slept.

We duck under the fabric, and I can instantly tell I'm right. The chief sits in the shadows on an old Igloo cooler. His iPad's screen casts a white light on his face, giving him an alien glow. His eyes are bloodshot, his posture concave. He stands when he sees it's us. Owl greets Danny with a firm handshake. "Good to see you, Dan. We can use a man with your skills."

Mr. Danny works for Fish and Wildlife in the next county over and knows his way around LaRue better than his son knows his way around the shooting range.

Owl senses Danny's unease. "Oh no. What now?"

"We don't know where Astrid is," Danny says.

Owl tucks his chin to his chest and mutters a curse before he collects himself. "You're sure?"

Danny explains the circumstances. During their brief exchange, Neil and I read Owl's open iPad screen.

7:00: Deuce starts 7 to 7 day shift.
7:17: Martin leaves home for school.
7:30: Martin arrives at GJHS. Confirmed by GJHS security Dale Owsley.
11:00: Martin's car leaves GJHS parking lot, turns right toward LaRue.
14:30: Deuce radios station for lunch break.
17:52: EMS responds to call. Blood on Hummer.
18:03: Chief/EMS arrive LaRue Campground. Deuce's cruiser / Martin's Hummer / Andy Bedford's Bronco located nearby.
18:53: Martin's shoe found at 36.745537, -88.082618
19:00: GJHS game canceled. Word out on social media.
22:20: Announce Deuce missing.
3:03: EM calls off volunteer search due to fog.

A series of questions follows the timeline.

Why did Martin leave GJHS campus?
What happened between 11:00 and 17:52?
Lucy?

Andy Bedford?

792 people signed in to help search for Martin/
Deuce. Scene permanently contaminated? Is this
a scene at all?

The iPad screen times out.

Two things stand out to me: Andy Bedford and my
own name. *Lucy?* feels like it's written in twenty-four-
point font. Neil points, as if I might not see. "I don't
know," I whisper.

Danny and Owl conclude their talk with the decision
to stay mum about Astrid's absence until they've reached
out to more of her friends. They reason there's no need to
create additional panic yet.

"Dad," Neil interrupts. "Panic is part of this. We're
in LaRue. Everyone in the county has PTSD right now."

Owl nods in agreement. "He's right. This feels—"

"—really bad," Danny finishes.

Danny does something I've seen Neil do a million
times. A weird thinking gesture where he twists his lips. I
think he's going to cry or scream or both.

Owl offers a calming statement. "Let's see what the
sunrise brings. You never know, we could all be eating at
Parson's by lunch."

He tries to smile and can't.

From Neil's stony-eyed stare into the middle distance,
I know he's imagining the worst.

Searchers arrive with the sun. Many from the night

before. New faces too. I don't see Robert anywhere, but his contingency is easy to spot in their fancy green puffer jackets.

Our SARs topographer lifts a mittened hand when she spots me at the tent; she's dressed in yesterday's clothes and has a smudge of hot chocolate on her collar. Volunteers circle up and pass around hand warmers and share gloves and hats. There are dozens of GJHS sports beanies and camo balaclavas. Deuce's mother, Donna Jo, leans on the bumper of Owl's squad car, looking dazed and confused. She's a gaming manager on a casino boat, and last we heard, she lives on a barge or something weird. Given her black pantsuit and vest, she came here straight from the boat. It's a good thing my mother isn't here; she'd likely give Donna Jo a piece of her mind for cheating on Owl all those years ago.

I'm handed a bright pink toboggan with stitching that reads *Compost Is Awesome*. I shove it over my head, my ears thanking me, and accept a hand smack to my arm as greeting from the giver, Andy Bedford. "You need that more than me," he says gruffly.

He smells like a frat party and a goat barn. That at least explains his name on Owl's iPad. He takes a cigarette from a pack in his front pocket, leans away to light the tip, and says, "I hate this place," with a few added expletives and a big, long drag.

"Have someone drive you home," I say.

Andy Bedford has more reason to hate LaRue than

anyone. He was the civil engineer of the LaRue Dam and the leader of Boy Scout Troop 1404. Either way his story's told, people died because of him. An investigation cleared him. The dam break was ruled a tragic accident, but Andy Bedford left society the same weekend my brother departed the earth.

"Can't leave. This is my lot," he slurs and weaves an unsteady path away from me, smoke billowing around his head. He bumps into Parson, who nearly drops a tray of bacon from the Landing. The two exchange brief words, but Parson recovers quickly and leaves the bacon at the hospitality tent set up by the Methodist church.

Among the milling crowd, there's a general hopefulness.

The fog's gone. The visibility's crisp. Nothing's as scary in stark daylight. Not even the blood on Martin's Hummer. You can almost convince yourself this is all a Halloween prank or a big misunderstanding. The snatches of conversation we overhear focus on the condition the boys will be in after a night in the elements. "Temperature stuck around forty," someone says. "Not great, but if they were dry, they're probably fine." They don't know Astrid is also missing.

Owl gathers the searchers in teams, thanks everyone for coming, and sends us out.

An hour later, the screams start.

Chapter Fourteen

I am not in the group that finds the bodies.

I'm a half mile away—Neil and Parson on either side—
working my hand warmer between my palms and calling,
"Martin! Deuce!" like everyone else. I'll never forget the
precise tone of the scream. Shrill. Female. Almost fake
sounding.

Then the word *bodies* cracks through the SARs' radios.

"*Bodies*? Plural?" Alarm rockets through my system.
My knees wobble. I dig my hand into a puny oak and bark
comes off in my palm.

Neil holds me up. "Breathe," he says. "Keep moving."
He leads us slowly in the direction of the scream.

Parson says, "I don't think we should go." He means in the direction the crowd is moving. He's shaking. His face is white. "It can't be—"

I stretch forward and take his hand. "Parse. We're all dying inside."

It's true. Martin's my stepbrother, Astrid is Neil's sister, and Deuce is Parson's best friend.

This man has coached me through the most intense moments of my life. He doesn't look like a man right now. There's a boyish fear coating him that I haven't seen in years. My rescue gene throbs in my heart. *Focus on Parson*, it says. *Focus on Parson*. My heart rate slows instantly.

He says, "What if it's Deu—"

"I don't know," I say and wrap my arm around his back. "We're all scared, but whatever has happened has already happened. Let's go together. None of us should be alone."

He gets a grip on himself. "You're right. You're absolutely right."

We are a wall, walking behind the crowd and up the hilly terrain.

The night before, we aimed our flashlights at the ground. We searched for trails of blood, a second shoe, signs of a possible head injury, footprints that suggested the guys traversed this way or that, evidence they stumbled into an old well or sinkhole. Anything askew in the landscape.

We did not know they were hidden away.

We reach the top of the rise. Below, the marsh covers

the valley. Locals call the area the Duck Pond because the entire field floods so easily, but it's not really a pond. Backwater comes in off the river and makes a knee-deep reflection swamp. This time of year the field is brown and gold and the sky, now a bright Carolina blue, glints on the rippling, mirrored surface.

LaRue is on the migratory path for Canada geese and home to various waterfowl. Every bird hunter from Kentucky to Canada knows LaRue's reputation, and the Duck Pond is a favored spot to set up blinds. Neil came to homeroom countless times with his duck call in his pocket. He'd honk the thing when the bell rang if he had a good day on the range. All the guys did.

A small crowd of law enforcement have waded out and are gathered around a brush pile in the water. I look harder. There's an artificial gathering of grasses and thatch. To Owl's left, one corner of a shallow wooden box shows off its camouflage spray paint.

"That's my blind," Neil says. "I was in it yesterday morning, checking for leaks."

There's nothing reassuring to say. The blind is clearly a scene of some kind. Owl's backing away the majority of the officers to establish a perimeter. The ping of my gut says someone is dead in that blind. And if that's true, if this isn't a horrible mistake, that someone was murdered.

No one in the gathering crowd around us says names. We stand on the rise, a collective of searchers. All around me, I hear phrases.

"The blood on the Hummer."

"The shoe."

"Whose blind is that? The Clarks'?"

They want to ask Neil, but they don't. They whisper a little lower. "You know, I heard he hated Martin." There's defense and a conversation and then they move farther away to another place on the hilltop. Neil hears too. He must. I wonder how long it takes a rumor to harden into a truth.

That all depends on what or who is in the blind.

Martin's fears. All of them come scratching at my skull. He was afraid something horrible, and preventable, happened out here during the dam break. He was afraid if he said that aloud, something horrible would happen again. It's impossible for me to think beyond that.

More searchers collect in the damp grass. Small clots of friends. More impatient conversations. No one knows whether it's right to go or stay, but they all stay. Waiting. I grip Neil's and Parson's hands. Neil's palm sweats against mine. Parson's is icy. Neil bangs his broken arm against a tree like a metronome.

Parson says, "I don't want to be here," but he doesn't move.

Neil starts a low chorus of nos. I prepare myself to shove my worst emotions somewhere else. *You have a compartment inside you that's on another planet*, I tell myself as I stuff fear and ache down and in. The compartment doesn't give me happiness, but it lets me breathe.

Blue whale breath. In through the nose. Out through the mouth. I will be fine. No matter the outcome.

I hear the ATVs behind us before I see them. Robert and Mr. Danny. The two men stand and lean away from the handlebars as they descend the hill. Robert stops first, his tires spinning and throwing a shower of mud in the air and onto his face. He breaks through the officers at the edge of the marsh. He's off-balance and splashes into the water on his way to Owl and the blind. An officer in thigh-high galoshes tries to stop him and can't. Mr. Danny arrives next but stays at the edge of the marsh. He recognizes the blind and that stops him midstride.

Someone behind us calls out boldly to Neil. "That your blind, Clark?"

Neil trembles violently. First his hand, then his legs. I slide closer until our hips press together. His entire body shakes. "Neil, what's in the blind?" I ask.

"Hurry," he coaxes the officers working the scene. "Hurry. Hurry. Please."

I want the reveal done fast and I want it slow. The officer bent over in the blind rises up and does his best to keep a neutral expression. He shakes his head at Owl and flashes two fingers.

"If that's Astrid . . . ," Neil says.

I know the threat in his heart. The voice screaming, *If that's Astrid, I'll die.*

I know because that voice came to me too.

On the day I lost Clay.

That Weekend

It was the Sunday afternoon of the long camping weekend. Mom's life with Robert Carlin wouldn't begin for several more years.

A month before, with no thoughts of rain, my dad talked all four camping families into splurging. "Let's reserve a pontoon," he said, "for the last weekend of camping season. We can motor between the LaRue Dam and Smithland." The splurge was a *splurge*, but everyone said yes. Although my mom said, "We have our own free paradise. Do we really need to go boating too?" She said this because my PoppaJack owned LaRue and the old campground. To which my dad boomed, "Carpe diem!"

Everyone in Grand Junction lived like we did—paycheck to paycheck, with more nos at the grocery than yeses—but my dad wasn't originally from Grand Junction and he was always trying to impress Mom's gang of high school friends. The pontoon rental money had to have been on the adults' minds because they talked about the weather in violent, incessant whispers, hoping the rain wouldn't prevent us from going. There was no return policy, and everyone seemed slightly on edge that Dad had gotten them into this now that it wasn't going well.

No sooner had we parked the car by the rental dock than the first streak of lightning crossed the sky. Owl wasn't sheriff yet, but he was quickly elected to sweet-talk the rental company into a refund or a reschedule date. He and Dad set off for the small swaying rental shack at the end of the dock, their shirts and ball caps whipping in the wind. Five minutes later they returned penniless. Dad fell into the driver's seat of our small sedan, slammed the door, and said, "No pontoon today," which we already guessed. To my mom, he said, "They're saying the forecast is nasty. Could get eight inches over the next twenty-four hours."

I remember her asking, "Should we pack up and go home?" and he said, "No. If we were in tents, maybe, but we'll be fine in the cabins." She said, "Well, thank God we're not here with Andy Bedford and the Boy Scouts, because Troop 1404 is gonna get soaked," and they laughed a little with relief.

The sky opened up.

The first raindrops hit the windshield like jets on a car wash and kept coming. Out my window, the world grayed. Dad didn't stop in the parking area next to the Boy Scout vans. He went up the access road and took PoppaJack's service trail into the back of camp. Our Ford Focus didn't have optimal tires for washed-out mud roads, so by the time we parked at the back of the cabins, Dad told Mom, "If we get out of here tomorrow, it'll be a miracle."

The idea of staying at camp longer didn't bother me. I secretly hoped we'd get stuck for a week.

In a group text, the eight adults claimed one cabin for day drinking and card games and sent the six kids clomping down, over the footbridge of Vespers Creek, to "the kid cabin" for whatever we could come up with that wouldn't bore us to death. After the treacherous ride there, we didn't give any additional thought to the storm except for how soaked we got moving from the vehicles to indoors. When the six of us arrived inside, we peeled away nearly all of our wet, plastered clothes.

To ease the loss of the pontoon and distract Clay from the thunder, Deuce made up a version of tag and cajoled Parson until Parson pushed back his chair and agreed to play. The moment Parson stood, Astrid flew over the back of the couch and into his back. "I'm on your team," she said and pulled on his ears.

Deuce tried to explain there were no teams, but

Parson whispered something in Astrid's ear that made her smile. There would be teams. There were always teams. Somehow the oldest boy and the youngest girl were always on one together. And where did that leave me? On a team with my little brother. We'd lost before we even knew the name of the game.

Deuce and Parson piled all the furniture from the main room into the bunk room so we had a proper arena. With the room set, Deuce handed each of us a flag football belt. Clay's royal blue flags dragged on the old floorboards. Our goal was to rip flags off each other while keeping our own attached. The last person standing with a flag won. Poor Clay stood there in the middle, looking fierce and tiny, convinced he could win.

We played for hours. Occasionally we glanced toward the ceiling when the pelting grew fierce or the lightning flashed particularly bright, but mostly we laughed and darted away from each other, hoping to be the last person standing with a flag.

Deuce's and Parson's attention was marvelous, far more marvelous than a pontoon. The day before they'd spent most of the day fishing, and the rest of us—Neil, Me, Astrid—were angry they'd gone off. They'd taken Clay, but not us. Neil in particular had a love-hate relationship with "the older boys." That's what the parents called Parson and Deuce. Instead of being included with them, Neil and I were constantly relegated to staying close to our parents or babysitting our younger siblings.

And Parson had changed over the last few months. He'd gotten serious about being a person, accomplishing things, having goals. There were fewer farts in our faces, fewer jokes. He constantly ditched us to fish. This weekend he'd spent nearly every minute on the lake with Deuce or bent over a table tying flies. Only Clay had passage to Parson; he crawled into Parson's lap while Parson worked on delicate knots. They sat that way for hours. I punched Parson in the back to get his attention, and he didn't move his gaze from the hooks and lines in his hand.

"Luce, you gotta let me work my plan," he said.

I sighed dramatically, afraid his plan would take him away from us, and at the time, he was my favorite.

"Your plan is boring," I said. "Fishing is lame."

"You won't say that when I open my restaurant."

"I will say that when you open your restaurant," I said, "because then you'll *always* be gone."

"I won't be gone. I'm gonna buy an acre from PoppaJack and you'll all be able to work with me when you get old enough."

"Won't catch me in a kitchen," Deuce said.

"Whatever. You'll end up in jail or begging me for a job," Parson teased him.

"Don't say that," Deuce snapped, and there was actual bite in the words.

Even at that age, I knew when the play stopped being play.

That morning the guys had come back from a predawn

fishing trip in a foul mood that stuck around until the flag game started.

To be inside their laughter and full attention for those hours of flag tag stopped the world.

None of us knew the forecasted eight inches of rain had been upped to a historic twelve. Eight would have been historic enough. Twelve was overkill. Once or twice, Parson peered out the front windows and said, "Dude, that's a lot of rain," to Deuce.

But rain was only rain. If we'd looked out the back, we'd have seen that Vespers Creek had grown from a ten-foot-wide stream to a forty-foot-wide canyon of rapidly moving water. Offshoots of Vespers had also swelled, and the footbridge to our cabin was long swept away.

Beyond that creek, a ruler-sized fissure opened up in the LaRue Dam, and the swollen Tennessee River pounded the weakening concrete with all its might.

Chapter Fifteen

Owl. Danny. Robert.

A cop, a park ranger, and an entrepreneur wait.

Three fathers in a marsh.

Three friends on the hilltop.

A valley of cypress knees, backwater, and a duck blind. The crime scene—and by now, I'm confident this is a crime scene—is a macabre fishbowl for the media. Reporters are arriving on the ridge with their cameras and setting up shots for a big reveal. Below, black equipment boxes are opened and protective gear is added. Every angle must be captured by a police photographer. The evidence logged. The perimeters set.

Who or what is in the blind is of the utmost importance and yet painfully delayed by details. The investigators dismantle the camouflaged elements atop the blind first. The thatching and cattails. Then the poultry wire that holds them in place. Sod had been added, and they peel it back like a moss sheet. The box is naked and exposed.

There appears to be blood on one of the two square cutouts in the top of the box. These are places for Mr. Danny and Neil to pop up and shoot from while still being disguised. Neil made this blind in his garage and then floated it along the creek behind his house and into LaRue on a pontoon. All the way to the Duck Pond, where he anchored it atop the trunks of two old cypress knees jutting up from the marsh.

Eight Kentucky State policemen detach and drag the spray-painted blind through the shallows to the edge of the marsh. They beach the box awkwardly and the photographer lifts his camera. When Owl is satisfied, he is the one who takes a DeWalt ripsaw to the top of the blind. Three officers help him lift the wooden shelf and place it on the ground. Owl waves for the same three men to crawl into the blind.

Beside me, Neil slows his rocking motion. Owl wouldn't need three officers to lift Astrid. She's a featherweight.

Deuce is at least 220.

How heavy is Martin? One forty-five? One fifty?

I assess Owl's reaction for any clue as to who is in the

blind. He's not reacting like a father, but maybe a cop wouldn't. He's careful to keep from looking at Danny or Robert. Instead, he tilts his head upward and meets my gaze with an agonizing expression. While he stands there, the three officers lift a body from the blind, over the wooden sides, into the arms of three other officers, who lay it thoughtfully on the sodden grass beach.

The photographer starts again. *Flash. Flash.* Owl steps away and buries his face in the fork of a tree. "Is it Deuce?" Parson asks, peering at Owl and then the body.

Behind me, Donna Jo starts to sob.

My voice catches in my throat. "Yes."

Deuce is Parson's oldest and best friend.

We sway toward each other.

You can hold someone without touching them.

Neil almost feels other, like he's slipping away. It must be surreal to watch the officers dismantle his duck blind. To lift his friend from its depth. To wait and see if his sister is next.

Two of the three officers crawl over the railing, back into the box, the process more familiar.

This time the body they lift out is smaller.

Robert collapses to the ground.

Martin is the second body in the blind.

Owl keeps his back to his team. Mr. Danny whisks Robert away to allow Owl's team to work. Robert wails and fights, but Mr. Danny is large enough to lower the sobbing man to the ground and keep him there.

After Dad left us high and dry for his high school girl-friend, Daisy, and before Mom married Robert, the two of us lived on a property owned by a farmer who let me bottle-feed calves. He also raised goats. Goats, as it turns out, know more about mourning than humans. When they die, they cry in ways that pierce your eardrums and your soul. Robert rivals a hundred dying goats.

Chapter Sixteen

My second brother is dead.

"I need to go to them," I say, my body on autopilot, the compartment inside me strong as iron.

Parson says, "Are you sure you want to see—"

Robert can't be left to howl alone. Owl needs me. And I need me to be someone who helps. A grief compacted is a grief delayed, and I take the delay.

The three of us slide through the knee-high weeds, down the ridge, to the flats of the marsh. No one stops us, and gratefully, none of the other searchers or media follow. When my stepfather sees me, he latches on. "Don't look," he repeats over and over. "Please don't look at him."

I have no desire to see what Robert saw. His agony paints its own picture of Martin.

But I want to get to Owl too. There's no chance of that yet. Robert holds me in a death grip.

Only Parson glances in the direction of the blind. Neil kneels, stoic and standoffish, scratching at the skin under his cast. I suppose it is its own form of pain to stand next to someone in more pain than you. To let them hurt and you be helpless, all while writhing in the shock that evil exists and it won't let you stay a stranger.

Deuce and Martin are dead. Why? Was Martin right? Or is something else going on? I don't see how anyone could fake this level of grief.

"Who did this to my son? Who did that to my son?" Robert asks of no one.

Behind me, Owl regains some composure and says to Mr. Danny, "I know a lawyer over in Paducah. Call him, since the blind belongs to you."

I pray Robert doesn't hear. He'll find out the blind is Neil's, but better that it doesn't happen right now.

Owl issues an officer to escort Robert and me to the access road and then drive us home. I have no choice but to go. To leave Martin in the valley beside the Duck Pond. To leave Owl mourning and Astrid lost.

The officer closes us in the patrol car, Robert in the front and me in the back. My stepdad tucks his head under the glovebox. Possibly to shield his face from the media; possibly because he's hyperventilating. I hear him struggling for breath. I hear him gag. I hear myself too.

In the weeds along the access road, Andy Bedford totters toward his farm, head kicked back, a flask at his lips. He gives me a nod that says he knows what happened at the Duck Pond. I rip the *Compost Is Awesome* beanie off my head and bury my face into the fabric.

Martin is gone. Deuce too. I can't believe it.

The access road ends at Highway 61, known locally as River Road. Robert built our house here, on the highest ridge above the Tennessee, looking down over the concrete infrastructure of the Grand Hydro Dam and Energy Project. My stepfather makes electricity for ten states, but that energy will never recreate his son.

He can't stop sobbing. I don't allow myself to start. Mom will need me.

The steepness of our driveway forces the officer to lay on the gas. He almost rams the gated entrance. "Sorry. Sorry," he says, trying to pull closer to the keypad. I tell him the code.

Mom's standing on the other side of the fence at the edge of our lawn. After the gate swings open and the patrol car eases through, Robert bursts from the front seat and toward my mother. They collapse in the grass, holding each other, their hands outstretched for me to join them. In a daze, I thank the officer and then I do my job.

I tell Mom that we need her.

I tell Robert there aren't words for his hurt.

I tell them Martin and Deuce would want us to get through this together.

And then I tell Martin, *I'm so sorry I left you in LaRue.*

Chapter Seventeen

The night before, Robert promised Owl he would bring someone to Grand Junction who knew what they were doing. That didn't seem like a real thing he would do, more like something he would threaten in the heat of the moment. There was no signal in LaRue and it was almost midnight. And who, from his corporate world, might specialize in our situation?

Robert should never be underestimated.

The orange Jeep arrives before the officer who drove us home leaves. It sneaks through the gate and parks. There's a woman in the driver's seat. A medium-size blond dog climbs over the console and waits in her lap for her to open the door. The minute she does, the dog launches to the grass and shakes.

Anyone with that dog is a good person. He's gorgeous.

"Galen, sit," she says, and the dog obeys. She smiles lovingly at him and then me. *I'm sorry*, her eyes say as she crosses our lawn, Galen trotting at her hip.

The woman calls across the yard with an equally apologetic voice, "Mr. and Mrs. Carlin, I'm Dana Jones. The missing persons investigator you hired last night."

Usually when Robert says, "I gotta guy," *guy* evokes the business equivalent of John Wayne: an old white dude with a big gun and a bigger agenda.

Dana Jones is the opposite: compassionate eyes, short torso, short legs, compact, the body of a rock climber or a triathlon athlete. She wears khakis, a down vest over a navy polo with *Jones Investigation Inc.* stitched above her breast, and a pair of aging KEEN boots. No jewelry, no nail polish. Her ponytail is equally no-nonsense.

Robert calms himself down enough to wave her forward. She shakes his hand with gusto, but my mother's she clasps and holds—a moment between two women, another *I'm sorry* spoken without words. I'm petting Galen, so we don't officially greet each other.

She says, "Galen and I caught a red-eye from a case we finished in New Orleans and came straight here. I called the locals when you didn't answer, and Chief Uri brought me up to speed on my drive in from Nashville. I'm incredibly sorry for the loss of your son. I don't mean to interrupt; I stopped to let you know I'm in town and will be staying at the Rose Cottage Inn." She extends her business card. "This is my direct number. I'll be ready to speak when and if you'd like to."

Mom says, "But we found him," like she can't imagine what Dana might do with herself now. She's not thinking about Astrid, but Dana is. That's clear, in her posture alone.

"You have my deepest sympathy for your loss," Dana says and nods once to herself, as if the task is done and to say more would be inappropriate. After a quiet command to Galen, she heads to the Jeep.

Something in Robert clicks. It's like watching a robot power up as he calls the investigator's name and says, "We can talk now. The sooner the better, right?" he asks, shaking his foot to wake it up and wiping his eyes with the sleeve of his jacket. When he stands, the elite businessman leaves the grieving father on the manicured lawn.

My mother doesn't have another version of herself.

I help her stand with Robert's assistance and wonder if I should run her a bath instead of letting her participate in whatever comes next. I telegraph my fears to Robert, but he doesn't read me.

Dana does. Following her hand command, Galen slips slyly under my mother's palm, forcing her fingers to graze his fur. She gives him an unconscious head massage and the dog keeps contact with her the entire trip across the yard. As he was trained to do. Mom is more alert by the time we're at the kitchen door. No one with two legs has ever managed to comfort my mother that quickly.

Dana smiles again at her dog. He's a special bit of magic; she knows I see it too. She says, "He's named after an ancient Roman healer. You're Lucy, yes?"

"Yes, and we'll take all the healing you and Galen have to give."

She appraises me and arrives at, *Oh, I see; you're not just a teenager,* faster than most people. Adults often respond with curiosity to Mom and me. The ones who size me up and are impressed are a hit of dopamine. They push me deeper into my rescuer role, and right now I'll take all the dopamine I can get.

Robert offers Dana a seat at the booth in our kitchen. Floor-to-ceiling windows showcase our lawn and, below that, Grand Hydro. It's a tailored view of zoysia grass and landscaping achievements that are marred by the industry beyond. Concrete, smoke plumes, transmission towers, wires. There's an old concrete batching plant about a football field away from our garage. A little reminder that the aggregate eating the river will likely dine again.

Only in the wide-angle view do you capture the fall colors bursting like forestry fireworks, the Tennessee River snaking through rocks and trees, the high steel-framed bridge going over the water. You can't see LaRue from the kitchen. You have to go to the front porch for that view and then to the side yard to see Grand Junction.

I assume that's why Robert keeps us in the kitchen. No one wants a view of LaRue today.

"Gorgeous," Dana says.

"We like it." Robert's voice quiets. "Martin says the gantry cranes look like the AT-ATs from Star Wars."

Mom exhales at the mention of Martin's name and then absentmindedly closes the butter dish he used every day on his cinnamon toast. She's nearest the window and rests her face on a pane, I assume to feel the cold air and ground herself for the conversation. Galen settles against her, his chin on her leg.

I busy myself making coffee, which gives me the time and privacy to google Dana Jones.

Wikipedia says she's former FBI turned private investigator. When she was with the bureau, she worked a high-profile missing person's case, known in the media as the Gemini Thief. According to the internet, that case changed the course of her career. She left the bureau and focused exclusively on missing persons. Apparently she's good at the work. The internet says she has a ninety-four percent success rate recovering missing persons.

Nutty aromas and stilted small talk fill the kitchen. When there are mugs in front of everyone, I slide into the booth next to Dana. She doctors her coffee and begins with a compassionate matter-of-fact speech that she's likely given before.

"Nothing will ever be the same again. I've seen these atrocities. Lived them with families like yours. You know that trauma cannot be replaced by money, sex, shopping, food, drugs, et cetera." She pauses. "And it can't be replaced by answers. Even when we find the truth, and I believe we will, trauma stays. And sometimes finding answers creates more trauma. Before I begin my work, you should know that nothing I do here will save you from walking in the pain you feel today, and it might make it worse for a time. For that, I'm very sorry, Mr. and Mrs. Carlin, Lucy." She syncs with each of us, pausing on me as she speaks again. "I used my flight to read everything there was and is to read on the Grand Hydro Dam and Energy Project and the previous LaRue Dam Break. I familiarized myself with the parts of your life that are documented. Your honors and award as well," she says to Robert. She continues by addressing my mom. "Am I correct in stating that your father, Jack Rickard, owned LaRue at the time of the flood and that you"—she moves her gaze to Robert—"purchased the property from him to build Grand Hydro after the LaRue Dam failed?"

"That's correct," Robert says.

Mom lets him answer for her. I can't tell if she's coming closer to us or moving farther away.

My palms break out in a cold sweat. I can feel Dana going exactly where I want to avoid.

Dana continues, "The location of Martin's murder"—we all flinch at *murder*—"cannot be lost on anyone. The same location that previously devastated your family, Mrs. Carlin. Nor can it be lost that Deuce Uri, a survivor of the same dam break disaster, is also a victim. And Astrid Clark, another survivor, is likely missing. This investigation, or rather, my approach to this investigation, will most certainly revisit that tragedy and the formation of your company, Mr. Carlin. That makes my first question rather difficult and simple at the same time. Would you still like to employ me as an investigator?"

I tense at the line of questioning and wonder how long before Dana reaches conclusions that are similar to Martin's, and what will happen when she does.

Robert is still cool and composed. He tests the temperature of his coffee with his lower lip. "I can't see how they're linked, but do what you need to do."

Mom rubs her fingers over the velvet fur triangle of Galen's ear and gives the tiniest of nods. I actually feel an odd burst of hope. Surely Robert wouldn't tell someone with a ninety-four percent success rate to go digging if he had any fears that his son's death was linked to his company's formation. If Martin were here, he'd be happy to know that. He loved his dad, and he wanted him to be perfect.

"Okay, good." Dana hesitates. "However, Mr. Carlin, my primary job here is—"

"—is to the find the man who killed my son."

A slight shake of Dana's head and a far firmer, "No," before she asserts, "My primary job is to focus on the recovery of Astrid Clark."

Robert's back straightens; his chin tilts.

Mom says, "Well, yes. Molly and Danny." A sob lodges in her throat.

Dana continues, "Justice is slower than it should be, but if my experience with missing persons—and at this point we have to hope that's what she is—has taught me anything, it's that I must put the presumed living before the dead. Doing this is not only an issue of morality but one of statistics. Assuming the murders and missing person case are linked in the present, and perhaps even linked to the past, locating Astrid Clark is the best chance of catching who murdered your son and Officer Deuce Uri. Justice plays the long game."

Robert is quiet. Dana has done her homework; she already knows he's a man who wants more than theories and moralities. He'll play the game until he wins.

"Do you still require my employment, Mr. Carlin?" Dana says, unwilling to proceed until he commits.

"Do I have another choice?"

"There are always choices, Mr. Carlin."

He licks his lips; his chin juts out as he swallows words and chooses something to say. "Ms. Jones, given what I know about you, you're going to pry into my company, looking for any possible connection you can find, whether I like it or not."

She nods confidently.

"Well then," he says, "I'd prefer to be the one signing the checks, so at least I know what you think you've found before you tell the media."

"I do not work with the media," Dana says.

She's offended enough that Galen checks in. When she stands and straightens her vest, Galen launches himself from Mom's lap to Dana's side. "I apologize for having this conversation so early in the investigation. You've lost your son, and that is an awful thing. I'll see myself out."

Mom clenches Robert's arm with a death grip.

"Wait," Robert says. "Can you find who did this to Martin?"

Dana doesn't hesitate. "Yes, I can."

That's all he needs to hear her say. "Okay. Do whatever you have to do. I'll stay out of your way."

Chapter Eighteen

Dana and Robert spend ten minutes on paperwork, bank routing numbers, and electronic signatures. There's talk of the funeral home and arrangements and the next interview. Galen licks the crumbs from the floor under the table. I sit, waiting and anxious. When the parameters of the relationship are laid out, Dana says, "I'd like to continue this interview for another fifteen minutes and then leave you to rest."

Mom and Robert agree, and I nod like my opinion might count.

Dana says, "I need to ask the three of you a series of questions. They will not be comfortable, and you should not take them as a personal affront. I ask everyone I work with the same things. If you are ready, Mr. Carlin, I will start with you."

Robert refills his coffee, reaches for the sugar bowl, and spoons an unhealthy amount into the cup. He signals for Dana to ask away. She fires fast and straight. "Mr. Carlin, are you involved in your son's murder?"

Wow. Straight for the jugular. She wants a reaction from him and doesn't get one.

"No, I am not," he says.

I start preparing my face for whatever she asks me. Because it's one thing for Dana Jones, Investigator, to look into Grand Hydro, and another for Robert to find out Martin was doing the same.

"And, Mrs. Carlin—"

"Joanny," Mom corrects.

"Sorry," Dana says and stays direct. "Joanny, are you involved in your stepson's murder?"

"No."

Mom sounds like an adult. I'm relieved. It could have gone the other way. I say no before Dana asks, and Galen nuzzles my knee.

"If you're all telling the truth, things are simpler," Dana says.

Her *if* stings.

"Next question. Do you know anyone who wanted Martin or Deuce harmed? Robert?"

"No."

"Joanny?"

"No. I can't imagine."

I hold my breath during their responses. I pray my face isn't as red as it feels.

"Lucy?"

"No." And that's true. I don't know anyone specifically. I don't even know anyone generally. Martin felt certain that his dad or his dad's investors would not want anything he found about the LaRue Dam Break to surface. And now Martin is dead.

My answer passes for Robert and Mom the same as theirs pass for me. Dana raises her coffee cup to her lips and above the brim gives me an inquisitive look. The tiniest gesture that says she will return to me at another time and re-ask the question. "One more for now. Why were Martin and Deuce in LaRue yesterday? And were they there together?"

Robert chews his thumbnail, thinking. "Deuce is a family friend of Joanny's, but I can't think of any specific reason they'd be together yesterday. Can you?" he asks Mom.

"I thought Martin was at school," she answers.

That leads Dana straight to me, where she was headed all along. "Lucy, what about you? Any insight into Martin skipping school or if he met with Deuce or maybe Astrid?"

I shake my head.

Her chin tilts; her eyebrows climb.

"You didn't skip with him?" she suggests in a way that says she knows I did.

Those stupid cameras at school. Owl must have told her my car left the parking lot right after Martin's.

"Well . . . ," I begin.

That wakes up my mom and Robert. Their bodies whip in my direction, their mouths askew and angry. I hold up my hands defensively. "Yeah, I skipped and—"

"With Martin?" Robert's eyes bulge.

"Yes," I answer.

"I can't believe you," he says.

"You'll understand in a minute," I say.

"I doubt that," Robert says, and there's an invisible family line that feels highlighted. I was his kid, and now I'm Mom's kid.

I begin. "Martin asked me to walk him through the day of the dam break. We walked to where the old LaRue Dam used to be and I talked him through the timeline. He made us take my route from the old cabin to the tree."

"Why would he do that?" Mom interrupts.

I start with the first truth. "That's what I'm getting to and why I didn't say anything yesterday. Martin decided during his history project that he wanted to search for Clay's remains. But he knew how that would go, and I didn't say anything because I thought you"—I lock eyes with my mother—"would lose it if you thought something happened to Martin when he was doing something for you. And I need you. Especially now."

She ebbs away. First her eyes. Then her body. Exactly what I was afraid would happen.

"He was looking for my Clay and now . . . My boys. My boys . . ."

We lose her all at once, and not even Galen can reach her where she is.

On her way out of the kitchen, she stops and braces herself against the doorframe. A portrait of Martin jars off its hook and crashes onto the concrete floor. The glass cracks and pieces skitter under the fridge and into the pantry. Mom screams and bangs the side of her head against the wall. "Clay. Martin. Clay. Martin." Over and over.

Galen looks up at Dana. I stand to comfort my mom, but Robert stops me. "Let me take care of her," he says cruelly. Then he wraps an arm around his wife and guides her along the hallway. Without taking his eyes off my mother, he says quietly over his shoulder, "Ms. Jones, I don't believe we require your services after all."

Chapter Nineteen

Robert's decision that we no longer require Dana's services after asking her to catch a red-eye flight and arranging paperwork does not agree with me. She's here and we need her. Justice might be slow, but Astrid is still out there. She's family. Maybe not Robert's family, but Mom considers the Clarks her chosen siblings. If she were in her right mind, she'd tell him that.

"It's not you," I tell Dana. "He doesn't know how to protect Mom right now." With a sigh, I add, "None of us do," and Dana says, "Most people don't know how to protect the ones they love. Especially not in the worst times of their lives."

I set my coffee mug on the counter a little harder than I mean to and the remaining liquid sloshes onto the table. Dana slides me a napkin. She doesn't appear to be the slightest bit angry or surprised by Robert's reaction. She pets Galen and says to me, "Thank you for your honesty. I know that wasn't easy to divulge, but they needed to know."

"They did," I agree, without adding, *And there's more where that came from for them to find out.*

Dana stands and Galen does the same, tail wagging. She says, "I'm so sorry for your loss. I'll let myself out," and leaves while I'm still at the table. Frozen in disbelief.

Martin and Deuce are dead, and Robert fired one of the best investigators in the country because, yet again, my mother can't handle the past. Clay has been dead longer than he was alive. And that is awful, awful, awful, but Martin is dead *now* and Astrid needs our help *now.*

Martin deserves more than my mother running off to her room. More than his father acquiescing to her grief rather than finding his son's murderer. Owl and Molly are my mother's oldest friends. I wish she could find the energy to love them when they're hurting rather than swim in a pool of her own tears.

"Wait," I call out the door.

Dana's already at her Jeep telling Galen to load in.

"Don't leave." I hear the desperation in my voice. "We need you. Astrid needs—"

I don't even realize I'm crying until I'm halfway across

the drive and Dana opens her arms and says, "I give a pretty mean hug if you need one." She sheds the formal tone and language she used with Mom and Robert.

I lean in and let her do the rest. My hands dangle at my sides as she encloses me in a fierce embrace. I give in to this; I tell myself to let the wall down. I lay my head on her shoulder and let her hold the weight of me. All the people who hug me are male or Mom. Everything is usually one direction: me hugging them. For once, someone soft and fierce is hugging me. For the first time in my life I think, *Maybe there's room to be both.*

"Please don't leave. I need someone—" *strong enough to do this.*

"Just grieve," she says, and tightens her grip and sways. "I'm not leaving Grand Junction."

Relief courses through my body. I don't know Dana, but I instantly know I need her. I feel suddenly awkward that I've let her hold me for so long. I wiggle out of her embrace, and we sit by the Jeep on the paving stones, with Galen between us.

She says, "Chief Uri asked me to stay. I'll consult for him instead of Robert Carlin." The formal way she speaks Robert's full name tells me she hasn't always been a fan and that perhaps some part of her is relieved he isn't her new boss. "You were holding back in there." She speaks matter-of-factly. "Was that to save you or your mom?"

Far below, a line of fog dances above the river, cloaking

the water in gray. "My whole life has been about saving someone."

"And your stepdad? Is his whole life about saving her too?"

"Maybe. I don't know."

Dana sighs and nods. "So it's not about his son?"

"He loves Martin, if that's what you're asking."

"Good. And you?"

"And what?" I ask, not following.

"Do you love his son?"

I hesitate, thinking of Martin, thinking of the last time we were together, and then speak from my heart. "Yes, so much. Martin is . . . Everyone loves Martin. You can't not."

"Then why is Robert more upset about your mom than his only son's death?"

"You said it yourself. You have to focus on the living, not the dead."

Dana smiles. "Touché. Piece of advice, Lucy?" She's asking me for permission and I give it, not at all sure I can handle what she might say next. "If you truly love Martin, and I believe you do, tell the whole truth. Get it all out, even if you think it might not be important. Even if you think it might hurt someone's feelings or reputation. We're in a critical time, and every detail might help us find Astrid alive."

"What if I cause more hurt?"

"Then you cause more hurt," she answers simply.

"But if there's something you can do to save Astrid and you don't act, you might cause even more hurt."

"I need to talk to Owl," I say. "And it's going to devastate him. It's going to devastate everyone."

Chapter Twenty

Galen and I share the front seat, and he is not great at sharing.

"He sheds." This is also Dana's apology for him lounging on my bladder.

Galen, as it turns out, is her service dog. They've spent a year training with Canis Major, a Kentucky company, and Galen performs all sorts of emotional support tasks. I am totally in love by the time we reach LaRue, and I like to think it's mutual.

I direct her toward Parson's Landing first, so we can cross the covered bridge and take the same route Martin would have taken yesterday. She wants to know as much of the area as she can before we talk to Owl. I don't argue. It gives me time to build up my courage.

"Tell me about Owl and Deuce."

Tears slide onto my cheeks as I sum up my friend and his dad in a few sentences. "They're a unit. Deuce is the kind of guy who got choked up when the baseball coach gave him his varsity uniform because it was Owl's old number. And Owl's the guy who got equally choked up on the day Deuce took the oath or whatever it's called to be an officer. They're simple guys. They love God, drink a beer at night, will do anything for their friends and twice as much for each other. If they're not working, they're fishing or helping someone."

"Sound like great people."

"The best," I say, and the hurt starts all over again. I am not good at being sad. Really, it pisses me off.

"It's truly gorgeous out here," she says, slowing the Jeep at the first trailhead and looking east to west.

I lower the window and breathe in the land. "It's my favorite place. Or it was," I add.

"Does Astrid like LaRue?"

I laugh. "Not like I do. Astrid likes . . ." I laugh again. "Air-conditioning."

"Not outdoorsy, eh?"

I shrug because I wouldn't say that either. "We all like the outdoors; she just also likes the indoors."

"Who is 'we all'?"

I tell Dana about the six of us, the kids' table, our

parents, the five survivors of the LaRue Dam Break, and how Martin fits into the picture. By the time she parks the Jeep, she's privy to the timeline of my relationship with Neil and everything there is to know about a Three-Position Air Rifle, even how much I adore Parson as a coach and how he had to work to bring himself to say, "Good job," every once in a while.

"Not an encourager?"

"He's complicated," I say. "You'll like him. And if you don't, you should still order the mac and cheese at the Landing; it's fantastic."

My stomach growls at the mention of food. Other than coffee at the house, I haven't eaten in hours. Dana's stomach growls on cue with mine. We smile and she says, "Talk to Owl and then food?"

Dana, Galen, and I find Owl at the command center at LaRue. From the look of him, he's doubled down, hasn't slept, and won't until he understands what happened to his son. Despite being midday, this second wave of fog has most of his searchers back in their vehicles waiting for the all clear. Between the television station, the hospitality tent, and lookie-loos, a solid crowd stirs around the scene, but he's alone in the corner on the cooler.

Owl spots me, sniffs, and wipes his eyes. "Hey, kiddo. I thought I sent you home to sleep."

"How are you?"

He lifts his shoulders and slides into his role as chief. "I've got at least two crime scenes that are both likely contaminated, one missing person, two murders—one of which is my officer—"

"And your son," Dana says with sympathy.

"Owl, meet Dana Jones," I say.

She extends her hand. "We spoke on the phone, sir. I'm sorry for your loss."

Owl shakes and rakes the back of his hand over his forehead, then resettles his cap. He's dog-tired.

Dana sees it and asks, "Can I be so bold as to ask when was the last time you slept?"

Owl lifts his exhausted frame from the cooler to a camp chair and urges Dana to sit. Then he hunches over his knees and says, "Please don't be the next person who tells me to go home, because the next person might get slugged." He has the presence of mind to say, "No offense, ladies."

Dana says, "I knew I liked you."

Owl points his red, chapped hands at me. "How's your mom? I can't believe she let you out of her sight."

"Sleeping," I say, although that's a guess. I left a note on the bar.

Getting my truck. Checking on Owl. Be home soon.
Love, Lucy

They haven't texted or called. Robert likely served them both a Valium. Maybe when they wake up they won't be as angry with me. When I ran upstairs to change into hiking boots and warm clothes, Robert was on the phone with his assistant, asking for all calls to be held, including those from the funeral home. He saw me pass in the hall and shook his head.

"You should be crashed out too," Owl says, and after a glance at Dana adds, "Forgive me for the lack of tact, but you look how I feel."

She rallies and straightens her back. "I bet I eat and sleep before you do. I, at least, have to feed my partner here," she says of Galen, who looks up with adoration. "Before I get to that, Lucy wanted to speak to you, and since her truck was still here, I brought her out. Then I promise I'll hit the motel and food. I would urge you to do the same."

Owl's radio crackles with an alert for him. One of his officers is escorting the coroner from the next county over to the morgue in Paducah. Chain of evidence protocol. Mention of the morgue and autopsies brings the heaviness of death to us all. I look at my boots, knowing I can't swallow the loss right now; I need to chew it like cud, let it fuel my need for answers. Still, that is Martin being escorted. My Martin. Martin who loves football, TikTok, and country music from the eighties. And my Deuce. Owl's Deuce.

"Tell me you've got good news, kiddo," Owl says as he clips the radio to his belt.

"Whatever I've got is not good." I proceed to confess in short, apologetic bursts. "I skipped school with Martin yesterday. I know you saw me leaving on the school camera. We came here, but when I left LaRue, Martin was fine. Wound up, but fine."

"Was Deuce here too?"

"I didn't see him if he was. I should have told you earlier when we were talking about the timeline."

"Yeah," he agrees, without trying to shame me. "Can I assume you didn't tell me for a good reason?" He turns to Dana. "This kid is gold," he says, cuffing my shoulder protectively. He clearly doesn't want my dishonesty to cast me in a bad light. It's a grace I don't deserve, and one I can't believe he has the energy to offer, under the circumstances.

I rock forward, gathering my courage, and then start by explaining the complication of Martin's search for Clay's remains, knowing Owl will understand. The last thing either of us wants is someone else looking for Clay, much less someone in my household who will remind my mother every day that Clay is dead. We did that for years.

Dana interrupts, confused. "Wouldn't finding Clay's remains be a good thing?"

Owl sighs. "Well, yeah, except, do you know how many people have looked? The dam break was a national event. We've had psychics from California, PIs from Michigan, podcasters, locals, cops. For Joanny, *finding* will be great, but *looking* brings it all up. And we're never going to find him."

Dana nods, but she's got that gleam in her eye—the

one I've seen so many times from others like her. *Don't tell me he can't be found when I am a finding expert.*

"Anyway," I continue. "Martin told me that once he decided to look for Clay's remains, he went to Planning and Zoning for a map. He wanted to be methodical about where he searched, and he wanted property records. I told him that was crazy because we were never going to find Clay's body with a flashlight and a Scooby-Doo van. You know," I say to Owl, "same as I do, that if those remains ever turn up, it'll be when someone dredges a tributary in Decatur or Mobile. That's if he didn't end up in the Ohio River, and then he might be swimming with the dolphins in the Gulf."

I lose the whole thread, thinking of Clay and where he might be and how equally pissed and grateful I was that Martin wanted to find my little brother. Dana brings me back through Galen. The dog presses the weight of his body against my calf and knees until I have to acknowledge him over the memory.

When I'm breathing normally again, Dana says, "Keep going."

I check to make sure no one can overhear what I'm about to say. "Martin found out that his dad tried to buy the LaRue property from PoppaJack before the dam broke."

That's news to Owl. "Jack never said such. And it's not like you can ask him."

That's true.

My beloved PoppaJack moved abruptly after the dam broke. He sold LaRue, the land he swore he'd never sell, for a song and relocated to Tampa. Six months later we found out the real reason for his relocation. His nurse, Salome, called Mom and read her a letter written by him explaining his diagnosis. Dementia. In the last paragraph he asked, begged us not to come. *I'm gonna forget what happened to Clay and I don't want to ask about him like he's still alive. Let me spare you that as a final act.*

I yelled into the phone, "I wish I could forget!"

I didn't know PoppaJack was on the call and lucid until his voice boomed out, "Never forget." That's the last coherent thing PoppaJack said to me. In retrospect, the man knew his daughter, and moving was an act of mercy. She hadn't been in a state to see her father like that after losing her son.

I didn't have to see PoppaJack for him to live on. He was the outlined boot treads in the dirt, the worry wrinkle on my forehead, the narrow set of my hips when I tugged on jeans. He would forget me, but forgetting him would be like forgetting my own name. I adopted the same tactic with Clay. They live with me like calloused skin.

"No, I can't ask PoppaJack," I agree. "But there are evidently emails that prove Robert lied about when he made the first offer on the land. Robert explicitly told Mom he'd never heard of the LaRue Dam until after it broke and made the news."

I'm not sure I can say the next part, but Dana pushes me forward. "Go on. You're safe with us."

I think of the officers lifting Martin's body over the wall of the blind and onto the ground. And of Deuce, and how much I love him too, and how I might destroy Owl and Robert with what I say next.

"There's something else. Something"—I grimace at Owl—"awful. Martin said he had evidence of Robert paying Deuce two thousand dollars a month since the dam broke. Roughly $216,000 total. Martin was convinced his dad or someone who worked for him sabotaged the LaRue Dam to build Grand Hydro. And because of the payout, he thought that person was Deuce. He was going to show me all the evidence last night after the game."

That Weekend

Later, the experts agreed we all would have died if lightning hadn't struck a tree by our cabin.

The Fourth of July contained all my experience with explosions prior to the lightning strike. The difference between gunpowder going off five hundred feet in the air and a three-hundred-year-old oak shattering cannot be overstated. The reverberation came through the floorboards into our bare feet. Our knees rattled so violently we fell on the floor. In the same instance we were falling, a branch missiled through the window like a dart. Its length split the room, part of it still outside, part buried into the opposite wood-paneled wall.

Parson had just been standing there. In disbelief he

reached up and plucked a yellow leaf from the limb above his head. The rain gusted through the broken window along with the smell of singed wood. Clay's large brown eyes widened with the fear we all felt.

Parson and Deuce ran for the cabin door and threw it open. What was left of the oak's trunk smoked; the rest lay in chunks around the yard.

The six of us stood together in the doorway. Rain smacked our chests and puddled on the floor. None of us backed away. We were spellbound, not by the smoldering oak but by the river of water rising toward us.

"That's the creek," Parson said.

"That's the creek," Clay repeated with the same intonation of fear.

If someone had taken a picture of the six of us right then, we would have looked like a horror movie poster. Clay and Astrid started to cry.

"I want Mom," Clay said.

Neil bent over Astrid. "Get your shoes. We're going now," he said with all the authority he could muster.

"You can't cross that," Deuce said.

"Can and will," Neil argued. "Astrid. Shoes." His voice was sharp and cruel.

"Mom," Clay said, pointing to the other side of the creek.

Mr. Danny and Dad ran from their cabin, slipping and sliding on the mud as they got near their side of the swollen creek.

"Dad, I'm coming across with Astrid!" Neil yelled.

"No!" Danny screamed over the storm, issuing us all directions.

Neil didn't listen. Parson and Deuce watched as Neil hoisted Astrid onto his shoulders and ran for the creek. She clung to his face like a monkey, screaming that she wanted down. No one stopped him. We were all still in shock.

Neil made it three strides into the water, to the deepest section, before he lost his footing. Astrid's shrill cry pierced our ears, climbing above the sound of the rain. Brother and sister went down. The red of Astrid's shirt was visible under the current. Parson tore toward the water's edge but Deuce held him back.

I thought they were gone. That I would never see them again.

Precious seconds later, Neil's head bobbed above the surface. He flailed, helpless against the momentum. By some miracle, Astrid clung to his back.

The lightning strike saved them. One of the larger limbs had fallen across the stream. The current slammed Neil into the wood. He screamed with pain but managed to get Astrid atop the branch.

Mr. Danny, who had been running along the shoreline after his daughter and son, waded out, anchoring his body against the branch. Each footing an eternity. Each movement a danger. The strength of the raging creek threatened to dislodge the branch entirely.

The limb slid an inch.

Another.

Another.

Precious seconds and inches. Danny reached Astrid. With the rain, we were too far away to hear anything, but I've wondered a million times what he said to Neil as he left his son there and started back to the shore with Astrid. How do you make a choice like that? Danny placed Astrid in my father's arms, then headed back into the water for Neil.

The limb shifted violently.

Neil lost his grip and slammed into an offshoot of the wood. We heard something in his body break.

"Hold on!" I screamed. The current pulled at the tree.

Danny's hand locked around Neil's wrist. With wretched slowness, he maneuvered Neil to the front of his body. The pressure of the water held Neil to Danny's chest as tightly as if he'd been tied there. Each step was a Herculean effort, but Danny dragged his son into the mud.

He leaned over him, knees in the mud, completely soaked, and peeled wild strands of hair away from Neil's face until his cheeks and forehead were pale and exposed. Then he kissed his son over and over. The relief so beautiful that I almost forgot we were all still in danger.

I've held that image my entire life. Especially because I immediately looked to my own father and watched him mouth the words, "Don't cross."

Those were the words. History has added more. I think what he was really saying was, *You're on your own, Lucy. I'm not coming for you.*

If we'd crossed then, we'd have had better odds than we ended up with.

This was all still excess rain.

The dam hadn't broken yet.

Chapter Twenty-One

"It was a natural disaster," Owl says sharply. I watch him choose his words. "And my son was a child when the dam broke. A child."

"He was what? A senior in high school?" Dana asks.

"Yeah," I answer because Owl begins a defensive tangent.

"I'd know if he was making that kind of money. I'd know. And Deuce would never agree to do something destructive and—"

"Kids do things all the time their parents don't know anything about," Dana says.

Owl ignores her and locks in on me. "Luce, you were

in LaRue when the dam broke, same as me." He laughs painfully, ironically. "Unless Robert is Mother Nature, Martin's full of hogwash. That dam failed, same as any dam of its size would with twelve inches of rain. This so-called property thing with Robert is probably nothing. The money thing with Deuce is a total farce."

Around the tent, heads turn in our direction. The fog reduces features to colorful blurs of motion, but everyone's hungry for news. There's no way to guess how many searchers and officers are in earshot. Maybe thirty or forty? Far fewer than before, but those left are chomping at the bit. Someone with a media badge yells out, "Chief, you ready for us?"

"No," Owl growls back.

I knew this would happen. Knew things would get worse if I told.

Dana grips our wrists, drawing us closer. She's kind and firm when she says to Owl, "Calm down. Let's take this discussion somewhere private." She flicks her head sideways to bring our attention to a lone reporter advancing on Owl.

"No comment," Chief says.

Dana adds, "There's nothing new. Just a bunch of hard emotions. You guys know that."

The reporter retreats into the fog, deflated.

Owl, more aware now, points to Dana's Jeep and lifts his radio and says, "Declan. Need you in the command tent ASAP."

An officer arrives out of breath seconds later. "Chief?" He straightens his shoulders and tucks a sandwich out of view.

"I need some air," Owl says. "Buy me an hour?"

"As long as you need." Declan settles heavily onto the cooler throne, pleased with his promotion, and says, "Weather Channel says two more hours of heavy fog."

Two more hours of delaying the search doesn't bode well for Astrid. I try not to think about where she might be and whether those two hours matter. I hope they matter. If they do, she's still alive, and that's far better than the alternative.

Galen pads ahead to Dana's Jeep. I join Galen in the back and Owl collapses in the front passenger seat. The energy drains out of him like water in a tub. Dana weaves through the parked vehicles at a snail's pace. The air is total soup again. Last night cars lined this stretch all the way back to the lodge. But they're mostly gone now. Maybe it's the fog. Maybe it's the murders.

"I'm sorry," I whisper in Owl's ear. "I'm so sorry."

"I know better than to shoot the messenger," he says and wraps his arm awkwardly behind the headrest to pat my head.

I lean into his hand. "Are you scared?"

"Terrified," he answers.

"Me too."

Owl's head snaps up and he says to Dana, "I don't

have any idea what your rate is, but I'll pay whatever it takes, for as long as it takes, to find Astrid."

"Yes, sir," Dana says.

"I can't take another . . ."

He doesn't say *death*. He doesn't have to.

Chapter Twenty-Two

The Landing is full. Searchers retreated to food and warmth.

I think we'll have to find somewhere else to go, but Parson's hostess, Maria, sees us walk in the front door. I'm here all the time. Owl is too. Without a word, Maria retrieves us from the back of the line and escorts us through the dining hall into a private meeting room. "I'm sorry," she says as she closes the door. I wonder if people will tell me that for the rest of my life.

Dana takes a seat. "Nice place." She gives a low whistle.

One whole wall is a window that looks across a field

of harvested cornstalks. The fog haunts the landscape, eating the field and the forest beyond. In good weather, the view stuns. As does the room. A raw wood table with a bright blue epoxy river running through the center steals the show. The centerpiece even impresses Robert's New York executives, and they are accustomed to beautiful things. More than one high-end weekender has offered to buy the table and chairs from Parson.

When Parson commissioned the piece, Neil and Deuce gave him so much crap. "Mr. Fancy" and "You're getting too top shelf for a country fisherman, bro" and "Tell me how you pronounce that cheese board thingy on the menu again."

"Char-cute-erie."

"Right. Charcuterie," Deuce had said, adding excessive twang.

Parson popped him in the ribs with a wash towel. "Food is everything, gentlemen, and I'll class you two up eventually." To Neil he said, "A trip to the Paris Olympics might even help with that."

Neil had grinned at that and tried every cheese Parson offered. Even the stinky ones.

That makes me think, I need to check on Neil. We haven't communicated since the officer escorted Robert and me away from the scene. Have they already questioned him about the duck blind? Do they suspect him? Surely not; his sister is missing.

I pull out my phone and text.

ME: Any word on Astrid?

NEIL: No. The fog's awful. Where are you?

ME: At the lodge with Owl and a private investigator.

NEIL: On my way.

NEIL: I'm sorry about Martin.

I'm not the only one taking phone time. Dana and Owl have their phones out too. We're basking in the Wi-Fi, and none of us are keen on the subject that brought us here. Only after a server arrives with three cups of coffee does Owl speak. "Lucy, start again and tell me everything."

I do, this time holding back only the tiniest of personal details.

"Evidently Robert's broker accidentally forwarded an email to Martin instead of his dad with instructions to move assets to maintain a certain preset account amount. That account memo was titled 'Deuce payoff.' Martin thought that was weird, but when he asked Robert, his dad said Martin misunderstood. *Deuce*, in that case, meant second payout, not that he'd paid off Deuce. Normal business stuff. Except Robert told Martin to let it go and not say anything to anyone because 'you know how rumors are.'"

"That sounds like Robert," Owl says, the judgment thick.

I continue, "Martin took his dad's word until he went to Planning and Zoning for the map of LaRue and someone in the office went on and on about how Grand

Hydro was a miracle because Jack Rickard told him for years he wasn't about to sell his land to Robert Carlin or Tamerlane. Tamerlane is a primary investor for Grand Hydro," I say to Dana, in case that wasn't in her preliminary research on Robert. "Evidently the Planning and Zoning person was under the impression that PoppaJack didn't care how much money they offered him."

"I see," Dana says, the picture starting to form for her.

"I would too," Owl agrees. "Except . . . twelve inches of rain. And big, huge investigations of LaRue Dam all landed on a single determination: the dam break was a natural disaster."

"I know," I say.

The server returns, which keeps me from continuing. Dana smiles kindly when none of us seem capable of words and orders three catfish platters and a bowl of scrambled eggs for Galen. When we're alone again, I answer, "But not according to Martin. He wouldn't tell me exactly what, but he thought he had actual evidence of the sabotage. He was scared, but he wouldn't let it go either."

Dana follows the train of thought. "If a corporation as large as Tamerlane, or even as large as Grand Hydro is now, were to have sabotaged the LaRue Dam to build Grand Hydro, and that dam broke and killed people, there's no way they would let Robert Carlin's son expose their crimes."

"Twelve inches of rain in five hours," Owl states again. "That's how LaRue failed. Andy Bedford had video evidence. All that came out in the investigation. There's a video inspection of the dam on the Friday before the flood. That's what cleared him in the federal court."

Dana straightens in her seat. "Andy Bedford? The scout troop leader of 1404?"

"Yeah, and the head civil engineer of the LaRue Dam," Owl says. "I mean, come on. Andy's a drunk now, but then . . . if he thought that dam wasn't perfect, he'd never have taken his troop camping in LaRue."

Dana's eyebrows twinge. "I'd be inclined to believe you, except Martin and Deuce are dead and Astrid is missing. Unless this is all a coincidence, which I don't believe in. Owl, can you tell us how they were murdered?"

Owl's eyes fill with tears and I stare into the fog. "Long-range rifle," is all he says.

Dana eyes the door, as if the server might return and we'll be overheard, and keeps the questions coming. "Lucy, why did Martin skip school yesterday? On the day of the big game. And who else knew you were going to be out there?"

"I didn't think anyone knew. He wanted me to walk him through the route we took on the day the dam broke and tell me exactly who was where when. But we didn't agree on him pursuing this and . . ." Emotion spears me. I can't catch my breath.

"Hey, it's okay," Dana says, calming me down. "There's no way you could have predicted this would happen."

I know that logically, but . . . "If he'd never done that project for school, he wouldn't have wanted to find Clay's remains, and then he'd never have gone to Planning and Zoning. I should have shut him down harder on looking for Clay. It's . . . If you knew him . . . He was so hard to shut down. He was all stupid and winsome."

"You couldn't have known," Dana says.

"But he did. Immediately," I say. "He knew he'd found something big and I didn't believe him."

Owl says, "Hold off on that for a minute and tell me when you left LaRue yesterday."

His question pushes me back in time for specifics. Grounds me in details. The meetup with Martin. The walk-through. The intimacy. The argument. What time was on the clock when I returned to the truck?

"One twenty," I say, fairly confident.

"Is there a time of death for the boys?" Dana avoids their names, but somehow *boys* makes it even more painful. That's what they were. Boys. Just boys.

Owl traces the blue epoxy river in the table and keeps his voice matter-of-fact. "Sometime between two and four based on liver temperature. I'm the coroner by default, not because I'm an expert. The state police will handle the autopsy and that will be more specific."

The door to the private dining room opens again and Parson steps through carrying four plates on a tray. The smells of batter, oil, and vinegar create flip-flops in my stomach. Parson places catfish platters on the table before us and Galen's bowl of eggs on the floor. His shoulder towel falls to the floor and he picks it up. To me he says, "I didn't know what to do with myself, so I came here to cook. If you want to shoot later, let me know."

I nod, thinking I might need the distraction, and introduce Parson and Dana. He asks to join us, and Dana performs a quick check-in with me and then Owl. In a series of nods, we agree to talk in front of Parson and tell him the whole story.

At the end of the telling, Parson says, "Hold up. You believe that crock of—" Parson stops. "Deuce and I were inseparable back then and he had nothing going on the side. I gave him money to take his EMT course. He wouldn't have asked for a loan if he had $2k rolling in each month."

Owl looks intrigued, maybe even hurt by the loan, but doesn't interrupt.

Parson takes a catfish fillet off my plate and pops it in his mouth. He chews and says, "I'd drop this and look into that big company Robert's talking to now. Spector. Maybe they don't like Robert saying no to building a pharmaceutical plant in Grand Junction. From the way they were yelling back here last week, that's a billion-dollar deal gone wrong." Parson finishes the thought. "*That's* a motive for murder."

Chapter Twenty-Three

Dana reaches a conclusion quickly. "Robert Carlin needs to be questioned. On the record. You need to get a warrant for his financials."

"Now?" I ask, appealing to Owl on Mom's behalf.

Owl says, "The judge will never sign that warrant on speculation. The media will implode. There's already a video of Robert watching us lift Martin out of the blind on CNN. He has a million sympathizers. I can't go after him. Not with opinion. Not with Deuce potentially involved. We'd need Martin's evidence to do that."

"I'm not saying Robert or Deuce did anything wrong," Dana says. "You told me to find Astrid. We need to know where to look. Is she out there somewhere? Could someone be holding her hostage?" She flicks her wrist toward LaRue. "How far does this go? All the way back to the dam break, or is it more recent, like Parson is suggesting? We don't have enough information, and every minute counts if we're going to find Astrid alive."

I feel the grip on my emotions grow slack. It's easy to predict how Robert and Mom will react. To see that future and fear it as much as the awful things we are living with now. Mom cannot lose Robert, and she might if the allegations surface and gain traction.

"Luce, focus." Parson helps me raise my glass to my lips. He's always been someone who knows how to steady my hand. Neil got me into shooting, but Parson coached me. Taught me to breathe. To focus when there was no earthly way to focus. He doesn't have my eye, and I don't have his low heart rate. If either of us had both, we'd have a gold medal.

I swallow the water and then reach for my coffee cup, wanting the anchor of warmth against my palms as my brain extrapolates the ways this might go and grow. The alibis. The theories. The consequences. Could Robert lose Grand Hydro? Go to jail? Will Mom have to support herself again? Meaning, I'll have to support her.

Dana says, "It's like I said to Lucy earlier—it's all going to come out at some point. Better to lean into the truth."

Over the years I've read the comments attached

to the coverage of the dam break. Probably the same news articles Dana read in preparation for meeting my family. Even if Martin's murder isn't connected, raising the possibility will bring all those images back to the front page. Photos of Clay. Side by side with Martin. My brothers.

If Robert *was* paying Deuce for something, whatever happens next isn't going to involve the truth. The narratives surrounding the disappearance and murders will grow audaciously wild. Speculation will create collateral damage. Investigations into Andy Bedford will resurface, and that stupid video of LaRue Dam, looking perfect and innocent, will be out there again. I hate the internet. It took Parson three seconds to throw in his own theory about the pharmaceutical company. A cloud of people will do the same.

Strangers will have theories about me too. They had them last time. Imagine reading the same girl was in LaRue both times.

Dana understands the circus that awaits us, and God bless her, she doesn't placate me or Owl. "Lucy, you can't see this from where you are, but you can't control anyone's narrative but your own. And the truth is, regardless of whether Martin was right or wrong about the dam break, if there's a conspiracy now or there isn't, you need to think about yourself. You were in LaRue near the window of the murder. Give a statement and volunteer what you know. Cooperate without exception. And, Owl, you'd better get ready for the gauntlet too. The state police investigation will include Deuce, and if Martin is right about Robert's payouts, this thing will get extra hairy. Lucy's done you a favor with her honesty. She's given you time to think rather than react."

Parson interjects, "Luce was here from two o'clock on. She has an alibi. There are cameras on the range."

"Thanks, Parse," I say.

He says, "But you should turn over all your guns as an act of cooperation."

"I don't own anything but air rifles," I say.

Parson knows that. He's still in his logic mode. "Neil should do the same. He was in LaRue yesterday and he's the best shot in the country. I don't know what sort of long-range bullet took them out, but I'd say that'll come up fast too."

I'm horrified by his conclusions.

Dana's face says, *Everything needs to be on the table.* She chooses her words carefully. "Parson's a hundred percent right. Lucy, if you genuinely believe Robert is innocent, ask him about the money before the police can. Do your stepfather the same courtesy you've done Owl."

Owl and Robert are vastly different men. For all the same reasons Martin didn't confront Robert, I don't want to either. If you intend to arm a bomb, you don't do it where you sleep. The minute I ask Robert about the bribe, it'll be *ka-pow*, lights out. Not to mention the effect it'll have on Mom.

I am positive Mom has Robert mentally separated from the dam break. The fact that he now owns the land is merely a coincidence. She won't believe he lied without hard proof, and in the meantime, she'll be revolted. But if Robert is involved, and therefore culpable for Clay's death, Mom will never survive. And I might be in as much danger as Martin.

"I hate this," I say and bite my tongue to keep from saying it's not fair.

I try to be generous with the idea that everyone has a hard life in his or her own way—but to be honest, my generosity's tapped out. My losses are over-the-top cruel. LaRue. Clay. Dad. Martin. Deuce.

I feel about a thousand and one years old. I want to be done. An undoing that's long overdue.

I don't lean into the feeling. Instead, I visualize myself on the shooting range. The weight and stiffness of my shooting coat. The heat. The smell. Ears stuffed with yellow foam. The shooting frame pinched against my nose. One eye blocked. The spotting scope in front of me. The familiarity of my stance—the way that turning sideways and closing my eyes with the butt of the rifle pressed against my shoulder empties my brain. You can't think when you're shooting. That is why I love it.

Tired has me by the throat. My eyes blur. The catfish fillets swim in and out of view. Still, we use the silence to consume food. That helps with the nausea roiling up my esophagus. When Parson's plate is empty, he rocks his chair onto two legs, closes his eyes, and props his muddy boots atop his very expensive table. V-shaped dirt falls out of the treads. I stare at the reddish mud.

Remnants of LaRue are always underfoot. We carry it with us.

I close my eyes again.

Martin is there. Practically in my eyelids. He looks as he did yesterday. Alive. Determined. Martin atop the dam morphs into Martin bleeding out in a duck blind. That Martin becomes a younger Martin, a roundish boy who stuck out his flabby hand and said, "You're prettier than I thought you'd be." Flabby Martin contours into the trim football player on the front page of the *Grand Junction Gazette*. *Gazette* Martin buckles the seat belt of my Nissan, tips his neck sideways with a precarious grin perched on his face, and says, "Luce, drive me somewhere I've never been."

The cycle wraps around itself, always looping to the duck blind.

Martin damaged. Martin dead.

Deuce. Dead.

Images, like moments, aren't made of equal weight. That last picture of them lying in the muck of the marsh will trump all others for the rest of my life. Like my last image of Clay.

Chapter Twenty-Four

Neil arrives and Owl leaves, saying he'll catch a ride back to the command tent. That we are to call him with any news and he will do the same. There's a strain between the two men as they pass each other.

We repeat the rigmarole of introductions between Neil and Dana. Galen's clearly the hit, but Neil's grateful that Owl has hired Dana to find Astrid. He's keeping it together, but only just.

The minute Parson sees Neil's casted hand he flips out. "What happened to you?"

"Hunting," Neil answers.

Parson gently taps the plaster surrounding Neil's wrist

with his fingernails. "Man," he says sympathetically. "How long will it keep you out of shooting?"

"Hopefully no longer than a month."

"Good." As an afterthought, Parson says, "Sorry. I shouldn't be talking about the Olympics. You guys probably don't care right now. I can't turn off my inner coach."

Neil and I exchange a glance. Do we care? Are we *allowed* to care about the thing we've been working toward forever? I'm not sure under the current circumstances. He isn't either given the screwed-up expression on his face. He works a box of orange Tic Tacs from his front pocket and lays them in my lap. The gesture coaxes weak smiles from us. Him and those stupid Tic Tacs. "I—"

Whatever he was going to say never becomes a sentence.

Dana plunges right into questioning Neil. "Can you make a list of everyone you saw when you were in LaRue yesterday?"

"I said I was hunting. I didn't mention LaRue," Neil says.

"Parson did, when he was bragging on your shooting abilities."

"Right." That puts Neil off-balance.

"So did you run into Martin or Deuce?"

"No," Neil says.

I don't interrupt or expose his lie. As a thank-you, he slides his foot to mine under the table and taps the sole lightly.

LaRue covers enough acreage the men could have all been there and not crossed paths, and yet it's small enough Neil had felt the need to promise me that he had nothing to do with anything that happened to Martin. At the time, we didn't even know that something had happened to Martin. He was missing, not dead.

Unless he was dead, rather than missing, to Neil.

The bodies were found in his duck blind.

No way. There is no way.

"What about Lucy?" she prods. "Can you confirm what time she left LaRue? Cameras will put her on the range, but it would be good to know when she left too."

"We didn't see each other until we were here," Neil says, thumb toward the hallway in the direction of the booth in the main restaurant. "That was probably five or so."

"What time did you leave?" she asks.

Parson answers for him. "You got here around four, yeah?"

Neil says, "I guess. I didn't look at the clock."

Dana arches her fingers in a prayer stance and then bounces her hands against the table. "So many people in LaRue," she says to herself. Then to Neil she says, "If you haven't already, you'll need to tell Owl your whereabouts. They'll want to talk to anyone near the scene during the time window of the murders. Maybe you saw a vehicle. Maybe you saw a hiker. Another hunter. Anything. All those pieces will be helpful."

Neil says, "The only thing I saw was the deer that did this"—he lifts the cast—"And I've already been questioned by the police because of my duck blind." He explains his connection to the murder scene to Dana and adds that he was questioned with his dad, Danny, earlier. "Dad's getting a lawyer, just in case," he offers. "Crazy that he has to do that since it's my sister who's missing. I need to get back out there."

I lift my hand to the window wall. "That weather plus pain meds is a bad idea, Neil."

"You sound like Owl."

"I sound smart," I argue, knowing how hard it is to sit here and do nothing.

"A lawyer is a great idea too," Dana says and yawns against her will. All of us follow suit. She says, "We need to get some real sleep to process this. Lucy, would you like a ride to your truck?"

Neil jumps up and pushes in his chair. "I'll take her."

Dana waits on me to nod my okay, which I give, then she raises her arms to full wingspan and expands her chest until the wrinkles in her polo are taut. For a split second, she reminds me of a younger version of my mother with her small frame. She sure has chosen a big job to go with that lean body. She says, "I'm meeting with the state police at four. The emergency management leader at five. Lucy, I'll call you with an update if there is anything I'm allowed to share. Galen, you ready?"

The dog lopes to her side, tail wagging.

The echo of her boots and Galen's nails clicking on the hardwood grows faint. Now that it's the three of us, I wonder if we might say more, but Parson stacks our empty plates and Neil says, "Okay."

It's his *I'm ready to go* okay. I've heard it a million times.

"Hey," Parson says to me. "When you were home, did you search Martin's room for his evidence?"

"Barely made it into the yard before Dana arrived," I say. "I will, though."

"What about you?" he asks Neil. "You been through Astrid's stuff?"

"No."

I can tell Neil hasn't even considered the idea.

Parson says, "There's at least another hour of fog before we can search outside. We might as well see if we can find something in either of their rooms, if the police haven't been there already."

"Mom and Robert are home," I say.

"Then we start with Astrid," Parson says. "Maybe we can figure out who she was meeting when she asked Wendy to cover for her."

Neil and I don't argue. We trudge behind our coach through the kitchen. When the exit door opens, a wall of fog slips inside. The water droplets are heavy enough my hair curls at the edges. We're across the parking lot and five feet from Parson's Ford F-150 Lightning before

I see the hulking truck. Which also means I hear a voice before I see someone leaning against the driver's side door. The man has his phone flat and raised to his lips like he might be leaving a memo or voice texting.

"Excuse me, sir," Parson says, assuming the stranger will step away.

He doesn't.

The man's clothes are off by an entire season and he has a sweaty look that suggests he's grown tired from standing. Jeans too long—the frayed hem wrapped under a pair of green flip-flops he's likely had for thirty years. His shirt, a Hawaiian design with overly large pink palm trees, doesn't cover all the skin of his belly. A handgun holster bulges at his side. If Jimmy Buffett starts a PI business, this guy will be first in line.

"Neil Clark?" he asks, hand thrust around Parson to Neil. "I'm an investigative podcaster for *Crew Time*. Like *True Crime*, but reversed."

Great, I think. Not finding him or the podcast title clever.

Before Neil takes his hand, I butt in: "We don't have anything to say."

Podcast knockoff Jimmy Buffett blows me off. "According to my sources, Martin Carlin and Officer Deuce Uri were murdered yesterday afternoon with a Ruger Precision Rifle, 6mm Creedmoor. Slugs between the eyes." He jabs his index finger into the wrinkles between his brows as if we need a demonstration of the location. He pauses dramatically. "Word is, you own a Ruger Precision Rifle, have a beef with the Carlin family, and are connected to the murder scene. Care to comment?"

Chapter Twenty-Five

I picture all the targets I've ever shot, the way bullets pierce the paper, and think of Martin's skull. Bile rises in my throat and I turn away, coughing, gagging with grief.

Whether from exhaustion or anger, Neil takes the podcaster's bait.

"Seriously?" His voice thunders through the fog. His fingers tighten into fists. "My sister is missing. My sister is *missing*! Get out of my face. *Now*."

Hitting a nerve, provoking conflict, that's this guy's goal. He's delighted when he says, "Missing or not, I've got leads, and they all point to you. Even if you didn't own a gun identical to the murder weapon, you're going to have to explain your documented vendetta against the Carlin family."

I brace myself, knowing what comes next even before he says, "Did you or did you not write a paper for your University of West Virginia environmental econ class that states"—he consults his phone for a precise quote—"'Grand Hydro should be shut down at all costs. The effects on the Tennessee River are criminal to the environment, and I fear that someone, maybe even myself, might have to do something radical in order to stop the Robert Carlins of the world.' End quote. So, Neil, does *radical* include killing Robert's son, Martin?"

Beside me, Parson's arm snakes up and around Neil's chest in the same second Neil lunges forward. Neil finds himself inside the cage of Parson's grip, with Parson in his ear saying, "Easy, brother. Easy. This dude's not worth jail."

Neil is a precise creature. Intentional. That's why he's such a good shot on the range. This unhinged, feral version isn't a side I recognize. Does Parson? If Parson loosened his hold, even a little bit, Neil would bust the podcaster in the face with his broken, plastered hand.

The podcaster takes a thoughtful step away from the truck, all while leaning forward with his chin, as if daring Neil to strike him. "From that response," he taunts, "I take it your *radical* does include hurting another human being."

"What's your name?" I snap.

"Seth Yarborough."

He has the nerve to thrust his hand in my direction. I snarl and he retracts. "Seth." I keep my voice even and sarcastic. "We would deeply appreciate you putting your investigative efforts into locating Astrid Clark and letting law enforcement handle what happened to Martin and Deuce."

"And I would deeply appreciate an interview after I share a copy of Neil's essay with law enforcement. I'll give you a chance to tell your story on air." He places a business card on the truck's bed rail. As he leaves, his flip-flop sticks to the asphalt, causing him to step out of the shoe entirely and stumble into the dumpster. He hurriedly jams his toes back into the foot strap and slinks away. Even with the flip-flop stutter, the round goes to Seth.

From the cause of death to the Ruger to the essay, he's done serious homework and must have an inside police source. He's also attached Neil to Parson enough to be waiting at Parson's truck. Luck? Or maybe he planned to speak with Parson first? Whatever he hoped, he got what he came for.

More of these encounters will happen. Seth Yarborough is merely the green-tinted sky, the warning of the coming storm. Neil will be first in the crosshairs of the media. The moment Seth shares that document, he'll be *a*, if not *the*, prime suspect.

The LaRue Dam Break of 2015 garnered loads of national attention. Since kids aren't media savvy, Owl coached us. He understood what people would ask before they asked. He understood the coverage would exist in perpetuity and had the foresight to understand we would not want to look back on our young, traumatized selves and cringe at our mistakes.

All the usual suspects turned up, each hungry for survivor and victim stories. Local hotels were so occupied with news personnel they couldn't initially support the homeowners affected by the flooding. As search and rescue efforts became search and recovery efforts, vans with small, mounted satellite dishes lined Main Street, and journalists with heavy black camera cases, tiny mics, and accentless voices became fixtures. They ate in our diners, visited our school, parked outside our homes. Videos of waterlogged yards, uprooted trees, and broken asphalt crowded social media. Drones and helicopters captured the widespread damage, but we were the human aspect: the kids who survived the break. And I was the girl who rescued Troop 1404 and lost her brother doing it.

I understood I was living history when the president of the United States came to Grand Junction. Barack Obama knocked on our farmhouse door, two Secret Service agents at his side, and in that slow, low, punctuated voice of his said, "Lucy Michaels, I'm sorry about your little brother. You were so, so brave." And then he hugged me. I tried to meet his eyes, but all I could think at the time was, *Even the president knows I failed.*

Our silence encouraged the big news moguls to move on to the terrorist attack in Paris. Thankfully, they didn't come back until Robert broke ground on Grand Hydro. That brought out all the bloggers, podcasters, and documentarians. In a world where everyone is one YouTube video away from *Good Morning America*, why wouldn't people shoot the videos with heartstrings and turn our survival story into the next miniseries paycheck?

All of them pissed me off. I actually kicked a reporter in the shins. He bought me an ice cream cone at Scoops and then held it above my reach when I didn't answer his questions. "If your little brother was with you, how did he end up in the water?" he asked, the mint chocolate chip cone a foot above my hand. He hammered away at me. "How do you feel about another dam going in? Is your mom dating Grand Hydro's builder?"

Man, I hated them.

They'll come again now. They'll ask all the hard questions. I want to run after Seth and kick him in the shins too.

Parson still has Neil in a reverse hold. "I'm letting you go. Behave," he warns.

Neil's cheeks are flush. He takes a long, deep breath and some of the tension releases from his shoulders.

Parson says, "I thought you were going to break his face."

"Me too," Neil agrees and awaits my judgment.

I have none for his response to Seth. Only for the essay that stoked the fire. "I told you to cut that line about Grand Hydro."

"I know."

He's mad about my "I told you so," but I don't care. *Don't write specific names or corporations.* I had been explicit in my advice. I'd done it selfishly, worried Robert would find out and leverage the information against Neil.

But Neil balked at the idea of holding back. If a dam break ruined your life, another dam isn't the answer.

The day Mom married Robert, Neil was sullen and wouldn't talk to me. I'd been looking forward to slow dancing at the reception. Instead, he told me all his secret concerns about Robert. Minutes before the wedding, he suggested I try to stop the ceremony. He wanted me to tell my mom how a man like Robert, with his environmental stance, was probably not a man of character.

I gave him a piece of my mind that included, but wasn't limited to, the fact that I didn't have control of who my mother fell in love with, and I certainly didn't have control of a multibillion-dollar hydroelectric project.

Not even for my boyfriend, the budding environmentalist.

In his defense, he was probably regurgitating stuff his dad taught him.

Even that line in the essay sounded like something Danny said. There's no real love between Danny and Robert. Though there might be now, given what they lived through this morning.

"I'm with Lucy on this one," Parson says. "You'd better get your apologies and sad face ready. They're going to eat you alive."

Parson loves Grand Hydro. Robert's success launched the restaurant beyond his wildest dreams. He stands atop the Ford's running board, door handle grasped firmly in his hand, and puts on his coach voice. "Come on, let's head to your house. We'll check Astrid's room and then you can take another codeine for that hand."

Once we're in the truck, Neil can't settle. He flips the Ford's vents up and down. "That essay doesn't mean I killed Martin. And Deuce. Gosh. I would never . . . Lucy, you know, right? You know I didn't kill them, don't you? I mean, I didn't like Martin or his dad, but I don't hunt people, and Deuce is like a brother."

"The idea's audacious," I say, hoping to comfort him, all the while considering his choice of phrase: *hunt people*.

The classification casts the crime, heinous as it is, in a new light. Ruger Precision Rifle. Long range. Was what happened to Martin and Deuce a *hunt*?

Parson starts the Ford and checks the rearview. There's only fog back there. He says, "Bud, regardless of what we know, the police will get a warrant for your Ruger."

Neil exhales.

I swivel. When you've grown up with someone the way we have, there are no poker faces. Neil's expression most closely mirrors guilt, and that scares me. "What?" I say.

Another sigh. Neil stares out the moonroof at the fog. "It's missing."

I give Neil a puzzled look. "Since when?"

He shakes his head. "Not sure. I noticed when I got back to my truck with the deer. It was gone from the back seat."

"You probably left it in West Virginia," I reason.

"No. I brought it home to sell."

That's news.

"Did you report it stolen?" Parson asks. "That's like a three-thousand-dollar gun."

"I didn't have time. My arm was broken."

That doesn't make sense.

Neil loves that rifle. The love anchored to quality and origin. When his grandfather died—the grandfather who taught him to shoot—he left all the grandkids an inheritance. There was never a minute Neil wavered on how to spend his. The Ruger Precision Rifle was arguably the best rifle on the market for his favorite style of hunting. Long distance. Big game. His grandfather would have loved the choice. Mr. Danny beamed at the idea.

Neil reboots the story. "It's not that I didn't have time.

I planned to tell Owl at the game, and then Martin turned up missing."

No, Martin turned up dead.

Maybe killed with Neil's gun.

Chapter Twenty-Six

I shove my phone at Neil and say, "Call Owl right now and tell him." Neil nods and makes the call.

I have an enormous early memory bank. Little snippets of my two, three, four, and up life. Things that must have happened within certain time windows because of where we lived, which dog was alive, whether Mom drove the station wagon or the Civic. Most memories are inconsequential. A weird blue shower cap Mom made me wear in the bath or the way water tasted from a certain pink Tupperware cup. Each snippet is an individual tile of a mosaic that makes up my childhood. Neil is not a single tile here or there. He's a primary color running through the whole piece of art.

I know him.

If he raises an eyebrow, I can write a five-page report on why.

But this? Nothing in my mental file suggests he's capable of gun negligence, and certainly not murder.

"I know it was stupid," he says to Owl. "To wait to tell you."

He's lucky Owl knows him well enough to give it to him through the phone rather than believe he's capable of murder. I massage the skin on my forehead, try to lessen the massive headache that has started to form.

"I can't shoot now anyway," Neil's telling Owl.

That's the dumbest response I've ever heard, and Neil isn't dumb. Not only that, he's principled. The guy turns around if a candy wrapper flies out his truck window on a country road. Even if it's a hundred degrees and he's late for school, he won't litter. Also, he won't buy dollar candy at Walmart to slip into the movie theater. Any guy like this reports a missing firearm immediately. In this world of school shootings and public violence, you have to. My Neil never, ever jacks around with gun responsibility.

Do I need to reckon with the idea there's a new Neil or—and I hate this idea—a Neil I never truly knew? He's off the phone and I'm hot.

"Don't judge me when you don't know the story," he begs.

"Well then, I'm asking for the story."

"And I can't give it to you."

I lay into him. "For Pete's sake, Neil, what if Seth Yarborough is right? What if it's not a gun *like* yours that killed Martin and Deuce; what if it's your gun? You were in LaRue during the murders. Your blind was where the bodies were found. You hate the Carlins. Everything he said is right."

Without a word, Neil launches himself out of the truck and slams the door hard enough to rock the Ford. He disappears into the fog. In response, Parson lowers the window so I have a four-inch crack of cold, hazy air.

"I'll get him," he says.

Five minutes later, my coach returns with Neil. Neil glances up from his boots, the side of his mouth twitching like he might lose it. He tugs the bill of his hat lower on his forehead. Before he is all the way into the truck, I start an apology.

"Hey," I say. "I'm tired and scared and sad and I don't like that you're making decisions that don't sound like the guy I know and . . . I'm sorry. I know you need support. This is a terrifying situation for you. I know Astrid is missing, and I'm the last person who should make this harder since I know how desperate it feels when a sibling is missing."

A sigh ebbs away.

"I came home this weekend to sell the Ruger for you, and that's all I want to say right now." He lies back in his seat and closes his eyes, the matter anything but settled, but clearly off the table for discussion.

I want to ask why but I don't. Parson keeps the windows cracked and the air twists the flyaways from my braids. The truck is drenched with pit barbecue smoke and the distinct smell of fall—of the fields and forests dying. Sinking deeper into the leather of Parson's Ford, I curl my knees to my chest and hide my face in the crevice. I inhale the grass from our yard in the denim fabric of my jeans. The smell of losing Martin.

That was only hours ago.

Martin will never drink Yoo-hoo again. Or listen to a YouTube video from MrBeast. Or leave a soda can in the corner of our shower.

That makes me laugh nostalgically in my head. Martin chose the guest room over the bedroom en suite that Robert's designer built specifically for him. His toothbrush showed up one day, his shampoo the next, his shaving kit the day after that. The little stubbles he refused to wash down the sink made me fuss daily. And why in dear heavens couldn't he install the toilet paper in the normal, humane over-the-roll fashion?

I cry quietly.

He'll never shuffle into my room and bounce on the side of my bed and say, "Let's go to the Humane Society, adopt a dog, and name it Cat. Wouldn't that be awesome?"

There's a slight shake to the center of my back, but if Parson and Neil notice, they have too much going on to comfort me.

"Neil." Parson uses a fatherly tone when he says Neil's name. "Do you think the Ruger was stolen here or in West Virginia? Like, could someone have taken it from your truck there?"

"No. It was definitely here. And—" Neil passes his cell to Parson.

Parson holds the phone at the center of the wheel and snatches glances at the screen as he drives. "I see the problem." He hands the phone to me.

Neil's phone is on TikTok. A video posted by Neil and dated Thursday morning shows Neil in full camouflage, lying on the ground with the rifle on its tiny tripod. The type reads, *Ruger Precision at 2300 meters.* He sights, fires. A paired video clip speeds up his walk between the rifle and target. The camera zooms in; he's within the bull's-eye. Military-level sniper skill. Type reads, *#sniperbaby.* And then Neil voices over the video, "Kill shot. Woot. Woot."

The skill required for that shot . . . Wow. He's one of the most impressive marksmen I've ever seen. I hand the phone over my shoulder to Neil and say, "Take that video down."

He shrugs helplessly. "Do I take them all down? Is it a crime to be a good shot? 'Cause if so, you're a suspect too, Luce."

"No," I say. "I have an alibi, and all you have is free time in LaRue until four."

Chapter Twenty-Seven

That was cruel of me. To point out the worst. It shuts us all down.

My brain is in a tailspin.

Where is Astrid? Whose blood is on Martin's Hummer? Martin's or Deuce's? Who stole Neil's gun? Was Martin right about Tamerlane and Robert paying off Deuce and the dam break and that's why he's dead? Is there any possibility Martin's and Deuce's deaths are random?

Those are the large-picture questions; the closer we drive to Neil's house, the more I consider the two attached solely to him.

Why did Neil make such a big deal of telling me last

night that he didn't hurt Martin? And why did he tell us that he didn't report his gun stolen because his arm was broken when he didn't break his arm until later in the evening, after he saw me at Parson's?

The *tick-tick, tick-tick* of the blinker brings me forward. We've arrived.

The Clarks have a garage they never park in and a carport they use as a patio. The driveway normally holds any number of vehicles, and I expected to find it crammed with friends and family. Instead, no one is home and anxious barks escape from Astrid's caramel-colored shepherd-pit mix.

Neil hushes Paco Taco with a scrub to his head and opens the Clarks' door with a code I know by heart. Without a thought, we kick off our shoes, launch them toward the mat, and pound up the steps toward the landing adjacent to Neil's and Astrid's rooms the way we did when we were much younger.

The house, a split-level, built in the 1970s, smells of animals, Febreze, and cigarette smoke. Not a scent I particularly love, but one I attach to the Clarks. The carpets on the upper floors are painfully original: golden shag. Between Astrid's and Neil's doors hangs an overlarge metal sign from the Dollar General that reads "Family First." Framed candid photographs and various awards are displayed floor to ceiling on all the remaining wall space. Neil actively avoids eye contact with the photos.

Astrid's door has crime scene tape stretched from

molding to molding. The yellow plastic clashes with the carpet.

Parson caresses the tape. "I wonder when they came."

Neil sinks into the carpet and massages the long tufts of golden shag. "What if we don't find her? What if people think I killed them? I'll go to prison. No Olympics," he says, and that almost breaks my heart in two.

Parson stands beside a crouching Neil. Parson somehow manages to look confident and lost at the same time. Splotchy red patches snake up Neil's neck and onto his cheeks, robbing him of all his handsome features: his smile, those lips, his perfect skin. His sunglasses slide forward in his hair and sit askew at the top of his head. Tears start to leak from his eyes and he pulls his sunglasses down. Parson awkwardly pats his shoulder.

I can't take it. I check Astrid's door. Locked. I leave the guys upstairs and head to the Clarks' garage, find the extension ladder that reaches the carport roof, and prop it against the gutter as Paco Taco barks his disapproval. In the course of my relationship with Neil, Astrid let me through her second-story window, the one nearly flush with the carport's roof, no less than a hundred times. Neil's principles never agreed with his mother's when it came to curfew.

Astrid's window slides open without a complaint. I climb through the opening and onto her lavender bedspread, taking a second to dust the leaves and shingle particles from my knees. Her room is maybe twelve by twelve, and most of it is taken up by the bed. What little space remains belongs to a computer desk and music center.

Where Neil has deer heads on his walls, Astrid has manga, music posters, and guitars. Strings of LED programmable lights are mounted to the molding; they're currently off, but if I switch them on, they'll be a chain of blinking purple joy, Astrid's favorite. The room feels warm and alive with Astrid's presence, and I bask in momentary hopefulness.

Neil and Parson hear me and call out, "You shouldn't be in there."

Still, when I unlock the door, Parson ducks under the crime scene tape and joins me while Neil peers at the seam where the golden hallway shag meets the navy blue plush of Astrid's room, like a tiger will eat him if he crosses the line.

"What are we looking for?" I ask.

"Anything that might tell us where she is," Parson answers.

"The police marked this off," Neil says. And then asks, "Should you maybe have on gloves?"

I have no idea what I should do at this point except try to find something they missed. A rectangular ring of dust on the lower desk shelf says the police removed her CPU from the aged desktop.

"Did she have a Chromebook and an iPhone?" Parson asks.

Neil nods. "They would have been in her backpack or in her hand."

Parson casts around for anything useful. "Does it look like the police removed anything?" He addresses Neil, who looks ashamed and admits that he hasn't been in here since early summer.

Parson turns to me and I sag onto the edge of the bed, thinking.

Normally when I pass through here Astrid's watching *Minecraft* on YouTube. That gives me one idea. I crawl across her comforter toward the bed's edge. The mattress presses against the wall, but I reach inside her pillow for what I know I'll find: a cushioned lap desk. Inside, an old iPad is tucked into a hidden pocket between the desk surface and the cushion. If it's connected to the same iCloud account as her phone, we'll have access to her most recent texts. I power it on.

"Brilliant," Parson says when her messages come up.

Neil flops down too, his hands raised, like he's afraid to touch anything. The mattress tilts inward with their added weight as they lean toward me and the iPad. Our hips and shoulders knock together as we stare at the screen.

The account connects.

We wait, holding our breath, as we scroll to the most recent messages. Nothing new has pinged through since Friday, yesterday, at 11:43 a.m. The last conversation stored in the iPad is between Astrid and Deuce. I read.

ASTRID: I know.

DEUCE: What???

ASTRID: The dam break. Where your money comes from.

ASTRID: Martin is going to tell. You should do something.

DEUCE: Meet me at VCB at 1:30?

ASTRID: K

DEUCE: Need a ride?

ASTRID: I'll kayak from the put-in at Greenwood Church.

Chapter Twenty-Eight

The exchange between Deuce and Astrid doesn't shed light on Astrid's intentions with the text—is she warning Deuce or threatening him? It does, however, place Astrid in LaRue. Which is what we thought, but seeing the text solidifies her location. Owl needs to know she's there somewhere and so is her kayak.

I reread the texts.

There's control and precision. If Martin and Deuce weren't dead and Astrid weren't missing, a threat between them, even the notion of a threat, would be ridiculous. Now the possibility has to be considered. Or Astrid might have been saying that Deuce should confess about the money because it was no longer a secret.

Either potentially puts Astrid in danger. Maybe for knowing some type of payoff had occurred.

Astrid's brilliant—the kind of brilliance that spins her brain at a different angle and on a different axis than most everyone else. She's also deeply opinionated about whatever she is deeply passionate about at any given moment. Everything from perfecting green food coloring in milkshakes to what the Supreme Court is doing to "ruin her life" to which Boston museums she wants season passes to when she arrives at Harvard.

She, like Neil, follows strange morality rules.

The whole Clark family does.

Hers are less predictable than Neil's. Like sitting one seat over from an assigned seat in an empty theater will make her panic. However, in the same breath, she'll make wild, psychotic suggestions about what should happen to certain politicians who disagree with her beliefs. She follows up most of her political commentary with an airy, "Am I right?" that makes everyone the slightest bit nervous about who might be listening.

I love her. She's family, and she's charming . . . until she's not. I look to Neil for some sort of interpretation, something to make sense of Astrid's texts. And then to Parson, who swore there was no money.

"I have no idea," Neil says.

"Me either," Parson agrees.

They're both sweating.

We read again.

ASTRID: I know.

DEUCE: What???

ASTRID: The dam break. Where your money comes from.

ASTRID: Martin is going to tell. You should do something.

DEUCE: Meet me at VCB at 1:30.

ASTRID: K

DEUCE: Need a ride?

ASTRID: I'll kayak from the put-in at Greenwood Church.

The exchange between these two doesn't completely compute.

Parson speaks first. "VCB?"

I run the letters again and again through my lexicon of Grand Junction and LaRue locations until I have a guess. "Vespers Creek Bridge?"

VCB isn't a known abbreviation for the covered bridge, but in this context, it makes more sense than anything else. But if Astrid and Deuce were communicating for the first time, VCB wouldn't mean anything. Had they had a previous conversation? Met up some other time? Were they in a relationship and we missed it? Not impossible. Astrid's beautiful, and underage, but attraction is bad at morals. And Wendy did infer Astrid was hooking up with someone.

I scroll backward in their text conversation; nothing

but a bunch of GamePigeon games. She either deleted messages, used a different app, or talked to him in person. Then I check Wendy's thread. There are fifteen messages that get progressively more panicked as the night wore on and Astrid didn't respond.

We're all considering what we know and, more importantly, what we don't.

Two hundred sixteen thousand dollars is reason enough to do something criminal, but Deuce has never cared about money. In my memory, all Deuce has ever wanted is to be a cop and impress his father. If Owl were a janitor or a zookeeper, Deuce would have bought a mop or a monkey. There's no way Deuce would get mixed up with Robert or Tamerlane for money. And he certainly wouldn't hurt Astrid.

Neil stands, and the absence of his weight sends me careening into Parson, who instantly scoots away with the iPad.

I grab Astrid's LED controller and switch it on, smiling when purple flashes on her walls. Parson runs his thumbs up and down the screen, reading and rereading the messages between Astrid and Deuce.

Neil stops pacing and looks over Parson's shoulder. "I can't tie Astrid to Deuce to Martin. Deuce is a million years older and Astrid and Martin weren't friends."

"They were friends," I say, thinking of Martin's fondness of and fascination with Astrid. He liked to turn her loose on a topic just to watch her go. He thought it was like setting a windmill in motion. At lunch, he'd look at her and say, "Five scientific reasons time travel could exist. Go." And boy, could she go. Everyone else at the table was lost in the first few mentions of an Einstein-Rosen bridge, but Martin stayed in rapt attention. I used to tease him about having a crush on her.

"Man, he was everywhere, wasn't he?" Neil says, and looks tempted to let his good fist fly against the closet door. Instead, he does the action in slow motion and stops inches from the wood.

I scoot off the mattress and stand on Astrid's clothes-strewn floor. Neil has his back partially to me. "Martin genuinely liked you, Neil." I know, I'm sure, because Neil was partially the topic of my last conversation with Martin.

Neil scoffs at my assertion and bends, busying himself with a collection of ponytail holders on Astrid's carpet. "Sounds like your saintly stepbrother could have been threatening Deuce. Our Deuce."

"So was your sister," I say, although not unkindly.

Neil clearly wants to fight, but something mounting in Parson's expression stops us both. He's watching something on the iPad with the sound off. When I say his name, he doesn't respond. I move toward the bed. "What is it?"

He lifts the iPad out of view.

Fueled with frustration, I rip the device from his

hands. There's a blurry, jolted-image video. Taken at 3:48 p.m. yesterday.

"What is this?" I crank the volume.

A distorted voice commands, "Underwater, baby."

Chapter Twenty-Nine

I slide the video cursor all the way to the left.

Rewatch.

Relisten.

The voice. The helter-skelter framing. A scuffling, crinkling noise. A flash of dark fabric, a bright red bloom, a snippet of gray daylight before the screen goes black.

That snippet. I rewind and slow the video.

Each frame tells me more.

The dark fabric isn't a solid color. I enlarge the image and pinch my fingers, rolling over brown, green, and black fabric. Camouflage.

The bright red bloom is next.

Slowed down, there's more than one color here as well.

I isolate the red, scroll forward, backward. A flash of peach, very blurred, maybe hair follicles, comes before the red. Then the red covers the lens.

I rewatch three times to clarify: the peach is the skin of her arm; the red, blood dropped from somewhere above her, a splatter landing partially on the lens.

Daylight shines next.

There's an infinitesimal portion of the screen not eclipsed by the blood and light. In that tiny space is the blurry outline of a man, caught from the waist up. He's in camouflage, his face hidden behind a bright green balaclava. But his frame reminds me of Neil's.

The phone smacks the surface of the water.

A gurgle.

A slow descent. The lens lands aimed at the creek bed.

But before it goes dark, shadows pass over the reflection and darken the image of the mud.

I turn the iPad volume up, hoping to catch anything else.

I do.

Astrid's muffled cry.

Spellbound and horrified, I move the video timeline backward again and watch from beginning to end. This confirms that Astrid turned the camera on while it was still in her pocket. Maybe she slipped it up her shirt. The rustling sounds support that phone movement.

She catches the voice.

"Underwater, baby."

If the devil were Southern, he'd sound like that. The pitch is low, too low to determine the age of the speaker. I rule out someone younger than me or old like PoppaJack. I force myself to listen to the audio with my eyes closed, isolating the sound. "Underwater, baby."

The slow, crusty way he says *baby*.

I rewind. Listen.

"Underwater, baby."

Have I heard that voice before?

I can't be sure. The voice is an imitation. I search my memories, strain my brain. Where do I know him from?

I nearly drop the iPad.

Orson Welles. The voice Astrid captured sounds identical to Orson Welles. Deuce is the only reason I know Orson Welles has a distinctive voice. He made me—all of us—watch *Citizen Kane* on our fifteenth birthdays. I hate the film, and every time Deuce brings up "the masterpiece that is *Citizen Kane*," I remind him that I gave him two hours of my life I will never get back.

The correlation makes me throw up in my mouth.

So does the number of times Neil has mimicked that voice.

Oh, Astrid. Oh no. This can't be. It just can't be. I look accusingly at Neil, but he's not reacting to the voice at all. His hand's stretched toward the iPad like he can reach through the device and save his sister.

"Play it again," Parson says.

Shaking, I hit Play and we watch one more time.

I focus on the green balaclava. Every football player at Grand Junction has one. They were all over the place at the search yesterday. One Friday night under the stadium lights, not long ago, Deuce said, "Man, Cleary County still gives out those ugly balaclavas for outdoor sports? We had those back in my day on the baseball team. Come on, Booster Club, step into the next generation."

Tears crowd Neil's lower eyelids and speed down his cheeks. His glasses fog. I wrap my arm around his waist and pull him tight to my side.

He starts to sob.

Parson's face hardens, his jaw stiff, his eyes filled with fury. "That brave girl. Too bad you can't see who that is. Play the audio again." He lowers his ear to the iPad.

I don't want to put Neil through it, but he wants to hear too, and I oblige. "Do you recognize him?" I ask.

Neil shakes his head slowly. His eyes glaze over.

Is he thinking about Orson Welles and all the imper-sonations over the years?

Surely.

It's all I hear now.

Parson releases a frustrated, angry laugh. "Video, audio, and nothing. Whoever this guy is, he got seriously lucky."

Chapter Thirty

Time stops while we watch the video.

My cell rings three times before I register the sound and answer. I'm not sure I can speak. In the split second of seeing Mom's name and hitting Accept, I ready myself.

"Where are you, baby?" she asks.

Baby.

I cringe at a word that usually makes me feel loved and seen.

"At the Clarks'," I answer, feeling guilty as I look from Neil to Parson, as though we've been caught in Astrid's room by the police instead of my mother.

"I woke up and you weren't here and I panicked. I wasn't angry with you earlier, baby. I was so upset."

"I know, Mom. I'm with Parson and Neil."

"Good. Poor Neil. Molly's here. They came over after the police left their house. She was comforting me and I was comforting her right back and neither of us knew what to say. We can't believe this. Their duck blind. Our boys. This is Grand Junction! How can this happen?"

The town's betrayal looms over us again and again. The dam break, now this. In between, we were lulled into safety with births, weddings, Fourth of July celebrations, school picnics, parades, state championships, new businesses, great days. The great days far outweighed our worst, but our worst are so bad they color everything else.

Evil came, left, and boomeranged.

It came with a rifle and a scope.

It came in a single word. *Hunted.*

It came with a voice: "*Underwater, baby.*"

I keep the description simple. "We've been trying to retrace Astrid's day yesterday. Seeing if we can come up with anything that might help Owl and Dana Jones locate her. We need to be, you know, doing something. I can't help Martin anymore, but Astrid . . ."

"I envy you," she says.

"Mom—"

"No, I do. I really do. You're so strong and I fall apart on you every time."

"It's okay."

"Is it? Is it okay to need you this much?" There's a rattle in her words. A sharp intake of air.

"Yeah," I say. It's strangely comforting. If she needs me, I'm the strong one, and if I'm the strong one, I have to keep going. Her needing me is the gasoline that powers my resiliency.

"But what do *you* need?" she asks. "You loved Martin too. And Deuce. But especially Martin."

"I did, Mom. I loved him a lot."

Neil's response to my statement is minor, but there. He tightens his left hand around his exposed right thumb and squeezes until his nail and the skin beneath it turn three shades redder than the rest of his arm. I lay my own hand on his to stop him.

"You must need something," she says.

"Answers. Astrid." *Neil to be innocent. My mother to never find out about Tamerlane or Robert trying to buy LaRue before the dam break.* "How's Owl?"

"Not good at all," she says, but given the fact that she doesn't elaborate, I'm fairly sure he hasn't approached Robert for financial records yet.

"Have you all talked to the police officially yet?" I ask.

"We have to go in the morning," she says. "Baby"—there's that word again—"would you come home for a while? I shouldn't, but I need you."

"I'm on my way."

After Clay, after Dad, when life was the two of us, *I*

need you meant she had a rock—a palm-sized three-pound stone—pressed to her skin, rubbing the rough edge against her body like sandpaper. On a good day, she targeted her thigh. On a bad, her forehead. She eroded the skin into dark, bloody patches. "Crying isn't enough," she told me back then. "This is how my soul feels."

I felt things too, but not like she did.

My feelings mostly held to logic; they ran like planes on charted flight plans. Hers ran willy-nilly. And Dad's . . . Well, I can't even begin to get my head around his. Before LaRue, I thought he was the strongest man on the planet. Turned out, he thought the same, and LaRue was his reckoning.

He left his children on the other side of the creek. And Steve Michaels could not continue to exist in that narrative. Logic told me he was hurting too, but I struggled not to hate him for leaving us. I never held that kind of hate for my mom, which didn't seem fair either.

"Mom." I speak so the guys won't hear. "Put the rock down."

"I don't have the rock," she says. "I'm not . . . I didn't mean I need you like that. I meant I want to see you. I want to hug you and hold you and know you're safe."

My heart floods with surprising, overwhelming affection. She called *for me*, not to ask something of me. "I've gotta go home," I say to Parson, and this time my voice quivers and my eyes fill with tears. "Mom, I'll be there soon." I end the call.

"Your mom in bad shape?" Parson asks.

Parson understands loss differently too. Maybe because his parents abandoned him to be raised by Auntie. Neil and Astrid grew up with both parents while the rest of us grew up with the idea that adults eventually timed out.

I save face and let him believe this is another time Mom needs me instead of the other way around.

Aside from Neil, Martin is, *was*, my closest friend, and I can't say that to Neil. Parson either. Although he's guessed, since Martin came to the shooting range with me every day. When Neil left for college, Martin stepped into his time slot. Riding through LaRue. Timing parachute sprints at the track—he really wanted to start varsity before the end of the season. Hiding out on the upper deck of the house in two BarcaLoungers, the Tennessee River below us, the stars above. On the weekends we stayed up until two or three in the morning talking about Paris and what we'd see when we were there (in the hopes that I would get there).

Robert took Martin to the Louvre as a child, and Martin was eager to see if his favorite places were as grand as he remembered. "Oh, you'll love such and such," he'd say. "They have chocolate eclairs that'll make you wish you had ten stomachs. Or at least, they did." He'd sound anxious and I'd feel his longing for me to love Paris the way he had.

"It'll be the Olympics," I'd said. "Even if the eclairs are terrible, it'll be epic." I'd meant it, and I'd also been slightly worried how I would divide my time between Martin and Neil when we were there. I couldn't leave Martin to his chocolate eclairs, and I couldn't imagine the three of us sharing a table in a patisserie. I wanted the three of us to move toward a way to exist together. I had room for both of them in my life.

There would never be Paris with Martin and Neil. Maybe never Paris at all.

"You should check on your mom and dad," I tell Neil. "This video. It's going to change the investigation. Encourage your mom not to watch it, okay?"

Neil's unresponsive. He's a shell of himself.

"Hey, this video will help your case." *No one else knows you can imitate Orson Welles.* "You don't have one of those balaclavas, and you were probably long gone from LaRue by the time this was filmed. No one will believe you hurt Astrid. You were probably at the Landing already," I say, trying to remind him of the one good thing the video would do: send investigators in another direction.

"I think I was still out there driving around then." Without a word, he goes and sits in the bottom of Astrid's closet with his back to us.

Parson slides Astrid's iPad into the band of his jeans at the small of his back. "Come on. I'll get you home and take this to Owl."

I let him guide me to the door. On my way out, I squeeze Neil's shoulder. "Call me later?" I say, hoping I can pierce his sadness.

He turns and lifts his eyes to mine, and then he reaches up and takes one of my braids into his left hand. He caresses the part below the ponytail holder, the part he calls my paintbrush. "Sure," he says, but I don't think he'll call.

During the drive between Neil's house and mine, Parson and I don't manage seat belts, words, or music. He barely manages stop signs. The iPad has to be dealt with. Owl needs to read the text conversation, watch the video, and share both with the investigative team. The Kentucky State Police. The FBI. Dana. The short scene Astrid captured will be studied frame by frame. Analyzed against Neil's body type and height. It needs to be shared far and wide to see if anyone recognizes the voice.

"You'll give Owl—"

"Yes," Parson affirms.

"You're wrong about the balaclava," he says quietly.

"What do you mean?"

"Neil has one." Parson unlocks his phone, opens photos, and finds Christmas two years before. The location isn't identifiable, but Parson and Neil pose in front of a large Fraser fir, axes raised. Both are wearing a Cleary County bright green balaclava. "And then there's the *Citizen Kane* voice thing . . ."

"Deuce!"

"I know," he says with the same worry I feel.

That's where my brain cuts off.

Where the exhaustion hits.

Pulling onto River Road unleashes a deep need for

sleep, or at least to close my eyes and shut myself away from the world. So many unknowns, but one thing I know for sure: I miss Martin. Even his stupid Coke can in my shower.

At home, I scurry from the Ford, wanting to get to Mom. Halfway to the back door, I turn, feeling so completely unfettered I'm not sure if I can make it inside the house without help. Parson idles the gigantic Ford, hands at ten and two; he stares sideways, toward Grand Hydro and the concrete batching company down the hill, and then he puts his head on the wheel. His body shakes with wave after wave of grief. I shouldn't watch as long as I do; I haven't seen Parson cry since Clay's funeral. Even the strongest among us break.

Inside the house, heavy metal notes of AC/DC, clanking weights, and grunts of strain and pain fill the downstairs. Robert is clearly in the home gym numbing his brain with a workout. Good for him. And better for me if we don't interact. I head upstairs in search of Mom. On the second floor, at the opposite end of the hall from mine and Martin's rooms, I find her boots beside the entrance to our Harry Potter closet. One of three closets shaped by staircases.

The designated Harry Potter closet is one of the few things Mom insisted on maintaining long after I outgrew my wizarding hopes and dreams. During pre–LaRue Dam Break days, Mom and Dad laid a futon mattress over the linoleum floor and hung Christmas lights from the steps overhead. In winter, when the house temperature dropped, they crawled onto the maroon pillow pile and made a place between their shoulders for Clay and me to snuggle. We read hundreds of library books—everything from *James and the Giant Peach* to Kate DiCamillo's entire works.

"Baby," Mom whispers, arms outstretched, when I peer inside.

Underwater, baby.

I quiet that voice. The evil of the day.

"Hey," I say, already on my knees, crawling toward the crook in her arm.

"You won't go, will you?" she asks, like I know the number of my days.

"No," I assure. I lay my face on her chest. I smell the skin between the collar of her T-shirt and neck and the fabric softener saturating her clothes. I feel the roughness of the GJHS embroidered letters of her sweatshirt. She hasn't changed clothes either.

"It doesn't feel safe to close my eyes," she says. "But I'm so, so tired."

"Let's read," I offer, and I pick up the worn copy of *Harry Potter and the Prisoner of Azkaban* and start chapter one. We fall asleep before Ron's attempt to phone Harry during the summer holiday.

Hours later, Dana Jones sends a text that ends a string of nightmares and begins new ones.

DANA: Call me. Judge issued an arrest warrant for Neil.

Chapter Thirty-One

I inch out of Mom's arms and close the Harry Potter closet door. Then I make my way to the roof patio to call Dana. She doesn't answer and I fire off a few quick texts.

> **LUCY:** Did Parson show you the video?
> **LUCY:** What happens next?
> **LUCY:** Neil did not do this.

Three dots appear. Disappear.

Three blue whale breaths. I ground myself with the surroundings.

It's Sunday morning. The day is warming, the sun a shade of yellow that belongs solely to fall. I shield my eyes from the glare off the water. The pumpkins on our lawn are starting to cave inward from their carvings. The birds crack mussels on the banks of the Tennessee River.

The fog's gone.

The searchers will be out. All we have to do is find Astrid and she can tell everyone that Neil didn't do anything.

I think of the video.

People should follow the creeks. They should bring in dogs and sonar technology. *Underwater, baby.* They should drag the river and the backwater. Find her kayak. They should check the Duck Pond for her body.

Dana's response buzzes.

DANA: He needs a lawyer. A good one.

DANA: I've seen the video. Chilling. Owl released to
social accounts. Robert put up a $100k reward
for evidence leading to arrest.

DANA: You'll be officially questioned. Robert too.
Come in.

LUCY: Can you and Galen be there with me?

DANA: I'll ask Owl.

DANA: There's something else. They found the
murder weapon.

DANA: It's Neil's.

I leave the roof and spend the next three hours search-ing Martin's room for whatever evidence he claimed he had. The room hasn't been formally searched yet, but it will be. I'm looking blindly for some type of paper or digital record incriminating Robert's former company. In my mind, that evidence is what killed Martin and Deuce, not Neil. The longer I search, the more I'm convinced Neil has nothing to do with this. Still, I can't find anything helpful. Now is the time to ask my stepdad about the $216,000 he supposedly transferred to Deuce. I can't wait any longer.

I have a terrible thought. Will the Olympic committee find out about the arrest? Can they boot Neil from the team for all this? I shouldn't be thinking about the Olympics, but it's hard not to. He can't go to prison.

He's going to Paris. We're going to Paris.

Before I change my mind, I march down our three flights of stairs to find Robert. He's sitting at the booth in the kitchen, flipping through a photo album. Martin's baby book.

Robert, so in the thick of memories, doesn't notice me until I put a mug of coffee on his placemat. "He didn't sleep all night until he was two," he says absently. "Before Lana had him, we sat through all these parenting classes that essentially added up to 'Don't shake babies.' I remember asking what sort of idiot shakes a baby. But I wanted him to stop crying so badly that I understood why the pediatrician put that advice in bold." Robert reaches for the coffee, tests the temperature with his upper lip, and laughs at the memory. "Terrible baby. A rotten baby. Then she died, and every time he cried it was like his little statement that he was still alive. I loved that cry then. It kept me going."

"Clay had colic," I say, remembering a time at the farmhouse when he wouldn't stop crying either. He'd been oneish. I'd been wearing Mom's Justin Bieber concert T-shirt as a nightgown, and in that period of time I wouldn't shower unless you bribed me with Star Wars movies. I'd wanted to shake him quiet too.

"I never thought I'd understand your mom like this," Robert says, more to himself than to me. His eyes drift up to the album, his despair raw enough to chap his skin. "Doesn't feel real."

"No," I agree and steady myself to ask the hard questions. "I need your help. I know you're still angry about earlier, but I can't wait."

Robert stops the coffee mug at his lips and peers over the rim. The *What?* unspoken but said all the same.

I lean toward the hallway to make sure Mom isn't lingering and then run my thumb over the worn corner of the baby album. This will hurt Robert, and he's already hurting. His eyes are bloodshot, the skin beneath puffy from crying. I understand the reality that faces him. He'll wake up every day for the rest of his life in a world where he's outlived his son; the same as I wake up every day knowing Clay never went to second grade or grew tall enough to ride a roller coaster or pop a pimple or drive a car or . . .

I play the conversation out in my head first. There

are a million ways he might respond. He could offer a rational explanation. Blow up with anger. Or heartbreak. The drumming of his fingers on the marble tells me his patience is thin.

"Tell me," he says, and for once he sounds like a father instead of a businessman.

The first words burst out. "They're going to question me. The police. They'll question you too."

"I know. You don't have to be scared."

"No," I say, because he doesn't know. He thinks he does, but he doesn't. "They're going to ask if you were giving Deuce money. Lots of money. Like $216k. They might even ask you if had anything to do with the dam break."

"Excuse me," Robert says, but there's something in his indignation that tells me he's listening.

I drop my voice to a whisper. "Martin and I were in LaRue on Friday because he thought you or Tamerlane had something to do with the dam break. He got an email from your broker about some money you were giving Deuce each month. He said he talked to you and you said that wasn't true, but then he found out you were trying to buy LaRue from PoppaJack before you met us. And he thought he had something on you, but he wasn't sure."

"I see." His words are measured, and I can't tell where he is.

"Martin got himself into something from your past

and maybe it got him killed, or maybe it didn't, but now Neil's been arrested for his murder. He needs a lawyer. We probably all need lawyers. Owl said I should tell you. Trust you. So this is me tipping you off or whatever."

"This feels more like you begging me for a lawyer for Neil and accusing me of a heinous crime."

"It is, but it's also for you. I don't care what you did. Well, maybe I do, but not right now. I know you would never hurt Martin or Mom intentionally, and I'm putting that first. Putting you first. But I need you to help Neil."

"Thank you," he says, and he sounds genuine.

"So you'll help?" I ask. He has the resources to get Neil the best lawyer in the country. "The Clarks probably can't . . ."

My words trail away.

Robert knows their situation. Danny, a park ranger; Molly, a preschool teacher. Neil's college tuition and Olympic pursuits have tapped every ounce of cash and credit they have. Before our fight, Neil told me his parents have more than thirty thousand dollars in credit card debt because of him and they want to downsize their house to pay off that debt. They evidently can't. The success of Grand Hydro exponentially raised the housing market in Cleary County. Three-bedroom homes that used to be eighty thousand are selling for three to four hundred thousand. With that market, they can sell, but they can't buy. Another reason Neil hates Grand Hydro.

"Do you know why the police are arresting Neil?" he asks.

Do I tell him about the weapon? Does he already know?

I opt for the truth. "His Ruger was stolen out of his truck on Friday and police are saying it's the murder weapon."

Robert acknowledges this information by raising his eyebrows. "Hmm. So Neil was home from school when Martin . . ." He doesn't finish the sentence.

"He was, and he was in LaRue hunting. While he was out there, someone took his other rifle from the truck and used it to . . ." I don't say Martin's name. "You can imagine how that looks with the duck blind and all."

There's an audacity in asking Martin's father to pay to defend the man who will likely be a main suspect in the murder, even if you don't add the fact that Neil hates Robert and that's probably public knowledge. I think of the hunger in Seth Yarborough's expression in the parking lot. He'll post Neil's essay and count the comments as they roll in.

Robert arches his back and stares at the vaulted ceiling. "I can."

Encouraged that he hasn't automatically turned me down, I keep going. "We don't want the investigation stalled on Neil because of coincidence. Every minute they focus on him, the real murderer gets away. Astrid doesn't have that time. If you saw the video I did, you'd understand. She's in danger. And Molly and Danny don't have the money." There, I've said it. I've asked. I tie it off with, "He could go to prison for the rest of his life. Please. Please. Help me."

Robert reopens the baby book to a photo of his first wife, bare-chested, a one-day-old Martin—tiny blue cap covering his head—pressed against her breast. "Did you know Neil graffitied Grand Hydro last summer?" he says.

"Wh-at?" I stammer.

Somewhere nearby, probably in the formal dining room, a cell phone rings. We listen as Mom answers. "Molly," she says and shuts a door behind her.

"There's no way," I say.

Robert returns his gaze to the baby book. He flips the page methodically, without truly looking. The photos this time are of him, Lana, and Martin in a bare-walled apartment. I latch onto my own coffee cup, take a long drink, and wait. The vein in Robert's forehead pulses. Then he laughs. He actually laughs. "You want a lawyer for Neil . . ."

"Yes, I—"

He lays his palms flat against the table as he tries to control his breathing. "Do you know what I want, Lucy?"

"No, I—"

"I want my son back."

"Robert—"

"And do you know what I think? I think until the police prove your boyfriend didn't murder my boy, all I can see is a jealous, angry, damaged kid with the means to murder my son."

"N-no," I sputter. "He might have hated you, but he'd never kill Martin and Deuce. You know that." I can't say more because Mom arrives in the kitchen with her huge gallon water jug tipped back to her lips, unaware of the tension.

I retreat toward the fridge, putting the island between Robert and me. Mom leaves the massive jug on the counter and falls into Robert's lap. She cups his chin in her hand and presses her lips against the stubble on his cheeks and stays there close to him. His anger doesn't so much deflate as hit a pause. He wraps his arms around my mother and holds her. "Baby," he says, and I shudder.

"Lucy." From inside his embrace, she extends her hand blindly in my direction.

I walk forward and place my hand in hers. She pulls me toward them into a *Golden Girls*-esque group hug. I smell the cigar Robert smoked this morning, the coffee I poured, and the anger. The tips of his fingers press roughly into the small of my back, a reminder that we aren't done with this conversation.

The hug breaks after several long, deep breaths from Mom. She wipes fresh tears from her face and says, "That was Molly on the phone. She, well . . . It's awful. The police have a warrant for Neil's arrest. They're at their house now and she doesn't know where he is. She hoped he might be here."

Robert casts around as if I might have stashed him in a cabinet.

"He's not," I say.

Mom crawls out of his lap for her abandoned water jug. She moves to refill the growler, and as she does, Robert's hand pins mine to the counter. He presses his mouth to my ear and says, "Neil Clark is never allowed in this house or on this property. And if I find out he killed my son, I swear I'll put a bullet between his eyes if I ever see him here again."

Chapter Thirty-Two

LUCY: Where are you?

LUCY: It's not safe to come here.

My messages to Neil don't show as delivered. He's either out of the service area or his phone is off. I have three messages from Parson.

PARSON: Owl has the iPad.

PARSON: Check out the police twitter account
    @ClearyCoSO Comments under Astrid's video.

PARSON: They're looking for Neil.

I open Twitter. There are multiple tweets from the sheriff's account and Kentucky Task Force 1, which manages search and rescue in central Kentucky.

The pinned tweet on the account is now a link to Astrid's video.

@ClearyCoSO

!! BOLO !!

Contact CCSO if you have any information regarding this video. Footage and audio captured by missing juvenile. Individual in camouflage wanted in conjunction with murder and kidnapping. $10,000 reward offered for viable tips. $100,000 for tip leading to arrest.

Below is Neil's University of West Virginia official sports photo. And the message:

Manhunt underway in Cleary County for Neil Clark; future Olympian wanted for the multiple murders. Clark is wearing camo sweatshirt, jeans, and camo hat. He's 6'1". If you spot Clark, dial 911 or call @ClearyCoSO

Before I force myself to read the other tweets, I scroll through the timeline I've already lived.

@ClearyCoSO

!! MISSING JUVENILE !!

The Clearly County Sheriff's Office is seeking
information on the whereabouts of Astrid Clark.
5'3", 98 lbs., brown hair, brown eyes. If you know
anything about her whereabouts, please notify
CCSO immediately.

An accompanying photo shows Astrid during a halftime show near the fifty-yard line, wearing her crisp
green-and-white band jacket and cap, hand raised in a stiff
orchestra movement. Total focus covers her pixie face.

@ClearyCoSO

!! INVESTIGATION UPDATE !!

Next of kin have been notified and the deceased
have been identified as Martin Carlin, 17, and
Officer Deuce Uri, 27, both of Grand Junction,
Kentucky.

@ClearyCoSO

Saturday, at 6:23 a.m., deputies and EMS
responded to reports of two murder victims
located in old LaRue Campground area. Both

were pronounced deceased on scene. This is
considered an ongoing homicide investigation.

@ClearyCoSO @KYTF-1

KYTF-1 asks all volunteers to return to their
vehicles/homes until the fog event has lifted. Search
for missing teenager will continue at first light.

@ClearyCoSO @KYTF-1

At 2300 (11 p.m.), KYTF-1 will deploy a team of
6 highly trained search and rescue specialists
to Grand Junction, KY. The team will assist in
the search and rescue efforts for a local missing
juvenile.

@ClearyCoSO

Friday evening at 5:07 p.m., CCSO responded to
the LaRue recreation area in reference to a report
of blood on the exterior of a gray Hummer with
yellow trim. This investigation is ongoing.

It's not what they say so much as the time that catches
my heart. Forty hours ago, Martin was still alive.

I return to the comments section below Astrid's

video, which has been shared 50.7k times and amassed well over one thousand comments. Is the volume what Parson wanted me to see? Or something more specific?

I keep scrolling and come to the tweet from @CrewTimeSY I expected.

Neil's essay. Posted in snapshots. Highlighted in bright yellow, the quote Seth Yarborough read to us yesterday:

"Grand Hydro should be shut down at all costs. The effects on the Tennessee River are criminal to the environment, and I fear that someone, maybe even myself, might have to do something radical in order to stop the Robert Carlins of the world."

Below *Crew Time*'s screenshots of Neil's essay, account @citizenx, with a bot image, has jacked the video from Neil's Instagram account and added commentary: *Neil Clark brags about shot equal to the distance that killed Carlin and Uri. #Murderer #videoevidence*

The videos sway the public opinion, but I've seen them before. I have context. What I haven't seen is @NurseTabatha. Her tweet reads:

!Tip! Neil Clark at Med Center Friday evening. Casted hand. Broken fingers. 100% sure from hitting someone or something. @ClearyCoSO Did either of your victims have wounds consistent with a beating?

Chapter Thirty-Three

One headline breaks my heart.

"Olympic Committee Suspends Neil Clark from 2024 Team."

I have a feeling I know where Neil is.

The local Methodist church owns property on Carter Pass Road, five minutes out of town in the opposite direction of LaRue. They dozed the buildings the decade before and left an old gym standing. Ball fields, broken asphalt tennis courts, and swing sets lie behind the gym. The newest part of the property, installed three years ago, is a sign at the highway that reads "Future Home of Cleary Community Church."

The future's here. The funds aren't.

Thanks to the dense woods surrounding the hidden entrance, drivers can't see most of the property from the highway. The church bushhogs the open areas once a year in July, but that mower is one of the only "regular" visitors. Even a curious bystander has to drive through the woods, past the gym, and around the old ball park trail to see where Neil and I usually hide our vehicles.

If he's not on the run or at the police station, he'll be there.

We claimed the hideout in seventh grade.

We biked out to Carter Pass Road, not wanting Parson or Deuce to see us hanging out in town and give us crap about being a couple. We stopped at the bridge and ended up dragging our bikes into the ditch. Two splashes later, we decided we were wet enough to walk in the creek. After a mile of walking through the ankle-deep water, we ascended the bank into the rear of the church property. That was like finding Narnia.

And it was the cheapest date in town.

We'd take peanut butter sandwiches and swing until we were nauseous and then lie on a blanket, watch the stars, make out, pick the grass, watch the groundhogs. Sometimes we had slingshot competitions with empty soda cans—a competitive break from air rifle. Sometimes we talked. The Future Home of Cleary Community Church was our sanctuary.

Please be there, I think. *Please, please be who I think you are.*

I text Mom I'm headed to the Clarks' and try not to think about the risk involved—of going somewhere without any way to call for help—or if I'm making a decision to abet a murderer.

He told me he broke his hand moving the deer. Is the nurse lying or generating drama? I need to look him in the eye and ask for myself.

The gated entrance is a simple post and chain barrier. As I've done many times before, I ease the Nissan around the first post into the grass and then speed along the secluded drive. When the land opens up behind the gym, I feel the familiar tug of nostalgia.

Neil's here. I make the turn around the third base dugout and spot his truck behind the old block bathroom building.

He sits on the tailgate, head down, legs swinging, boots looking heavy. Like the police said, he's wearing jeans he's had for years, a camo sweatshirt, and a favorite camo Carhartt cap with a fishing lure attached to the bill. He raises his left hand, fingers dancing slowly in the air. The familiarity of that wave fills me with love and sadness.

How many times has he sat here waiting for me to get to him? A hundred? Five hundred?

I don't know what to say when I park next to his truck and get out of the Nissan.

"You came," he says, a slow, sad smile on his face. "I knew you'd come eventually."

"I hoped you'd be here," I say.

"They have a warrant for me."

"You can't hide."

"I'm not. I wanted to see you before I turned myself in. There's something I need to tell you myself. In person."

I take a half step back and hope he won't notice, but of course he does.

Neil starts at the beginning.

"I drove home from West Virginia Thursday night after practice. Went straight to LaRue and was there when the sun came up. I figured I didn't have anything until Astrid's game, so why not hunt and then crash during the day? I ended up tracking a buck trail several miles farther than I anticipated. Worth the work too. I got in an amazing shot, and you probably saw the beast in the truck bed on your way in—"

I hadn't, but I don't interrupt.

"A real monster. Took me two hours to drag him to a clearing where I could get my truck. By the time I hoisted him into the bed, I was tanked. I rinsed off in the creek and lay down on the front seat. The plan was for it to be a thirty-minute nap." He laughs. "Woke up close to one thirty. You know how I am when I first wake up," he says.

"A bear."

He continues, "I left the field, tired and starving and driving too fast. I planned to go to Parson's for breakfast, but I spotted Martin's Hummer in the trailhead parking lot. I pulled over to brag on the deer I'd bagged, and he said that I'd just missed you. Well, that pissed me off right nice so I got out of the truck. He was clueless, not reading the room at all, and asked me about the dam break. Did I think it could have been sabotage? Had I uncovered anything about his father during my econ paper research? I wasn't hearing any of it. All I could think about was you and why you'd skip school to meet Martin." Neil looks off toward the ridge, where the land drops away into the creek.

"What?" I ask.

Neil's weighing something. I reach out, thread the fabric of his sweatshirt into my hand, and tug slightly. "Tell me," I urge.

"Then he apologized for being in love with you."

My jaw drops. "He did not."

"Oh, he did, and, Luce, I lost it."

Lost it?

"What else did he tell you?" I ask, thinking of my last moments with Martin before I drove away.

"He promised me he wouldn't let either of you act on his feelings."

I want to reach into the past and slap Martin. This scenario is kryptonite. I suddenly don't know whether to pull away or keep Neil talking. "Define 'lost it.'"

"I punched him hard." He points to his left cheekbone and then his nose. "Twice. Three times. Blood went everywhere. The cartilage in his nose snapped." Neil shivers at the memory, mouth agape, eyes fixed somewhere beyond my head. "I didn't break my hand on a deer. I broke it on Martin's face."

Now I don't hide that I'm scared. I back away and try for words. The only thing I manage is his name.

Neil keeps talking. "I was stupid and awful. He's here with you all the time and I'm in West Virginia and he has money and he's . . . him. And you clearly love him. And then he was agreeing with me about his dad and it was too much and I snapped—"

"Neil, what did you do?"

"I didn't mean for any of this to happen."

Oh my gosh. I can't think straight. "What do you mean, you didn't mean for this to happen? Hitting him? Killing him?"

Neil's eyes narrow at me and I feel judged.

"No!" He's appalled. "Breaking up with you. I never meant to break up with you, Luce. I really thought you'd change your mind about taking Robert's money and you'd trust yourself to qualify at Walther. But then you didn't back down, and I don't know, my brain said the wrong thing and then it was too late."

"You sent me Tic Tacs," I say.

"I said good luck."

"Goodbye and good luck," I correct.

He sighs, like the goodbye was good manners and I'm being stupid. "Anyway. I thought we were on pause until the Olympics, but then Parson said you were hanging out with Martin all the time and I thought maybe we weren't on pause. Maybe you were done with me and, Luce, I need you." He's babbling, talking fast. "I've been in a bad place."

I've seen his lizard brain make mistakes before. The day of the dam break. When he hoisted Astrid above his head and charged into the rapids with no thought to what would happen.

My heart catches in my throat. "Neil, are you confessing to mur—"

"I'm confessing to three punches. That's it. Martin was alive when I left LaRue. I never even saw Deuce or Astrid. But I left there and drove around because I knew you'd go nuts when you saw his face or his dad would, like, sue me or something."

"You're positive he was alive?"

He looks at me like I'm an idiot and then like he doesn't want to tell me the next part. Slowly, Neil removes his fishing cap and runs a hand through the wilds of his oily, dark hair. He scratches his scalp, like he can't believe what transpired. "Positive. The dude walked over to his Hummer, opened the passenger door, got a frozen packet from his lunch, and then proceeded to wrap my hand with gauze from the glovebox first aid kit."

I laugh because of course Martin did.

Neil's not laughing. "Blood's pouring out his nose and he says it's nothing and he wants me to be able to compete in Paris and I won't be able to if I broke my hand. And then we can't get eclairs or some crap like that."

Raising the plaster cast to eye level, Neil says, "Guess I got what I deserved there. You probably would be better off with him. Anyway, I wanted you to hear it from me and . . ." Neil slides off the tailgate and opens the driver's door of his truck. He pushes the lever that lifts the seat forward and pulls out a hard-sided black travel gun case that I know by heart. It has the Bigfoot stickers I bought him plastered front and center.

He opens the latches and smiles sadly as he lifts the lid. His Walther LG400 Alutec Competition air rifle lies on a bed of dark gray foam. "All yours. And so is this." From beneath the dark dappled foam, he pulls an envelope. Inside is a printed email with flight confirmations to another tournament in Alaska. "I've been saving," he says. "I knew you were anxious about Walther, and I was hard on you about Rio. So I got you another option, not because I don't believe in you, but because I needed you to know I understand you too. I was a jerk about Robert. He's a jerk, and I don't like him, but I was awful to you."

I can't accept this. It's too much. "You need your rifle," I say.

"Probably not," he says, and I know he's seen the Olympic dismissal too.

"Did you tag Grand Hydro last summer?" I ask.

He looks away and I know he did. "I told you I was stupid."

Neil reaches forward, holds my braid, my paintbrush, and I let him close the space between us. The heat from his body mirrors mine. He tightens his hands around the small of my back and lowers his chin into my shoulder. Tiny kisses land on the narrow strip of exposed skin near my neck. He plants a line of those kisses up to my ear. "Luce," he says, and I remember the first time he kissed me.

The summer I turned thirteen. Three days after my birthday and two days after my braces came off. We were at his parents' house. We'd been "boyfriend and girlfriend" since Christmas and he'd given me an E. E. Cummings poem and a necklace with gold trinkets: sun, moon, and stars. He'd saved to get it from a kiosk in the mall. I should have kissed him then, but I was still twelve and scared I didn't know anything about kissing. The idea of his tongue inside my mouth sounded gross, but I also wanted to know what it was like.

One half of their garage has a ratty, unbalanced pool table surrounded by couches. We gravitated toward the garage because it was the only place on the property Astrid wouldn't turn up. She was scared of the crickets that bellowed their existence from the cracks in the walls. We sweated buckets that summer hiding from her. The only place hotter than hell is a closed garage in July. We didn't care. We crammed ourselves onto the same couch cushion. "I think I'm ready," I'd said. "You're sure?" he'd asked, leaning closer. I nodded and he said, "I'm going to start slow and I'm going to start right here." He put the tiniest of kisses next to my left ear.

I shivered. Maybe this wouldn't be gross after all.

Millimeters from that first kiss, another light sweep of his lips. The electricity thrummed through my body.

He tiptoed his lips across the plane of my cheek until he caught the corner of my lip. By then, the anticipation devoured me.

I tilted. He tilted.

And then I was having my first kiss. Like so many things in my life, I researched this moment long before it arrived. I read articles and rewatched one of my favorite influencers go through kissing dos and don'ts. Maybe Neil did the same: I was fairly sure the tiny kiss thing came from *Teen Vogue*'s account.

We'd gone into the garage that morning after we fed Paco Taco at eight thirty.

We kissed all day without stopping to pee or eat or drink. The next day my jaw was so sore I couldn't speak.

We'd never get the chance to kiss like that again.

He says, "I'm really sorry about Martin. He didn't deserve what happened to him."

"You don't deserve to be blamed," I say.

"No, but they say it's my gun and they're going to find blood from my knuckles on him. You and I both know what that will mean."

I do and it's devastating.

"I'll go with you to Owl's," I say.

"Don't do that. Tell me you believe me."

And without a doubt, I do.

"I believe you," I say.

That Weekend

The rain kept falling.

It never slowed.

It wouldn't stop.

My feet slid in the mud as I reversed along the bank of the creek Astrid and Neil crossed. Deuce righted me and we stood by Parson while Danny yelled something. The wind was so loud; even though we were about fifty feet apart, I only heard every other word.

". . . To . . . Mounds."

He tried again. A dead branch fell from a tree and landed on the roof of the cabin. The limb exploded, obliterating all other sounds.

"Indian Mounds!" Parson yelled back to confirm.

Danny's eyes swept up and down the rampage of water. He looked over our shoulders in the direction of the Tennessee. He must have had an instinct that if the creek was swollen, the river might be too.

"Go. To. The. Mounds," he yelled again. "Highest. Ground."

Deuce slung Clay on his back. "We need to run, Luce."

I understood as we set out for Indian Mounds that we were in a dangerous situation, but I was glad we weren't crossing Vespers Creek after watching what happened to Neil and Astrid. "I want to go in the cabin," I said to Parson. "Why can't we go inside the cabin and wait?"

"Yeah, I like the cabin better than outside," Clay said. His hair was plastered to his head. Mud streaked around his bare calves and feet.

"We're going to the Mounds," Deuce said.

We ran. The rain was cold, the mud colder still. I stayed beside Deuce, my short legs pumping to keep up. I smelled the sweat on him from our tag game.

The guys tore through brambles and the brambles tore through our skin. I was bleeding somewhere on my legs. The treads of our shoes filled with mud. There was no traction. My clothes clung to my body, the cotton growing heavy.

Deuce hit a patch of mud and slid, nearly dropping a screaming Clay. I slipped on the same patch seconds later and ended up facedown on the soggy ground. Parson was ahead of Deuce and Deuce and Clay were ahead of me. Neither of them realized I fell. They yelled at each other in the storm. Screaming words that didn't make sense to me. They couldn't agree on the direction. There was another fork in the creek this way. No, it was that way. If we didn't make it, it was Deuce's fault. No, it was Parson's.

We pounded through the woods, searching for any place the land rose. We'd been on low land since we left the cabin, the Mounds still farther away than we imagined.

Deuce turned out to be right about the creek forking. A smaller stream, Beaver Creek, broke the banks somewhere behind us and filled the area. The rain slapped the surface, making the creek look alive.

"Let's cross there." Parson pointed toward a place where the water appeared to be no deeper than ankle height. Although the water was shallow, there was no footing. The rocks were slick with moss and algae. I fell twice and slammed my knees so hard I bit through my tongue. I felt the water jerk me sideways.

Parson lifted me by the waistband of my jeans and set me upright. "Keep going," he commanded. Blood gushed from my knee. When we reached the other side, water oozed and squished beneath us. Our feet slid inside our shoes.

I was reaching out to Deuce for help when a gust of wind threw me sideways and a *crack* pierced the air. I looked up. A limb the size of a small tree broke away from its trunk and teetered.

I covered my head, screaming as it fell. It hit the ground, and I felt the reverberation.

The rain kept falling.

It never slowed.

It wouldn't stop.

Where Deuce and Clay were, a branch that must have been forty feet long sprawled across the ground. Dozens and dozens of limbs. Leaves everywhere in bunches, attached and unattached. The earth was littered with green, brown, and red confetti.

"Deuce! Clay!"

"Lucy!"

Clay lay flat in the mud, inches from being struck. I deadlifted him from the ground and held him to my chest while he yelled, "Deuce. Deuce."

Deuce's black-and-white-checkered Vans were visible through the greenery. He didn't answer Clay. He didn't move at all.

"Help me," Parson screeched.

We grabbed the branch and heaved. Our hands slid on the wet bark. It didn't feel like we made any progress. Parson grabbed another limb and tried to use it to counterlift the branch.

It didn't move.

The thing that was moving: the creek.

We now stood in ankle-deep water.

"You need to take Clay and go," Parson said.

"No."

"Yes," he demanded and pointed. "Go that way until you reach the Mounds. And stay away from the Duck Pond."

"No."

Parson shoved Clay into my arms. "*Now.* I'll get Deuce. I promise. Go." He pushed at the small of my back and I took a step to keep from falling. I took another.

We were alone then.

Clay and I and the big brown forest. Brown for what felt like miles and miles. No Mounds in sight.

The rain kept falling.

It never slowed.

It wouldn't stop.

I looked over my shoulder. I couldn't see Parson and Deuce anymore. We were all alone.

Except we weren't. I remembered then the conversation between my parents.

"Should we pack up and go home?"

"No. If we were in a tent, maybe, but we'll be fine in the cabins."

"Well, thank God we're not here with the Boy Scouts."

The Boy Scouts were out here too.

Chapter Thirty-Four

After Neil leaves, I sit in the Nissan, my body limp against the steering wheel. I don't know what to do with myself now. Walk randomly through LaRue searching for Astrid? Cry? Pray? Find Dana and beg her to stay in Grand Junction and help me prove Neil is innocent? Go back to the house and search for Martin's evidence?

What happened out there in LaRue?

Is it still happening?

Is Astrid alive?

The truth is a person could look day and night for years and not stumble across any leads or clues. We found that out after the dam broke.

Neil didn't do this. And whoever the killer is frightens me differently now. None of this was random. Someone found out what Martin knew and set Neil up.

I take stock of what I know.

Martin investigated cash payments he believed Robert made to Deuce and swore he had some kind of evidence about damage to the dam from Tamerlane. Where is that evidence now, and who else did he tell he was looking into this?

He must have tipped off someone at some point.

He came to me and asked for my recollection of the timeline. Did he do the same with Astrid, Deuce, Parson? Did he ask Andy Bedford for his reports on the dam or his account of the flood? Andy wouldn't have divulged that. Did Andy kill him? Andy's never sober enough to walk straight, much less shoot straight.

I only agreed to walk through my terrible memories because he wasn't going to stop asking. And maybe because he was Martin. As we walked the path in LaRue, he witnessed the freshness of the emotions I carry. The fear. My guilt. He reached out and touched my arm and held on while I said, "I'll never forget the water. The way it came for us."

The wall of water was the sharpest and most exaggerated of the memories. Always a gigantic, towering wave. Sometimes so large it was a cartoonish rendering, the way an amateur might draw Moses parting the Red Sea.

"My God," he'd said, and I felt like someone finally

saw me in a way no one else ever had. Everyone else was too close. Everyone else had their own terror to reckon with. His response was for me. Intimate. It didn't make excuses or ooze with pity.

Moments ago I argued with Neil like I hadn't known Martin was in love with me.

I didn't want to hurt Neil. But I knew.

Martin was too good at being uncloaked, unguarded. I didn't know anyone else like that. I didn't know anyone who could look right at a person and say the kinds of things most people kept in their heads.

"Luce," he'd said as we laid our backs against a tree. We were at the end of the tour of LaRue and I was spent. I'd relived my final moments with Clay, something I'd only ever discussed with a therapist.

"Luce," he'd said again, and I rolled my head toward him. He kept almost painful eye contact with me, and then it all came out of him. "I'm in love with you, but I'm not going to let it ruin us, okay? I promise I won't. I'll keep my mouth shut after this, but I need to say it in case there's even the slightest chance you feel the same way. I'm sure you don't, and that's okay. I'll be fine, but I think I might die if I don't tell you. Sometimes I can't think about anything else."

I wasn't sure what to do.

I felt like I did that day when I was thirteen, in Neil's garage.

Rather than answer, I turned toward him. He had a

baby face. Smooth blond facial hair. Soft. So different from Neil's dark scratchy stubble. He'd had a haircut the day before and the trim around his ears was sharp. His lips were pink and narrow, the upper lip almost disappearing into his mouth, but he had a wide divot below his nose. That feature, along with dimples, gave him the appearance of eternally smiling. His eyes were sky blue with tiny flecks of gray.

I was sort of in love with him too. Every conversation, every drive, every game of Bananagrams on the kitchen table. They were all part of this moment as a destination. I didn't know if he was my next beginning or a roadblock with Neil, whom I loved terribly, but I knew he was important.

I guess there's a point when everyone understands, for better or worse, that humans have the capacity to love more than one person at a time.

That's an expansive, troublesome, terrible thought.

"Kiss me," I said to Martin.

And he did and it was awesome, and I knew we were totally screwed the minute his mouth was on mine, fitting perfectly. We moved like synchronized dancers who had been practicing for years. He's the one who pulled away, with me still leaning toward him, wanting more.

He laughed and said, "Well, I might not be able to forget that."

And I laughed because what else was there to do?

Likely because it was a safer topic than us, he asked,

"Do you think you missed anything that day? The day the dam broke."

"I'm sure I have. I was a kid. And traumatized," I added, as though trauma were an afterthought.

Whatever I missed got Martin and Deuce murdered.

I turn my attention to Deuce.

He was a young cop. Maybe he was involved, but maybe not in sabotage. Martin might have come out and asked him about the payout the same way he spit out being in love with me.

And Astrid . . . well, she was fairly young at the time of the break.

Two Astrid facts stand out in my mind from that weekend: one, the kid was a dang monkey, jumping from the couch to Parson to the couch again, always yelling in his ear for him to "Play with me instead of Deuce," and two, the moment immediately after her water rescue, she screamed, not for her parents or Neil—who clung precariously to the limb across the creek—but for Parson.

I dig into the memory, unable to land on anything consequential. She had a childhood obsession with Parson, we all did, and she babbled endlessly about fishing techniques to show off for him. She was good at everything, even then, so he was actually impressed. In my memory, she was slightly scared of Deuce. Maybe because Deuce was so physically strong.

Martin and I didn't talk about Astrid on Friday. She came up in the timeline, of course, but he didn't have any questions specific to her. He focused primarily on Deuce and perhaps some on Parson near the end. Nothing in his language suggested that he'd talked to her already.

"Deuce is the only one getting money from Dad," Martin had said. "And from your account, Parson and Deuce were inseparable that weekend. Meaning, if Deuce was being paid off, and Parson wasn't, there was a reason. Think back again. Were they ever apart? That might be the key to the money."

By then I was tired of revisiting the worst day of my life and flustered from our kiss. There were a million memories, but none were relevant. I shook my head. "I don't know."

"Will you ask Parson?" he'd pleaded.

"I will," I'd said.

"Now?"

"No. I'm not calling him now. Even if I wanted to, there's no signal."

He kept pressing until I snapped at him. "No matter what conspiracy theory you cook up about the dam break, no one but God controls the rain that fell. Let this go. You have a great relationship with your dad. Don't muck that up."

"Luce, if you've seen what I've seen, you wouldn't say that."

"Then show me."

"Okay. I will after the game tonight."

I hadn't believed him. I hadn't even taken him seriously

enough to go straight to Owl when Mom sent those initial texts that he didn't show up for the game.

He's dead because I didn't believe him.

That's two brothers dead because of me.

Part Two

I can't go on. I'll go on.

—SAMUEL BECKETT

Whatever evidence Martin planned to show me, I never find. I turn our house upside down in the days after the funeral.

Meanwhile, the police have all the evidence they need.

Neil is arrested and arraigned.

In a speedy trial, he is tried and convicted for the murders of Deuce Uri and Martin Carlin.

If I'd been on the jury, with no link to Neil, I'd have found him guilty too.

Astrid remains missing. The police locate her kayak through a pawnshop in Memphis.

Her video has been watched more than twenty million times.

I make the Olympic team in Alaska, on my last chance, and win bronze in Paris. Parson and Owl travel with me. Mom and Robert are in the stands. Distant, but there. The eclairs are better than Martin described.

Owl retires and spends every day searching for Astrid.

I plan to never return to Grand Junction.

Instead, I will shoot until they don't need me on the team or I fail miserably or people laugh in my face, and then I'll throw my rifle in the ocean, drive until I see a sign for "Free Kittens," and pick one fuzzball from the heap of purring engines. I hope it's a calico, a boy, and he doesn't mind living in the desert and going by the name Dog.

Part Three

Two Years After the Murders

*There are a few times in life when you leap up and
the past that you'd been standing on falls away
behind you, and the future you mean to land on is
not yet in place, and for a moment you're suspended
knowing nothing and no one, not even yourself.*
—ANN PATCHETT

Chapter One

I am living in a motel in Colorado when I get a text from a number I haven't seen in a month.

DANA JONES: I have a lead on Astrid.
DANA JONES: Come to Zionsville.
ME: I'm on my way.

I shoot off the text and am halfway to Zionsville, Indiana, everything I own in the bed of the Nissan, before I realize I'm moving backward in time. Dangerous territory.

Still, it's Astrid. I keep driving. What choice do I have?

Dana's investigative office and apartment are housed in a decent-sized space over the carriage house of a rich friend she met at SIU law school. I know because I turned up here uninvited after Neil's trial.

She wasn't unhappy to see me, but she was confused. She opened the door and I sidled in with my overnight bag. Galen wagged his tail and I said to him, rather than her, "I couldn't stay there, could I, buddy?" The next morning I waited, argument prepared, for her to send me away. She didn't. Instead, she handed me a job application for the Zionsville library and told me to ask for Lisa.

That was the second beginning of my life.

Lisa hired me part-time on the spot, and within the week Dana agreed to let me do contract work for Jones Investigations. Social media searches. Camera footage collection. Open records research. Two jobs gave me enough money to keep me shooting at a local range, Neil's rifle at my shoulder every day.

The only good thing left to believe in.

Accuracy and the Olympics.

I got good at being Dana's assistant.

Good at following Neil's appeals from a distance.

Good at watching Astrid's video a hundred times a day, hoping to spot something no one else had. I'd find myself alone in a hotel room in some competition city, ordering a salad and soda water on DoorDash, watching and rewatching . . . "Underwater, baby."

That wasn't Neil's voice.

It still isn't.

I take the Zionsville exit after midnight and am at Dana's by twelve twenty. There's no sneaking into the carriage house. Galen hears my feet on the side steps, my key in the lock. He meets me at the door with a squeaky yawn, nose in my thigh, tail swinging a million miles an hour. "Hey, buddy," I say and bend to kiss his face.

Behind him, Dana stands in the hallway, her oversized T-shirt inside out. "Welcome home, stranger," she says.

That makes me smile.

I guess she's the closest thing I have to home these days. Definitely more than the motel I left this morning. It hadn't even had a coffeepot.

"You want to sleep or talk?" she asks, moving toward the kitchen.

"Sleep," I say. I've been on the road fifteen hours.

"Sweet."

She takes my bag and flicks off the lights. I follow her to the bedroom and fall theatrically face-first on the mattress. I'm fully clothed on top of her comforter and have zero ambition of digging through my bag for a toothbrush. In seconds, Galen curls behind my knees, and the last thing I hear is Dana saying, "Traitor," before I'm out.

The next morning we sit opposite each other at her tiny bistro table with steaming mugs of tea that is too hot to drink.

"What would you say if I told you Astrid's alive?"

This sounds more like a trivia game than a real question, so I play along. "I'd say that's great." Then a beat later, I add, "I'd also ask how and where." If there's one thing I've come to believe over the last two years, it's that Astrid died in LaRue.

Dana smirks; she knows I don't buy the theory.

"Michigan City," she says.

"Where's that?" The name sounds familiar, but I can't place why.

She takes a drink and looks toward the stove. We're waiting on the oven to heat so we can make canned cinnamon rolls, the closest either of us gets to a homemade breakfast. "Upstate Indiana. Near Chicago. There's a federal prison there."

"Right," I say, feeling stupid. Neil's prison sentence began in Eddyville, but he was moved to Idaho in the first year due to an overcrowding issue. He told me once in a letter that he might ask for a transfer to Michigan City to get closer to home.

"I think she's living there," Dana says.

I don't roll my eyes, but my tone sounds like this is the dumbest idea Dana has ever had. "Come on," I say. "Why did I really drive here from Colorado?"

"I'm serious. I think Astrid's alive and teaching violin lessons as Ashley Smith."

"No way." I push back from the table, open the oven, and throw the cinnamon rolls inside.

Dana lifts her phone, taps on Facebook, and shows me

the screen. An account for JoanaandCarson Willoughby. The album's primary picture is of Willow, an elementary kid with a violin tucked under her chin, red dress and shoes clashing with her red hair. I scroll through the subsequent fifteen pictures. Near the end, she stands with a petite woman in her early twenties. Her hair is back in a severe bun, not a hair out of place.

The caption reads, "Ashley Smith is our hero. The best teacher in the world."

Unless Astrid has a twin, Dana's right.

"How?" I say, followed by, "No way."

"I have no idea," she says. "But if Astrid's alive, it changes everything."

Chapter Two

There isn't the shadowiest corner of my imagination that allows for this outcome. Still, Dana and I finish the cinnamon rolls and I indulge her. We toss around ideas of how Astrid might be masquerading through life as Ashley Smith. In Dana's line of work, she's seen weirder circumstances. Witness protection. Stockholm syndrome. Runaways. Women sold as brides to men from other countries. I'm suggesting, "Maybe she had a severe head injury," when the doorbell rings.

Dana opens the door and Owl's there, leaning against the doorframe, a computer backpack in his hand, sunglasses resting on his balding head. He's tan and ruddy.

Thinner than I've ever seen him, and stronger. We talk on the phone every Sunday night, but his references to how much he's hiking and his new set of weights didn't prepare me for his new look. He's whittled. Like someone carved a bunch of muscles into a sculpture.

He's sizing me up too. Comparing my weekly phone voice to the young woman in front of him. To the me from a year ago, the person he put on a plane with a peck on the forehead and a twenty-dollar bill in case I needed a snack. I left Paris for Greece and then Greece for Portland. He flew home to Grand Junction, and we haven't seen each other since.

He doesn't have the same tact as Dana. He stares at the hollowness of my cheeks, the sharp line of my jaw, the haircut I've needed for months, and says, "Dang, kid, you're supposed to take better care of yourself than this." To Dana he says, "Tell me you fed her something like donuts and bacon."

"Cheap cinnamon rolls," Dana says with a laugh.

I fall into his open arms. "Hey, Owl," I say from inside the warmth of his T-shirt. Home, the good parts of it, are alive again.

"Let's go see our boy," he says and smooches the top of my head.

I raise an eyebrow and look to Dana for an answer. I assume she called him about Astrid, but that doesn't seem to be the case. Dana throws her hands up in the air like she's been caught. "Party in Michigan City," she announces. "You and Owl have a one o'clock with Neil, and I have an appointment with Ashley Smith about my daughter . . . Kaitlin"—she invents the name from the air—"starting violin." She makes a screechy violin sound that causes Galen to bark at her.

"Transfer lottery finally fell in Neil's favor," Owl explains.

"Wait! He's there and he's willing to see me?" If so, that's more surprising than the transfer and an impromptu trip with Dana and Owl.

"So far he's willing to see me. We'll see about you when we get there," Owl says. "We weren't really sure you'd leave your fancy Colorado motel for us."

"Funny," I say, even though it isn't.

Due to overcrowding, Neil has spent the last three years in the South Boise Prison Complex in Idaho. A twenty-six-hour drive from Grand Junction. That's a long way from his folks and Owl. A long way from anyone who still loves him. I've only seen him once. Not because I haven't gone. I've tried. I've wasted plane trips, and money, trying.

After Paris, he agreed to a single visit. I flew to Boise on a red-eye from Boston; I'd been on tour with the US Team. He gave me thirty minutes of our allotted hour with a rule that I was not allowed to talk about anything except Paris and the competition. When I left, he told me, "Come back again in four years with the gold."

He sort of made me hate him.

And I think that was his plan.

Chapter Three

The drive to Michigan City is hard candy and Ed Sheeran Radio. Dana likes lemon drops, Owl prefers Red Hots, and I'm sucking on Gobstoppers, trying not to break my teeth in two. We're all nervous and crunchy and have vastly different air-conditioning needs.

Dana makes me drive. She and Owl pore over everything she has on Ashley Smith. Which isn't much considering the commonness of the name. This particular Ashley Smith, *the best violin teacher in the world*, has no criminal record, no credit cards in her name, and no property. Dana can't even find a lease.

"Maybe she lives in a motel," I say unhelpfully. "Or maybe she's not Astrid Clark."

I've moved from surprise to impossibility on this
Astrid/Ashley idea. I can't imagine a world where Astrid
teaches children. The violin, sure, yes, but kids? Hard no.
If Astrid is still alive out there, she's in a NASA think tank
or on Wall Street.

Owl's a little annoyed with me. He huffs when I make
these comments. I get it. He needs hope and I need reality.
He spends hours in LaRue every day looking for Astrid's
remains and trying to find any clues that might explain
who murdered his son and Martin. So the idea that Astrid
might be alive somewhere is the most hope he's had. I'm
not trying to make light of that; I'm simply preparing him
for the disappointment of another dead end.

Dana, posing under a fake Facebook account, reached
out to the Willoughbys and asked for Ashley's number.
Joana didn't hesitate to share. Any chance to talk about
her little prodigy's miracle worker is a golden moment.
Ashley responded promptly too, with a text as no-
nonsense as the bun on her head. Again, so different from
Astrid. The Astrid we know might have debated the time
and given a lecture on how time zones came to exist.

They're meeting at a Starbucks thirty minutes before
Owl and I see Neil.

"I'm sorry I'm being negative," I tell Owl.

"What about me?" Dana says, smiling. "Do I get an
apology? My daughter's violin career is at stake."

We all laugh, the tension broken, and she asks Owl
for updates from Grand Junction.

"Wilma's opening a gift shop next to the Chamber. You know Parson—another day, another franchise. What's he at now, three restaurants?"

"Still two," I say, but he has plans for three more.

After the trial, Parson didn't seem to want to go home either. He drove to Zionsville off and on before the Olympics to make sure I was still shooting and fundamentally sound. Each time he crashed on Dana's couch and the three of us would sit up late, talking about Neil's case and any new lead Dana and I tracked down. When Paris came, there was no question about who would go. He was right there with Owl, whispering advice in my ear and refusing to say "Good job" aloud. Of all of us, he's changed the least.

"The Clarks are having a hard time," Owl says and doesn't elaborate.

"And Mom?" I ask.

"Oh, you know," he says. "Still wishing you'd come home once in a while."

"She knows Robert doesn't want me there."

My open support of Neil during the trial was the straw that broke my ability to live at 101 River Road. Or even visit Grand Junction.

Our side of the courtroom was so empty a New Yorker cartoonist compared us to people who still thought Kanye should be president. My mother stood with us privately. I told myself she had never been strong and I shouldn't expect her to be strong enough to stand up to Robert, but secretly I'd hoped she would. I hoped she would choose her best friend, Molly; I hoped she would choose her daughter. When she didn't, part of me broke away like an iceberg.

To Robert, I was the reason the media wouldn't leave him and Grand Hydro alone. Investigations hadn't amounted to anything more than bad press. Martin's theories hadn't proved true yet, if they ever would. There was no evidence Robert had paid Deuce anything, much less $216k.

We might have worked it out, but I couldn't shake the coldness in his voice on the day I asked him to help Neil. That wasn't something I'd ever get over.

Sometimes Owl and I would get lost in a grief cloud and wonder if Robert killed Martin and Deuce, but then we'd remember the way he cried over Martin's body and how the one time we got him onto the range at Parson's, he couldn't hit the broad side of a barn.

We arrive in Michigan City with an hour to spare. The main drag offers plenty of fast-food joints. Owl chooses McDonald's and, too nauseous to eat, I stomach a Diet Coke. We leave our table at McDonald's and stroll into a force field of heat. An air-conditioning unit hidden behind a short brick wall drips and steam lifts off the concrete. It must be a hundred degrees. Owl's St. Louis Cardinals cap has a salt line from sweat.

We drop Dana a block away from Starbucks and arrive fifteen minutes early for our one thirty appointment at the correctional center. Owl, a pro at security, has us waved through the outer gate in record time.

"Showtime," I say. I'm not even sure what I'm hoping for. To see Neil. To be rejected again. It's almost easier if he says no. It's what I've come to expect.

The guard inside checks his list. "Owl Uri?"

"That's me," Owl says and hands over his ID.

"And . . ." The guard, *Collins* is on the Velcro patch at his shoulder, delays a brief second before saying, "Lucy Michaels?"

"That's me."

"Step over here to be patted down."

Neil has agreed to see me.

Chapter Four

The prison isn't air-conditioned.

I breathe into the collar of my shirt and count it as a breeze. We're seated at a small cafeteria table among other inmates and their visitors. One child has colored a picture of a dinosaur and he's singing the Barney song.

My smudgy palms coat the plastic table, and I draw my initials in my own sweat. Five minutes pass. Ten. Maybe Neil has changed his mind.

Then the door opens and he's there. Owl nudges me with his knee; I can feel him smiling beside me. Neil's taller than I remember. Stockier too. His beard looks like an honest-to-God adult man beard. It is so ridiculous it reminds me of a Halloween costume or a No-Shave November gag. He looks like his father.

A sad smile creases his cheeks as he walks our way. We live in a world where if he moves incorrectly, we will be separated by a man with a gun and a nightstick.

Owl stands and they shake hands. Then Owl gives him a lingering hug and I hear him whisper, "That's from your momma." Neil tugs his sweat-rimmed shirt over his eyes. When he emerges from the cotton, not crying but almost, he looks at me.

I can't read him anymore, so I wait.

His arms release from his sides and lift slightly. That's an invitation and I accept.

Our hug is brilliant, with no remnants of his last terrible dismissal in Idaho. With Neil, I always feel like I have to hold two conflicting emotions within a magnet's grip of each other: hate, for how much he's hurt me; and love, for how much he's tried to protect me from loving him.

His chest swells against mine as he breathes me in. His smell is no longer his mother's lavender washing powder but his own. Familiar. I can almost imagine him stopping at my house after a morning hunt, covered in muck from lying in a duck blind.

A tear lands in my hair. It plops like a raindrop. Like that sweat coming off the air conditioner at McDonald's earlier. Once upon a time, an abundance of water, a wall of water, ruined my life. Today, a single drop almost does the same.

The guard yells, "Clark!" and we separate.

I expect small talk. Instead, Neil says, "I got a birthday card from PoppaJack."

"That's strange," I say.

"Yeah," he agrees and then lays the card on the table.

The card's colors and font are dated. *Happy Birthday* is written on a sash across the breast of a dog wearing pineapple sunglasses. I remember this card. I mailed it to him when I was a child. PoppaJack has likely pulled the card from an old stack in his desk drawer. Inside, I see my name and Clay's in our childish fonts. On the left side of the card, the handwriting switches to PoppaJack's.

It reads:

Neil, your sister phoned. She said you didn't hurt anyone. Happy birthday.

Love,

Jack Rickard

(PoppaJack)

I reread the few sentences again. Under the table, Owl clenches my knee.

"PoppaJack has dementia," I say, uncertain of how to feel and what Owl wants me to do.

"Neil, you can't take this as what it—"

"I know," he says. "But it sounds like he could have, you know, seen Astrid."

Owl intervenes. "Son, he might have a new nurse or

an occupational therapist. Heck, it could have been a delivery woman from Amazon. You can't think—"

"You're right," he says. "But this felt so, I don't know . . . strange."

I can't believe anything can eclipse time with Neil, but this card does. My brain is a million miles away, and if I'm reading Owl correctly, his is too. Or maybe less a million miles and more like three blocks over at the local Starbucks.

For the remainder of the time, Neil peppers Owl and me with everyday questions. He wants to hear about the cases I research for Dana, my last competition, friends in Zionsville. I ask him about his life, and he says he works in the prison library and plays pickup basketball. We laugh about both of us having library experience on our résumés.

When time's almost up, Owl stretches his long legs and promises Neil he'll visit again soon now that he's back on our side of the country, then he walks toward the guard at the door and buys us an extra five minutes of time.

Five minutes that start with an apology from Neil— for his asinine behavior in Idaho—and end with him taking a box of Tic Tacs from his pocket and sliding them to the center of the table. "They had them in the commissary," he says. "They won't let me give them to you, but you know they're for you."

Same old Neil.

"Fat Potter, it's time," the guard yells.

"Fat Potter?" I ask.

"Their favorite nickname for me here. Harry Potter. Like I haven't heard that before." Neil rolls his eyes the way he used to do at the boys in eighth grade. "I'm struggling, Luce. I try not to need you, but today I wasn't strong enough to turn you away."

"I know."

One last long hug and the guard escorts him away. The ankle chains clank as he follows the taunting guard. "That your girl, Fat Potter? She know you got killer magic in you? You little Voldemort? Or does she think you're innocent? I'll bet she does."

Chapter Five

Owl and I leave the prison with his long arm draped loosely around my back. He is so strong and I lean against him.

"What do you make of that card?"

"I'm not sure you can make anything of it at all," I say.

"Sure would be nice to have hope."

"Sure would," I say, but I'm not falling for hope, not ever again.

He powers on his phone and squints at the screen. "We've missed a bunch of messages from Dana."

I'm seeing the same thing. Seven messages in total. None of them what I want to read.

Ashley Smith didn't show up to their appointment.

She also disconnected her number.

Whoever Ashley Smith is, she doesn't want to be found and we spooked her.

Fifteen minutes later, Dana hops in the truck with three cups of coffee and some egg bites. I crank the air and we talk in the Starbucks parking lot. Despite the disappointment of the meeting, she's buzzing with energy. Ashley's no-show tells her we hit a nerve. This woman, whoever she is, is a lead worth following. Dana's equally interested in the birthday card, but agrees with the probability of it being nothing more than PoppaJack's mind locked in another time and place.

"If you have doubts, you should go see him," she says.

I'd already decided I would. The moment I saw the card. "What are you going to do next?" I ask.

"Well, I've got a case in Tennessee, but after that I'm going to start investigating violin teachers in Boise for evidence of Ashley Smith there. Michigan City can't be a coincidence. If Astrid's really alive and masquerading as a violin teacher, maybe she's trying to stay close to Neil."

This theory makes as much sense as anything.

Dana looks to Owl. "What's next for you?"

Owl shoves a toothpick into the corner of his mouth. "Oh, you know me, back to LaRue."

We drive then.

I pretend to sleep for most of the trip. I drift in dream-like memory back to those three perfect camping week-ends before the dam broke. The curiousness of being a kid. The way October felt like July one day and December the next. The smell of campfire and burnt marshmallows. I think of Owl hanging hammocks and us rolling up like caterpillars inside them, spinning and spinning until we fell out into a pile of leaves on the dusty ground.

I remember Deuce hid me under a blanket during a game of hide-and-seek. While Neil searched, Deuce leaned over and teased, "Sleep, little sister, sleep," and my gosh, I loved it when he did that. To be someone's in that way only a sibling can. You're young; you're formative; you're lateral. In the strangest innate way, you carry a secret that neither of you can understand or voice; a guttural knowledge that you will outlive your parents and the resulting bond between the two of you is different from the bond between them and you. I had that with Clay and Martin and occasionally Deuce. And they're all gone now.

Owl treats me like his kid.

Now he, more than my mom, throws his protective force field into the ether for me. I don't know if that would have happened if Deuce hadn't died. The tenderness of our relationship has solid roots without our shared griefs, but those have surely welded us together. If I could ever bring myself to go home to Grand Junction, I would walk through the woods in LaRue with him. I would turn over rocks and look for bones. I would hold his hand and say, "Let's find who killed your boy."

But I can't. I can't go back there.

Heartbreak smacks me in the face at the county line.

Owl will never leave. But part of me wishes he'd move somewhere else and call and say, "I've got a bedroom for you if you ever need one." I doubt I'll ever marry, but if I do, he'll be the one to give me away.

I listen as he tells Dana about his retirement and how Parson offered him a fluff gig at the lodge being a maître d'. "Can you believe that?" he asks Dana. "Like I'm so hard up for money that I would want to do that." He has choice words for the work offer that his preacher would not approve of. "All I need is a walking stick and a break in this case."

Rain or shine. Cold or hot. Searching is his only priority these days.

If I were to go missing, my mom wouldn't look for me. She never looked for Clay. After the police listened to my and Andy Bedford's accounts and told her he didn't survive and they'd likely never find his remains, that was that. A dusting of the hands. A decision to pause my brother's life in the past without even so much as a skeleton.

The way people cope with loss fascinates me. Like how does Owl find the gumption to search every day for Astrid, who isn't even his own daughter, while my mom crawls into bed with her head under the pillow rather than look for Clay? Even stranger, that same man loves my mother so much he forgives her every day for not loving me the way he thinks she should. That doesn't even get into Molly and Danny's grief response and all the complicated emotional subsets of having a son accused of murdering his missing sister.

When he's sure I'm asleep, he asks Dana how I'm doing and she says, "I think she's fine as long as her compartments stay intact."

Owl understands without asking a follow-up question.

We arrive at Dana's apartment exhausted and starving. She invites Owl to stay, but he turns her down. He ventures inside long enough to pee and visit her guest bedroom, which has the cardboard diorama of LaRue I built in the months I stayed here after trial.

I can't believe she kept it intact.

Owl's equally surprised. "Thank you," he whispers, standing over the many squares of yellow marked *Searched*.

"It's not a cold case for me," she says.

We have a final hug and he leaves without another word.

"Thank you," I call after him from the door. "I'll let you know about PoppaJack."

The minute the door closes, Dana, Galen, and I sink into her couch. The dog wedges his body into a position to touch us both. I stroke his head, amazed at how easily my affection swells in the presence of this sweet creature. Dana orders food like the apocalypse is coming tonight and then falls back against the couch.

"So?" she says, and even though I can't see her through my closed eyelids, I know what she's asking. *Neil.*

"It was crazy hard to see him."

"I'm sure. I kept praying he would actually let you in."

"Me too," I admit.

I know Dana's history the way she knows mine. Precious confessions discussed over ten-mile runs, hours at the range, wine and tacos. She's never been in love. People have been in love with her, but she's never done more than talk herself into or out of those relationships based on pro and con lists. Eventually there are more cons than feelings. She says the difference between us is I'm a turtle and she's a frog. I take my home with me; she figures out how to make a home with whatever she's working with that day: lungs or gills. Both equal lifestyles of isolation.

"Can I tell you something awful?" I ask.

"Anything," she says.

I make myself form the words I've wanted to say since the trial. "It would have been easier if he'd died in LaRue too. I don't mean I wish he was dead. I mean, if I had to choose between him being in prison and him dying in LaRue, I might actually choose the dying, because if he was dead, I could let him go. Like this, I feel like I'm abandoning him."

There, I said it. The worst thing. From the worst place in me.

Dana sees the tornado of emotions and accepts me without judgment. "What if you give yourself a deadline? Maybe even multiple deadlines."

"Say more."

"Go see PoppaJack. If there's nothing there, come back here and we'll burn the diorama."

"We can't do that."

"We can. You can stop looking for justice."

"I can't. Think of Owl." I pause. "Think of Astrid."

Dana shoves me with her toe. "Think of Lucy."

The doorbell rings and Dana launches off the couch to the door. Our General Tso's is here. I look into Galen's mile-deep eyes. They're my favorite cavern in the world. I hold his velvety triangle ears and stroke the fur in my fingers. "Okay," I say, and feel like I'm agreeing to run a marathon on stilts.

If there's nothing at PoppaJack's, I'll do something for me.

Chapter Six

The next morning I leave Dana snoozing and hit the range on my way out of Zionsville. If I want to keep my sponsorships and make good on my promise of a gold medal, I can't afford to miss practices.

I would like a new air rifle. Shooting Neil's competition gun keeps him fixed in my everyday life in a way that nothing else does. A former teammate offered to trade after Paris; it might be time to call her and see if she's still up for that deal. I'm not sure I can afford a new one unless I can finagle a new deal from the Walther rep, and I don't know that I'll ever fire a gun without thinking of Neil. That feels like God looking at a rainbow and not remembering He created the sun.

Two hours of shooting later and I'm on the road.

This time to Tampa.

I'm wearing my boots for the occasion of seeing my grandfather, and they feel heavy on the gas pedal. I drive I-75 south until it basically runs out and find a motel close to his retirement home. I am the Guy Fieri of crappy hotels. I actively choose the dumps and dives. The places that need paint and smell of smoke, that sell by the hour and hide their crimes in thin, cheap bedspreads. I don't know why exactly. I leave them feeling worse about the world, but a little bit better about myself. Dana proposes it's because Robert is filthy rich, and maybe she's right.

I am up with the sun and at PoppaJack's at a time that makes me nervous to ring the doorbell.

PoppaJack's nurse, Salome, answers on the third buzz and recognizes me from the framed photos on his walls. She's happy I'm here for a visit and babbles about his condition. The living room smells of cedar and menthol, the kitchen of freshly burned toast. Where once his aromas came from hiking in the woods and aftershave, they now belong to mothballs and Icy Hot.

PoppaJack has dozens of pictures of Clay and me. Dozens more of Mom and my grandma, whom I never met.

The nurse catches the tremble of my lip and removes a photo from the wall for me to hold. "You okay?" she asks.

I laugh. "I haven't been okay in years, but I can do this."

I open the door.

The man in the bed doesn't resemble my grandfather. Doesn't resemble a man. He's a bag of bones under a lightweight white quilt. I cross the room to stand beside him and slide my hand across his forehead. He has a fuzzy shock of white hair that's much thinner than I remember.

"PoppaJack," I say.

He stirs.

I kiss his cheek and his skin is the texture and temperature of refrigerated wax paper. The sensation is wildly uncomfortable. I'd like to leave the room, but his eyes are open. Staring.

They smile for the rest of his face and there's recognition.

"Joanny," he says like he's been waiting on her to come. "Is everything okay with the baby?"

I nod. He's in another time and place.

"What did Owl say?" he says.

I lean closer. "What?"

He whispers, "Did he agree to keep the baby a secret?"

"Did Owl what?" I ask. "Which baby?"

PoppaJack's head lilts to the side and he smiles wildly. "The baby girl."

Time stops.

Did Mom have an affair with Owl? Is PoppaJack

saying I am Owl's kid? This could be nothing, nothing at all. Or it could be so much more.

I try to get PoppaJack to say something else, but he falls asleep.

I leave the room in search of his nurse and find her sitting at the kitchen table. "Can you give him something to wake him up?" I ask. "He said something important and then he fell asleep."

Salome smiles sadly. She stands and takes a glass from the cabinet and fills it with tap water. I take that as an invitation to wait. "It's good that you came." It feels like she's working hard to keep the judgment from her voice. "He has so few visitors."

"He told us not to," I say. "I'm not supposed to be here now."

"You were a child. He talks about you. All of you."

I pull the woven-backed chair out and sit opposite her. "What does he say?"

"Mostly stories of nothingness." She pushes a basket of sweets in my direction. "Would you like a Little Debbie? He loves these so much."

"No," I say more sharply than I intend.

"You look like you could use a Little Debbie."

Salome's not going to stop unless I agree. I want to keep her talking, so I accept the basket with Zebra Cakes and Oatmeal Creme Pies and choose the Zebra. I take a demonstrative bite and say, "What does he say about a man named Owl?"

"The cop?"

"Yes," I say.

"He likes him better than Robert. That's a popular topic around here. And I really don't know why. Robert is perfectly lovely."

I'm not expecting that opinion. "When did you meet Robert?"

"Oh, he comes every year in January and pays."

"For what?"

Salome lifts her hands into the air. "Me. The condo. Jack's insurance and medicines. Everything."

That's astounding. I almost don't believe her.

"He could do all that over the phone," I say absently. "Why come here?" I think about how important Robert is to Grand Hydro and how he tries not to be away from home and Mom.

She considers this. "I suppose he could, but I don't think he likes to send cash in the mail. He usually visits for an hour, writes checks, and adds money to the safe in case we need anything."

"Wait. Robert uses a safe here?"

"Oh yes, in the spare bedroom."

I take a second Little Debbie from the bowl, knowing it will please the nurse. I change the conversation to her and ask if she likes her work. "This must be a lonely job," I say. She tells me about her daughter, Gloria, in the Peace Corps. I move the topic in this direction for thirty minutes and listen to her stories of Gloria, who is creating a written language for a native tribe of Africa. "There'll be a picture book eventually," Salome brags.

When I have listened long enough and gotten us both Cokes from the fridge, I work my way back to Robert. "Salome," I say cautiously, "since I'm here, I could look things over, let Robert know if PoppaJack needs anything."

"As long as I can watch," she says, only mildly suspicious.

"Oh, absolutely." I silently curse her loyalty and my negligence. If I came more often, she'd trust me.

We move in tandem to the safe and I kneel beside her as she dials the combination. The safe has shelves, and I don't know what I'm looking for now any more than I knew in the days after the murder. But I feel the ping in my gut that says this is where Robert hid whatever Martin found. Not in our house. Not in his office drawers. Here, where none of us would ever think to go or look.

The stored paperwork is neat, fairly standard, and boring. Life insurance policies. Bank accounts. Envelopes of cash with various labels. Paperwork from the sale of LaRue. I'm thinking there's nothing here until I reach to the back of the top shelf. My fingers close around something hard and plastic with an elastic strap.

I bring the object into the light.

A GoPro camera with a flash drive taped to its side.

Knowing the task ahead will not be easy, I scream with delight, putting on my happiest voice. "Oh my gosh,

I can't believe he kept this. Salome, is there a computer here? We have to watch these." I'm up and searching the room with wild interest for a desktop or laptop. "I have to see these photos. They're from our last camping trip with Clay."

Salome nods, the smallest of smiles on her lips. "There is one in Jack's room."

For the sake of my memories, she offers me privacy.

Chapter Seven

PoppaJack's snores shake the bedside lamp.

Owl has a secret baby girl. I could be Owl's kid. Is there evidence on this drive of that too? My breath catches in my throat. Only one way to find out. I slide the flash drive into the USB slot and click anxiously into the new folder that appears on the desktop.

There are two files.

One labeled *Tamerlane*. The other *Dam Footage*.

Four documents are in the *Tamerlane* folder.

One is a series of emails, twelve in total, between Tamerlane Assets and Jack Rickard. All sent prior to the dam break. They offered to purchase the LaRue land tract from PoppaJack and are heavy hitters about it. He refuses and the amount grows nonsensically. All the way to $25 million. They're indignant. One of the emails says, "Environmental studies show no signs of oil or sellable minerals. The land will be preserved from development. Trust us, you need to sell now." It's like they know something he doesn't.

PoppaJack writes back, "I don't trust anyone who says 'trust us.' The land's not for sale. Not now. Not ever."

The second document is the record of sale for LaRue.

Robert, not Tamerlane, purchased the tract for a mere $375,000. Multiple property assessments are included. Each conclude the dam break drastically reduced the property value, and by the time Robert made his offer, LaRue had fallen well below the previously assessed value. Comically below Tamerlane's initial $25 million.

The third document includes emails sent between an anonymous account to Andy Bedford. I skim and then reread. Skim and reread a second time. Andy Bedford is offered, and accepts, the job of blocking the LaRue Dam with a metal grate. Two hundred fifty thousand dollars upon installation. Another $250,000 when his assessment report is filed with the army and the EPA declares any failure is an act of nature.

In January of the year the dam broke, Andy states that his associate has placed the grate over the sluice gate. He predicts that by April the following year the dam will have failed.

He records the first transfer.

The January after the dam break, Andy submits his assessment and requests the second transfer.

This is the reason for the safe. The reason Robert comes here in secret every January. I knew the moment I read the first screenshot with Andy Bedford's name.

The fourth and final document is Robert's resignation from Tamerlane. It's signed and notarized in October, before the dam broke in November. With the resignation, he has included a letter detailing other documents in the file and how he blackmailed Tamerlane into giving him enough money to buy the land from PoppaJack and invest in Grand Hydro's construction.

I can barely breathe.

If anyone released these documents, so many people would go to prison. Robert included.

This is what got Martin and Deuce killed.

I email the folders to myself.

I click back to the front and choose *Dam Footage*.

The file is dated the day before the dam break.

The video starts.

A much younger Robert is out of focus and filling the screen. He's got the long hair man-bun he had when we first met. He's wearing a wetsuit. The sun's blazing, but the trees are orange and red. The water of the Tennessee is already cold.

"Hi. Robert Carlin here." He's self-conscious. Maybe nervous. Maybe cold. "Behind me is the LaRue Dam, located on the private property of Jack Rickard. This dam controls a minor offshoot of the Tennessee River, Vespers Creek, primarily for flood control and to create a hunting reserve that is a source of tourism in Cleary County, Kentucky.

"I have acquired information that Tamerlane Assets hired two men from Grand Junction to block this dam's sluice gate with an additional metal grate. They're hoping to create slow, imperceptible damage that will eventually cause this dam to fail. If the plan succeeds, that action will create catastrophic flooding in the reserve and make a case to remove this dam and create a hydroelectric project four miles upriver on the Tennessee. The new hydro project would be located on the same land. I'm going to show you the grate now."

Robert straps the camera to his forehead and eases into the water, inhaling sharply at the temperature. The next few minutes are painfully slow. He swims and makes mention of the strong current. "This is going to be harder than I thought," he says to the camera.

In the distance, three person-shaped shadows appear on the berm. Two tall individuals, one short. I can't tell who they are because the camera lowers into the water.

Robert, now within touching distance of the dam's concrete wall, fills his lungs with oxygen and dives. You can hear someone shouting, "Hey! Hey! Don't do that, man. It's dangerous."

The voice sounds like Orson Welles. Like Deuce.

Robert moves easily through the water, like he's being propelled. The sluice gate comes into view, and with the light from the GoPro, you can see someone has attached industrial-strength hard cloth over the water tunnel. You can also hear the suction of water and, simultaneously, Robert's struggle.

He gurgles and the GoPro catches the stream of bubbles.

It feels like he's been under the water a long time. His arms flail into view, and then I hear something crack. He jerks backward and stops moving. The camera shows only the water now. A passing school of fish. A sunken log.

Moments pass.

How long has he been under the water? One minute? Two? I check the feed. He's at a minute and thirty-eight seconds on the camera.

His body billows slightly with the suction of the water through the grate.

Then the camera view moves again.

It takes me a moment to realize that it, and thus him, is climbing, not sinking. Something is moving him. The water lightens through a spectrum of greens until the sky brightens the water to almost clear.

I hold my breath, watching, scared, even though I know how this ends. My stepfather lives.

Still, Robert should be dead. He was under the water for a long time.

The camera jolts again, changes position completely.

Now white daylight and blue sky fill the screen. Framed in the center of the GoPro is a gasping, amped-to-the-gills Deuce. "I gotcha," he says over and over. The view wobbles, the dam growing farther and farther away in the screen. Deuce must be rescue swimming with Robert. There's splashing next, then the heaving effort of dragging him onto the beach.

Deuce is off camera momentarily. He's gasping for air and screaming for help. The camera shakes and then falls to the side and shows the hair on Deuce's knees. Deuce is in full frame now. He rights Robert's head and begins giving him mouth to mouth, cussing through the effort and fear.

The camera jolts as Robert coughs.

He's alive again.

Deuce is in Robert's face again, wiping my stepdad's hair out of his eyes and shaking him. "Hey, man," he says, leaning even closer. "What were you doing down there? Trying to get yourself killed? You can't go near the sluice gate. The suction will kill you."

The camera cuts to black.

Chapter Eight

The Little Debbie Zebra Cake threatens to come up. I fold myself over and hold my ankles. *Blue whale breath*, I think.

But there's no way to breathe.

I can make mental sense of the footage and the contents of the folder, but slotting this information into place is revolutionary and revolting. Robert knew. He's always known. He even documented the crime.

Martin was right. About all of it.

The dam break wasn't an act of God; someone planned and paid for the wall of water that carried my brother away. Tamerlane.

The entire time he dated my mother, Robert knew what his company did to her son, to Troop 1404, to me. Robert sat at our little farm table that first Thanksgiving, held my mother's hand, and raised a glass of sparkling grape juice to the life Clay would never live, while knowing exactly who took it from him. Worse even, he sat glassy-eyed at another family table and lied when Dana asked if he could think of anyone who would want to hurt his son.

Robert was the person with a motive to hurt Martin. And if not Robert, anyone and everyone caught up in the LaRue Dam Break cover-up.

Did Robert kill his son to keep this story hidden? To cover his own tracks? Or did he pay someone else to do it?

Andy Bedford? His associate?

Or someone from Tamerlane?

Salome calls out, "Lucy, it's time for Jack's medication."

"Give me another minute, please." I step to the door and quietly turn the bolt.

Fear roars at the surface. Salome is a harmless care-giver, but I already feel watched, like Robert might have seen me open these files. Salome's heavy body traverses the carpet, back and forth to the kitchen, in a loop. I only have a few more minutes.

I perch at the edge of PoppaJack's bed and force myself to hold one thought at a time.

Then I play out a scenario where Martin confronts his father about the dam break and the emails. Robert doesn't behave violently; he barters like a businessman. Which is exactly what he did with Tamerlane after the dam failed. Not a man who rants and raves and demands justice. Instead, Robert leverages the information and builds Grand Hydro right out from under them. Maybe that was his plan from the beginning, or merely a side effect. His documentation, even his demeanor and desperation on the video, does make it seem like he refused to be involved in breaking the LaRue Dam in order to build a new dam upstream.

The trouble with that scenario is Martin didn't confront his dad with these details. He told me instead. Told me he found evidence and was scared. This flash drive must be what he was going to show me after the game. We were going to figure out what to do together. Only I didn't listen. I was too busy protecting my mother to understand what he knew about his father.

That doesn't mean Robert killed Martin himself. I honestly can't imagine that.

And at least two other men knew what happened to the LaRue Dam because they caused it: Andy Bedford and his associate.

The flooding. The deaths. Sweet Clay. A double homicide. Neil's incarceration. Everything.

Andy could not have known the dam would fail so quickly; the speed was an act of nature. No one could have predicted twelve inches of rain in five hours, but they had to have known they were at least hurting PoppaJack's land. Maybe they lulled themselves into believing no one would be in LaRue when it broke. Andy didn't think of the hunters. Of PoppaJack. Of the five-year-old kid who loved glowbugs and couldn't pronounce his g's.

Andy Bedford is a drunk who narrowly escaped prison. His footage of the dam inspection kept him from going to jail, but the dam break ruined his life. Even when he was exonerated, the town still blamed him. He lives on a farm and sells compost for a living. From engineer to crap salesman. Would he care enough about the remainder of his life to kill Martin and Deuce? Robert might have paid him to care.

Because, at some point, Robert knew Martin knew. He must have. The moment he went to wherever he hid this flash drive and found it missing. He would have searched Martin's stuff, found it, and at some point, after the funeral, moved it here, to PoppaJack's safe. The one place no one would ever in a million years think to look.

Still, whoever committed the murder had to be strong enough to move Martin's body from the Hummer to the duck blind. Andy's not exactly the picture of health. He would have left a trail. Unless . . . Well, he could have moved it using the creek, the same way Neil moved the blind into place.

That's when my insides explode.

This evidence can get Neil released.

If I can prove someone else is guilty, Neil will be set free.

Chapter Nine

There's still so much I don't know. I wish I could talk to Deuce.

Deuce saved Robert, but how did he know Robert was in danger if he wasn't the one who put the metal over the sluice gate?

It's likely that Martin was right again. Deuce was Andy Bedford's associate and Robert paid him every month to keep quiet about the grate damage. His testimony alone would have confirmed that Robert knew about the plan to sabotage the dam. There had to be something there.

Robert came into our lives the following year, and

Deuce never showed any familiarity toward him and vice versa. That had to have been hard to fake; our families were together all the time. And why fake it for nothing?

The fridge closes and Salome's feet are on the carpet outside the door again. My questions will have to wait. I can't afford for her to call Robert. I say, "I'm coming right out," and push the chair under the desk, hoping she will hear through the door.

Before I disconnect the flash drive, I check my email to confirm the files have arrived, then I forward everything except the GoPro footage to Dana and Owl. That file is too large to send. I save it and everything else in an untitled file on the desktop and upload it to the Dropbox account with all my Olympic videos. Then I put the GoPro back in the safe and open the door to PoppaJack's room.

"Did you have a special time?" Salome asks.

"Memories are hard," I say, then thank Salome for allowing me privacy.

Salome wakes PoppaJack for his medicine, but he falls asleep after he swallows the pills. "I'm sorry," she says.

"Me too," I say. I turn to Salome for one final piece of information. "Did you help PoppaJack mail a card to Neil Clark?"

"Oh yes. In Michigan City. The correctional institute."

"Right. Do you remember why he wrote that card?"

"He was having a good day and someone called, said she was from home, and asked to speak with him. I let him take the call; he has so few contacts," she says with pity.

"He didn't say who it was?"

"No, but she sounded young, and maybe like she didn't know Jack's current condition. He told me what he wanted to say, and I mailed the card that day."

"Thank you," I say, regretting how set my mother was on no one from Grand Junction finding out PoppaJack had dementia. "He'd die of embarrassment," and "Let him keep his dignity," Mom used to say. There's no way to know if Astrid told him what to write on that card, but I'm fairly sure she didn't know PoppaJack was impaired.

Salome and I say goodbye on the stoop and I promise to visit again soon.

I can't tell who is dangerous anymore. Astrid? Robert? Tamerlane? Andy Bedford?

Outside, I look around, suspicious of palm trees and azalea bushes, expecting someone to confront me about what I now know.

I try Dana first. She doesn't answer and I scream with frustration.

Then Owl. The call cuts to voice mail instead of ringing through.

My next step is to call Parson. Maybe he was with Deuce when he rescued Robert. He doesn't answer.

Who else would know?

Someone from the camping weekend. I can't call

Mom, not yet. I try FaceTiming Molly, Danny, and finally get Wilma. It's nearly 11:00 a.m. and she's in her shop arranging a pyramid of local honey. "Lu-Lu, how you been?" she greets.

"Can you step away? Somewhere private?" I ask.

Her face scrunches with worry and starts a long, dizzy—for me—walk to the alleyway. I can tell she's behind the Chamber from the building's facade. "You look white as a sheet, honey bear," she says. "You start talking right now and I'll do whatever I can to help."

"I'm fine," I say. "Listen, the weekend of the dam break, didn't Parson and Deuce stay in your cabin?"

"Yes."

"This is weird, but did Deuce say anything about rescuing someone, or did he ever mention later that he met Robert the weekend of the dam break?"

"Your stepdad, Robert?" Wilma asks, raising an eyebrow.

"Yeah."

Wilma strains, like she's looking into the past through eyeglasses with a severe prescription. "Let's see. The boys fished all of Saturday. I remember that. Now, Deuce was in a bad mood that night, but he said that had to do with his dad." She squints harder. "Then we had that business with the pontoon. And . . . sorry, Lu-Lu, I've done loads of therapy, but there are things about that weekend that are plain gone. I remember Parson cooked for us all. And you know what, I think maybe Owl and Deuce were fighting about Deuce being a cop. That's about all I know about the boys. Why are you asking?"

I can't tell her what I've found at PoppaJack's. I don't even want her to know I'm in Tampa. With her big mouth, that would get back to Robert fast. "A therapy thing."

There's a flicker of something that's there and then leaves. "What?"

"Nothing."

"Come on, Auntie. What was that look?"

"Well, I was thinking. You asked if Deuce met Robert the weekend of the dam break. I don't have any idea if he did, but Owl did."

"What makes you say that?" I ask in a measured tone, even though I'm starting to feel light-headed.

"Well, later on, when your momma met Robert, Owl had a fit about it. I asked him why, you know, trying to get him to admit that he had a thing for your momma, which he swore he didn't, even though he did, plain as day. Anyway, he said that wasn't it. He told me he met Robert on the dock the weekend the dam broke and he didn't like him one bit. I think he was in the marina when we tried to rent the pontoon."

"Hmm."

"Those two were always off to the races. Robert and Owl, I mean. With your momma between them. And then the money fiasco."

"What money?"

"Oh, Owl had a bunch of money, post the great

divorce of Donna Jo." Auntie says this like it's a historical event, and I suppose to that group of friends it was. "You know Donna, gambler through and through. Evidently she got lucky on the boat and unlucky in the courtroom. Owl ended up holding a chunky chunk of her change and he wanted to invest in Grand Hydro and Robert wouldn't let him. Even though he let the rest of Joanny's friends. That's ultimately how I had enough to open my new shop. Anyhoo, Owl didn't like Robert, but you didn't have to be an analyst to see the wisdom in investing."

"You all invested in Grand Hydro?"

"Well, yeah, honey. Who wouldn't?"

"Do you have any idea how much Owl wanted to invest?"

"I want to say it was $250,000 or some astronomical number. I only know the amount because he ended up investing in Parson's Lodge instead."

"Thanks, Auntie," I say and hang up.

Two hundred fifty thousand dollars?

Owl could have been Andy Bedford's associate, and I just sent him all of Robert's files.

Chapter Ten

I'm in the truck again and I can barely hold my phone, my hand is shaking so badly. I want to throw up all that sugar in my stomach.

Dana calls. She read the files.

I listen on autopilot as she regurgitates all the mental conversations I had in PoppaJack's bedroom about who, what, when, and where. We have similar conclusions, which isn't surprising. She's trained me to think like her. When she finally takes a breath, I tell her there's more and that I might have made a huge mistake. The conversation with Wilma rips out of me, to which she says, "Owl? No way. Not possible."

When I don't answer, she says, "Lucy, can you hear me? Lucy! It's not him."

I can't make myself speak.

"*Lucy.*"

"I'm not saying it's him. I don't want it to be him." I stumble over my words like I can't believe I'm saying this aloud either. "I'm saying $250,000 is—"

"Astrid," she says. "What about Astrid? Why spend all these hours looking for her if he killed Deuce and Martin? Come on, Luce. You know Owl."

"I thought I knew them all."

"You do. You know Owl. He loves you."

"People are more than one thing," I say. "Think about it. He called off the search because of the fog. Couldn't he also have controlled where we went and then made sure there would be scads of people around when the bodies were discovered the next morning? Wasn't he in one of the teams that found the bodies?" I don't remember.

"But he's Owl," she says.

"We all pitied him. Plus, he had Neil. Whoever did this had to know us all well enough to set up Neil."

Then I remember what PoppaJack said to me about the baby girl Owl had with my mother. He is a man willing to keep secrets. That doesn't make him a murderer. But it adds to my knowledge that there's more to Owl than he's shared with me.

I wonder then, did my father find out about Mom's infidelity? Is that why he didn't swim across the creek for me and Clay? Maybe he thought we weren't his and we weren't worth it. Is that why he left?

"I sent him the files," I remind her.

Dana momentarily loses her composure, which tells me she's not as certain of Owl's innocence as she wants me to believe. "Okay, here's what we're going to do. I'm going to call Owl and tell him I sent the files to a friend in the FBI and see how he reacts."

"Okay," I say.

"Go find a range and shoot for a couple of hours and then head this way. I'll call you back as soon as I know more."

"Okay," I agree.

"Don't give up on Owl. Please," she says before she hangs up.

She's right. There are plenty of other people to be angry with. But disappointment is different from anger. And if there's a world where Owl did this, maybe I don't want to know the truth. Maybe I won't answer the phone when she calls, or ever again. Because he, as a cop, might have believed that a new dam would bring prosperity to the county. A prosperity we desperately needed at the time. No one could have seen that rain coming. It could have been a terrible accident.

I stuff all my fear, anger, and disappointment into that inner compartment in my soul and find it's very hard to close the lid.

Instead of finding a shooting range and hitting the

highway, I go back to the motel where I spent the night and rent another room. I lie on the mattress, smelling the cigarette smoke from the room next door and listening to a couple fighting on the stoop outside. She wants to eat at Waffle House; he wants Cracker Barrel. *Oh, for such a simple fight*, I think and close my eyes against the noise of the world.

I should call Dana and let her know I'm here, but I can't muster the energy. Instead, I turn my phone off entirely, and for the first time in a long time, I ask myself whether I care if I ever wake up.

The world is not a good place. It is grossly unfair and audaciously evil, and yet it's the container of my life. Something in me hates it, but something stronger in me thrums, *I will not be beaten*. How much tragedy can one life hold?

Well, for today, at least this much.

I turn off the light and sleep.

Chapter Eleven

When I wake up, I don't know where I am. The scratchy comforter reminds me. Tampa. Then the rest of it, I remember that too.

I reach across the bed, slide open the curtain over the air-conditioning unit, and see the security light blinking in the parking lot. The digital clock says it's 9:00 p.m. But which day does this 9:00 p.m. belong to? I feel groggy enough I might have slept through a whole day. It wouldn't be the first time I've done that to escape trauma.

I do a starfish stretch to wake up. My skin itches for a shower. I reach for the back pocket of my jeans for my phone. It's not there. I find it loose in the sheets after several nervous seconds of searching.

When I power it on, message notifications cover the length of the phone.

Twenty-two from Dana. More from Owl, which makes me seize with worry. Parson, my mother, Wilma. Another from a reporter. My Olympic team thread from 2024 has thirty-four texts.

Whatever this is, I probably don't want to know.

I give myself a five-second count of ignorance before I unlock my phone and tap on Dana's name. The first text says, I need you to call me. Then she elevates to, I'm calling the police if I don't hear from you. That one was thirty minutes ago. I dial her number without looking at anything else, my heart thumping.

"I was asleep. I've been asleep. No one came after me," I say before she can speak.

I hear her exhale with relief and then again, though not with relief. "You don't know yet, do you?"

"Know what?"

She switches the call to FaceTime. I have no idea what I look like, probably a hot mess, but her puffy, red eyes tell me the news is bad.

"Luce, I'm going to say this and then I'm going to come get you. You're going to stay right where you are until I get there. Promise me, okay?"

"You're scaring me," I say.

"I know, but you have to promise me. You have to."

"Okay. I promise." My heart quickens. Heat rises in my throat in anticipation.

"Five hours ago, Neil killed himself in prison."

"No."

"He confessed to murdering Deuce and Martin. He said he was the reason the LaRue Dam broke. He said Andy Bedford, his swim coach, talked him into putting a metal wire piece over the sluice gate for Tamerlane."

"No. That's not possible."

"There's more," she says.

"Luce, he told them where to find Clay's remains. His suicide note says he found the body when he was hunting. He told the police right where to go. They're there now on the scene. They have the skeleton of a child."

"Someone got to him," I say. "Someone got to Neil."

She doesn't argue and she doesn't agree.

"I spoke with your mom," she says. "I'm gonna get you home to Grand Junction."

I suppose I say something coherent about my address because hours later, although I cannot say how many, Dana knocks on the motel room door. I open the door, wearing yesterday, smelling of yesterday, and too broken to stand for more than the seconds it takes me to turn the handle. Dana joins me on the floor and swamps me with a hug. She's always been a good hugger, full of empathy, but this is more. This is anguish, and the hug is as close as she can come to bubble wrapping me away from the world. Galen lays his chin on my shoulder and I feel his steady breath on my neck.

Afterward, the three of us begin the fifteen-hour drive home.

Chapter Twelve

I gave up crying after Neil went to prison and I mostly haven't picked it back up. Like crying is a soda addiction that can be left behind with enough willpower.

It is safe to say that today is the day I run out of willpower.

When Dana stops at a Target to get me clothes, a stranger pulls a Kleenex from her purse and lays it atop a stack of Red Hot Chili Peppers T-shirts. My own personal dam has broken. The compartment inside me has been demolished with a nuclear bomb. I don't know if this is relief or grief, good or bad, but it all rockets out like vomit, like a living thing, a release of emotional muscles that have been clenched for twelve long years. My Clay is home. My Neil is gone.

There are too many tragedies to process. I barely remember high school chemistry, but separating these emotions seems like pulling apart atoms. Each molecule—Clay, Deuce, Neil, Martin—another explosion.

"I can't go home. I'm already tired of feeling," I say to Dana, who is crouched beside me on Target's industrial carpet. She wraps her arms around my back because we both know we are going to Grand Junction; whether I can or can't, we will. We must look strange: a mound of weeping women in aisle seventeen.

"Is this much bad possible?" I ask.

She offers a simple, unfortunate reply. "Yes."

"How do you keep going when—" My voice breaks.

"You just do."

"The bad isn't even over."

"No," she agrees. This is the thing I love about Dana. No buttercream icing to cover a cake of blood. When she speaks again, her voice tips toward controlled rage. "Someone did this to people you love, and we're not going to stop until we figure out who that is."

"You don't believe Neil's letter?" I ask.

"Maybe. I don't know yet."

I hear the *crack* of her jaw, the sound she makes when she's grinding her teeth side to side, when the rage is about to break free, and then, "I do know the evil stops here.

One piece of justice at a time. Think about Clay. He's home again. That's piece one."

A laser of heat hits my gut. Clay is home. I never thought this day would come. But in the few moments I've allowed myself to explore a future where my little brother's body was somehow discovered, Neil was always with me.

Neil. Owl. Deuce. Mom. Wilma. Danny and Molly. Astrid. Parson. The camping crew, together again, in finality, as we lay our boy to rest.

What's finality now?

Tamerlane caused the dam break. They hired Andy Bedford, and Andy Bedford manipulated a kid on a junior swimming team to help him. Robert knew. Martin found the evidence. Deuce saw the grate the day he saved Robert. Neil killed them. Neil's dead. Astrid's teaching violin lessons.

That's not finality; that's a Scorsese film.

Chapter Thirteen

The Nashville skyline fills the horizon. We've been driving for hours, stopping only for gas, energy drinks, and Galen's bladder. I work up the courage to ask the question that's been playing in my head the last hour. "Do you think God heard me?"

"Heard what?" she asks, but she must know: the conversation we had on her couch after my visit with Neil. My awful confession.

"Me wishing Neil was dead so I could let him go. I said it and then he died, Dana. What does that mean?"

"I'm not sure where God is in your story, but I'm pretty sure you're not His cocounsel on mortality issues.

You can absolve yourself of any form of thought-death. The real question is, did he truly take his own life?"

She's choosing to redirect toward questions that might someday have answers. I let her.

"How are we supposed to know?" I can't keep the anger from my voice. The old anger. He shut me out of his life. I've seen him twice in two years.

Dana rests one hand on the wheel and the other in Galen's shoulder fur. "You know him best."

"Knew."

"Do you think he's capable of death by suicide? Or what he confessed to in the note?"

I think of Neil in Michigan City. The cruel taunts from the guards. Fat Potter. The way he'd aged. And then, the last words he said: *I'm struggling, Luce.* "Maybe the suicide," I say to Dana.

That isn't what she expected to hear. "What are you thinking?" I ask.

"That this is all fairly neat and tied up, and I don't believe in bows when it comes to murder. Especially not after you found those files. They're not enough to exonerate Neil, but they would have been enough to reopen the case. Then, within twenty-four hours, Neil is dead, names himself the associate, and Andy Bedford is arrested. That's a heck of a bow."

"Do you mean Owl?" I ask quietly, wondering if his law enforcement connections might allow for such an arrangement.

Dana knows everything I found in PoppaJack's condo from my email, and somewhere, miles ago in Alabama, I told her what PoppaJack said about Owl being my father. She didn't receive the information well. She came to his defense faster than she was driving, and we'd already gotten one speeding ticket. "You can't trust the Alzheimer's to know your DNA. You don't look anything like Owl."

"I know," I'd said and scrolled through my phone photos until I found one of us next to each other. None of our features matched.

"I think," she says, "we have to put it on the table that someone, and I'm not saying it was Owl, only that it might have been, coerced Neil into confessing and then killed him."

I do believe it's easier for me to wrestle with the idea that Neil's last emotion was fear rather than sadness, because maybe I don't want sadness to have as much power as evil.

"How would we ever prove someone got to Neil?"

"Astrid."

"Astrid," I repeat.

If she's alive, she's the key to this.

"Trouble is," Dana says, "I can't figure out how she survived whatever happened that day in LaRue. Why do all the damage that has been done and then let Astrid go? Why leave a huge loose end when you tie up all the others one by one? Unless she helped."

"Come on," I say, exasperated by the idea. "I know her."

"You know all of them," she says.

I sigh.

"Someone let her live, and if that's true, she's alive for one of three reasons: one, she's willing to remain quiet; two, she's involved; or three, she's too scared to talk. So is there anyone she loves enough to remain quiet about murder?"

Truth is, Astrid wasn't close to many people. She had tons of friends and bandmates, but after Neil left for college, she probably spent more time with me and Martin than anyone else. "Neil, maybe. Her parents."

That sends us into silence.

"He could have done this," I say. "Like he said he did. And maybe we've been looking under rocks so long we can't stop turning them over."

I play out that awful Friday in LaRue two years ago with Neil as the murderer. Astrid's there. An unexpected witness to his actions. Maybe she even feels responsible for asking Deuce to meet her there. Did Neil intend to kill her when he put her in the water? *Underwater, baby.* Orson Welles. Then he couldn't, so he sent her away.

I am unable to accept this theory, and I sound as intolerable as I feel. "There's no way."

"Somewhere there's a way. Three people are dead," Dana growls, and Galen puts his wet nose on her neck. This makes her take a breath. "We need another opinion, and

I'm not sure whose it should be. I have friends in the FBI, but no one who can drop everything and come now for a case that looks open and shut. And then there's the fact that he knew where Clay's body was. All that time."

"If he was coerced, that piece of information could have been fed to him. It could have even been the leverage someone used to get him to take his own life. Like, I'll release Clay's bones if you confess to the murder. That might have tempted Neil," I say honestly. "He would know how much that would mean to me. And he might have believed that I . . . well, that I wouldn't move on if he was still alive."

Dana nods once at the theory. Not like she accepts it but like it's viable. "But by who? Who did the coercing?"

"Someone who has spent hours searching LaRue?" I ask, hating that this has circled back to Owl.

"Okay, Luce, let's say you're right. Who do we talk to next? Who can we trust?"

"Parson?" I offer. He was around for the whole timeline.

She considers this, already nodding slightly, when she says, "Maybe." There's an air of authority in her voice when she speaks again. "Okay, here's my best game plan. I work behind the scenes and locate Astrid. You should grieve, cry, get angry. Be normal." She gestures to the puffy skin under my eyes. "Tell everyone Neil's death is too much and you're ready to put all this behind you and go after Olympic gold. Then, if there is still someone out there, we don't give them any reason to target you. Then afterward, when we're back in Zionsville, you get a DNA test or ask Owl if he's your father, and we start again on the investigation from ground zero. But, Luce, for the next few days, you can't disappear on me and Galen. No turning off your phone. No solo investigations. No hiding in terrible motels. I should know where you are all the time. We're not going to tell anyone about the evidence you found at PoppaJack's house. And when Owl asks, I'll confirm that Neil was the associate."

"Is Andy Bedford talking?"

"I'm going to pay Andy Bedford a visit and find out."

I say nothing, but I know she's right.

In my head, I make a different sort of vow: if I figure out who did this to my family, I'm going to drown them in the Tennessee with my own two hands.

Chapter Fourteen

Going home after a long time away is expressed less in historical facts and more in the stories we tell and retell ourselves, like a game of telephone, played only by one person. Prevailing memories transform into one or two prevailing emotions that become one or two prevailing statements. You hear it from people in small talk all the time. Statements like: *I grew up in Alaska. My family loved baseball. We had a pool. My parents owned a llama farm.* As if a million memories merge into something far simpler. Something that can be shared on an elevator ride to the second floor.

For me, I can spit out my childhood in a single phrase: Grand Junction is the place my brothers died.

Who was it who said you can never go home again? Jesus?

There's a green highway sign at the Grand Junction city limits that reads "Hometown of Olympic Bronze Medalist Lucy Michaels." Mom didn't tell me they had installed that. Wilma must have been behind the effort. Little green signs are a Chamber of Commerce thing. And what other options did they have? *Grand Junction. Natural disaster and double homicide location. We're not the safest place to live.*

The minute we leave the main highway for River Road, Galen hops to the back seat and paces across the bench. He can sense the end of the trip is near. We're all aching to be out of the truck. It's almost five and the humidity is not slowing down. Normally I keep contact with Galen on long trips; not this one. Even my clothes feel like an unbearable weight.

We had the windows down most of today. My forearm is sunburned and my butt is numb and sticking to the leather seat. Then the Tennessee River comes into view, and I forget about nearly everything else. It's odd to love a thing that hurt you, but we all do it. I have two stories about that river. It's gorgeous and resourceful, *and*, at its worst, it tore us all apart. I don't miss living here.

Galen strains his ears toward the open window and whines. Then I hear the *pop, pop, pop. Pop, pop, pop. Pop, pop, pop. Pop.*

"Easy," I tell Galen. "Someone's target shooting." I often talk to him like he's a human.

There's a cadence to the firing. Ten more shots pop off in a row. Pause. Another ten shots. The caliber is lower. I've heard this thousands of times, caused it, but I didn't expect it to be part of the welcome wagon. The target shooting is coming from up the hill at Mom and Robert's house.

We turn onto the long drive and gear down to make the climb easier in my aging Nissan. A Lexus and an Acura block our garage doors. Owl's SUV has been left off to the side. Like maybe he didn't want to pull near Martin's old spot. Dana coasts into the grass and parks.

From the backyard, the gunshots come again. Then laughter.

Galen's whine grows louder, and to save his ears, Dana allows him to wait in the truck. She's not about to turn him loose. I tell Dana how in the old days we'd host potluck suppers and shoot cans and targets, the kids begging for a chance to compete with the adults. "You had a very different childhood from most people," she says.

"Not the people around here."

We follow the cobblestones around to the backyard. On the way, it's easy to picture Danny and Owl trading shots while Mom, Molly, and Auntie Wilma sit around the patio, swapping stories of their lost boys. To my surprise, Parson, Danny, Robert, and Owl are nowhere to be seen. The three women have dragged camping chairs into the yard and set an ammunition and wine station on the glass table. Mom loads a clip, a half-empty glass of red within reach. No large water jug today.

Auntie and Molly pass the handgun and wineglass between them. They're laughing. Or maybe they're crying. It's hard to tell. Peals of something are coming out of them. Molly has the gun and slaps the clip into place with certainty. There's no doubt where Neil got his eagle eye. The center of the paper target is completely gutted at the end of her ten reps. The afterburn smell is as familiar as a turkey roasting in the oven.

"Hi," I call gently, unwilling to startle any of them. Who knows how much they've had to drink.

"This is not what I expected," Dana whispers.

"Me either."

"Lu-Lu!" Auntie yells with delight.

Mom drops the clip and hurdles a potted plant to reach me. She's not as light on her feet, but she's so very her. There's an energy in her movement that's unique, a way she pauses as she arrives in front of me, like she's making a jump shot in basketball, flings her arms wide, and then flies toward me until our chests collide and my spine pops from being held so tightly. I mimic her movement, the us of us so ingrained there is nothing else to do but allow her to swallow me whole.

I am eaten by love.

And then by guilt.

I haven't been here for her. The thought afterward: *She hasn't been here for me either.*

Maybe we're both okay with that. Maybe grieving is never about fixing someone else; maybe it's only surviving the sadness by whatever means possible. There are so many ways to lose the people we love and so many different types of homecomings.

"Baby," she says.

"Hey, Mom." My emotions are warm and soft like melting wax.

"Thank you for being here," she says over my shoulder to Dana. "I didn't want her traveling alone, and to know she has you as a friend means the world."

Mom releases me and turns our focus toward Molly and Wilma. Wilma is rotund, her face flush from the wine and heat. She opens her arms and says, "Lu-Lu, I haven't seen you in a month of Sundays. Sure am glad you're home. Did you come in on Lake Road? Did you see your sign?" She's giddy, so giddy no amount of sad occasions can cover how happy she is for having pulled this off.

"I did," I say, and turn to Molly Clark. In the rightful universe that sign would have Neil's name on it too. "Thank you for the honor."

"Girl—" She stretches the word for a long time. "We are so proud of you."

I don't break eye contact with Molly.

I never know how to address her, and the problem has gotten worse over the years. If she'd only been part of the camping crew, I would have merged from a polite Ms. Clark to her first name the way I did with everyone else, but she was mother-in-law material, and I never got comfortable enough to call her anything. This lack of name is its own distance. I should call her something. Especially now. I don't, though.

"I am so, so sorry," I tell her, and Wilma and Mom fold around her.

She offers a demonstrative nod, an acceptance that I'm here and also that my words are not enough. She shrugs off her friends, turns back to the target, and reels off ten more shots. She doesn't miss.

Her action sends the group into silent awkwardness. No one appears to know what to say or how to hold their bodies. In some ways, Molly has more claim to my mom than I do. They've lived every year of their lives together, and I've been in the picture less than half of those.

I'm not sure if Molly's rejection means I should leave. I look to Mom, who shakes her head and says, "This is all so hard," and then she returns to Molly's side for support and says, "But we're going to walk through this together. No matter what."

Auntie nudges her hips into the space between Dana and me and throws her heavy arms over our shoulders. "It's by the grace of God those two stick together, ain't it? The grace of God," she repeats. "But there they are, tighter than bark on a tree. I mean, Lu-Lu, your momma said from the beginning that if Neil killed Martin, she wasn't gonna lose Molly too, and she hasn't changed a jot or tittle."

Dana raises an eyebrow as if to say, *Does she always*

talk like this? Or maybe, *I have no idea what that means.* Either would be fair. Wilma's more quintessentially Southern than bacon grease in green beans.

Wilma's still on the subject of Mom and Molly. "'Course no one knows what it's like to lose a child without a body to mourn like Joanny. She's about the only one who can reach Molly about Astrid. And now Neil, in a new way. They know a different momma-shaped pain than most people do. We'll have to pray we can do this again one day to celebrate Astrid."

"Do what exactly?" I ask.

Wilma says, "Did she not tell you what we're doing for the boys? All of them. Which was a thing at first, but it's settled now. Your mom insisted."

I shake my head, expecting to hear something dramatic like they're burying stuffed animals the way she did originally with Clay.

"Well, now, here's the plan." Auntie lowers her voice as she shares, like she doesn't want to interrupt whatever Molly and Mom are saying over by the gun and wine table with her painful logistics. "We're not gonna do a traditional funeral for Clay's recovery because we don't want to be hounded by the press. The media's here in force. That's why Robert's not here right now. He and the guys are holding a press conference on the far side of the dam to give us time alone."

Good call. Three grieving women with guns isn't a good combo.

"We're just the camping crew, gathering in LaRue tomorrow, there at the campground. We're plantin' all sorts of bulbs that will flower in the fall and spring. Forever."

"Hmm," I say, taking this in.

"We all need a reminder that there is still beauty in broken places."

Inwardly I question if Auntie pushed for this option so she could put that phrase on a town brochure.

"Everyone will have a chance to speak about all of our boys," she adds. "We're still debating on whether we do it for Astrid. We think we will and then we'll do it again if . . ." *They ever find Astrid's body*, I think.

I wonder what they would plant if it turns out Astrid is teaching violin as Ashley Smith.

"And Owl's okay with this too?" I ask, hoping for some insight into his behavior.

"Wilma," Molly calls. "It's your turn to be a show-off."

"Shooting calls," Auntie says, then tips her empty glass in our direction and stalks away.

For as long as I can remember, Wilma has carried a Mark IV pink and silver Ruger in her purse, right next to her police scanner.

"I can see why you took up the air rifle," Dana says. "Everyone here shoots."

"Yeah. They're good at it."

Wilma replaces the target Molly demolished, walks thirty paces away, turns with flare, and fires. She's right on the money.

That Weekend

I had never been a hero.

I always shied away from being the first or last one at anything. I lived in the middle. The middle at school, the middle in sports, the middle in the camping crew. Middle, middle, middle. The middle was good to me.

There was nothing middle about running in the wrong direction of floodwaters, but I'd never be able to look at myself again if I left LaRue without making sure the Boy Scouts knew how to get to Indian Mounds.

Clay didn't kick and scream when I turned the wrong way. He had no idea where we were. He simply trusted me to do the right thing. PoppaJack made me memorize the footprint of LaRue. The Boy Scouts would be set up on the plateau area near the Duck Pond. That's the best place for a big group to camp.

I was about four minutes from there, maybe five with Clay's little legs. The rain fell fast, but it couldn't fall that fast. We would not, could not drown in four minutes. I arrived at the ring of tents wearing only one shoe, my wet clothes clinging to my skin. "You have to get out!" I screamed.

The shadows of boys were visible inside their zipped tents. The nylon billowed in the wind, taking a beating.

I was right. They didn't know the creek was up.

"The area's flooding," I screamed. "You have to get out!"

Andy Bedford unzipped his tent and peered out. He told me later it was the sight of me that did it. That and the rain. The sky poured like a heavenly fire hydrant.

"Out!" he yelled with authority.

The boys emerged in seconds. They loved Andy and they trusted him. That's what gets you out of a tent in seconds. Love and trust are what send you running in the rain, not a one-shoed girl with a little brother on her back and blood on her face.

We ran for Indian Mounds.

The dam broke on our way up the hill. The ground beneath us crawled with vibration.

Andy stopped running so abruptly I ran over him. "That was the dam!" he yelled.

The wheels turned fast in Andy and in me. Our eyes cast around for solutions. There was only one. PoppaJack told me once that if the dam ever broke it would swallow this area like it hadn't eaten a meal in days. "Up," he said, pointing at the strongest tree with low branches.

You can't shove someone up a tree, but Andy did. We climbed like wild monkeys up as many branches as we could. "Hold on," Andy said. "Hold on."

He meant to stop climbing. We were out of time.

I wanted to be higher but there wasn't a higher. There were only feet and bodies and breathing and rain.

Clay fought me. "Stop fighting. Hold on!" I screamed over the downpour. I shoved his body against the trunk and wrapped his fingers around the closest branch he could reach. I couldn't fit behind him.

"Find a branch now!" Andy screamed at me.

The water came.

I glanced to the right, to the valley we'd run through. The wave moved, uprooting everything with it that wasn't deep in the earth.

Clay and I were maybe fifteen feet off the ground. Some of the boys were much higher. Their shoes were on my head. Mud dripped from their soles onto my face.

I didn't know if the tree would hold. Or if the wave would be above our heads. All I could do was wrap my hands around the closest branch and squeeze.

The wave slammed into me at thigh level. The mist from the impact covered my body.

I held on. I held my breath. I held my life to the bark.
The water ripped at my legs.

If I could stand in the middle of a thundercloud, the
sound would be a whisper compared to the water that hit
our tree.

Chapter Fifteen

The house smells of vanilla candle and citrus cleaner. The old booth in front of the windows, where Dana first sat to get to know us, is gone. In its place is a table that Parson must have commissioned for my mom. There's a sun-colored epoxy river down the middle. Beautiful oranges and yellows that are picked up in accents all around the room. Nearly every square inch of horizontal surfaces is covered with food. Everything from sandwich trays to Crock-Pot roast to red velvet cake. The South knows how to funeral.

When I look past the food, the first thing I notice is that the house appears more lived in than it used to.

Dishes are in the sink and magnets are askew on the fridge. We weren't allowed to put magnets on the fridge when we were teens, and really, we weren't supposed to touch any of the appliances without wiping them down afterward. I'm glad to see they've eased up. Through the window and across the yard, the women are crying and reloading. The familiar *pop, pop, pop* rings out again and again. The dam below is as stoic as ever. The media circus is a tiny speck in the distance.

I wonder what Robert's telling them.

Dana grabs a slice of ham and folds it into her mouth. I walk toward Robert's office and say, "We can check Facebook and see if they're on."

Dana scrolls on her phone and pumps up the volume on the press conference.

Robert's voice fills the hallway. "No, I do not believe Grand Junction is cursed. The atrocities we've experienced have been connected by law enforcement. There is no reason to believe our citizens or my employees are in any current danger. Next question."

"What about Astrid Clark?" a reporter asks.

"My thoughts and prayers go out to Molly and Danny Clark during this exceedingly difficult time. Unfortunately, Neil left no clues as to the location of his sister's remains. You've already heard from the chief of police on this matter, and my opinions are congruent."

A hand shoots up. "According to the visitors' log in Michigan City, your stepdaughter visited Neil Clark a few days before his death. Do you connect her to his decision to confess or take his own life?"

"No," he says. "My stepdaughter has nothing to do with this."

Another reporter calls out, "Owl Uri is on the same log. Did he have anything to do with the confession?"

"No." Robert is clear on the matter. Forceful and believable. He's eloquent. And as they ask more questions, he pivots around the hard places with ease. He's giving away nothing without shying away from the tough questions.

"Are we going to take advantage of our privacy?" I ask, turning the lock on his office door.

"Absolutely," Dana says, and pulls two pairs of gloves from her back pocket and flings one at me. "I'd like to know everything I can about Robert Carlin before I interview Andy Bedford."

The room has been arranged for video conferencing. Multiple screens and cords and blinking Wi-Fi boosters take precedence. There's a massive desk, which I searched right after Martin died, in the center of a circular red rug. One side of the room is filing cabinets. The other, a bar with a variety of bourbons. To the right of the bourbon, a closet.

"The key to the closet is under a bottle of Blanton's," I say and walk toward the desk. "That's the one with the horses on top."

"As if I don't know my bourbons." She picks up one

of the six squatty bottles with the little running horses at the top. Three attempts later, she finds the key. I settle in Robert's chair, choosing which drawer to open first. The shallow middle drawer is neat as a pin, a miniature version of Office Depot's supply aisle. The three drawers to the right vary in size. I start with the lower file drawer.

The documents appear to be typical household files: insurance, bills, remodeling quotes. Robert has a stash of blank thank-you cards with the Grand Hydro logo and various keepsakes. I thumb through the contents quickly and see nothing that might pertain to Tamerlane. Nearly everything in here is less than ten years old.

I change to the middle drawer. If the middle drawer was Office Depot, this is an Apple store. Every version of the iPhone or iPad Robert has ever owned and its subsequent cords, adaptors, and earphones are here. There's a pair of Bose headphones that have never been opened that I'm tempted to take. Moving up to the last drawer, I find only printer paper and Grand Hydro envelopes. I call up dozens of memories of Robert sitting here writing or typing notes. Mom used to beg Martin and me to pop in here and tell Robert good night before we went up to bed. During the many times we indulged her request, Robert would half look up from a card and say, "Good night," before returning to his work.

"Struck out," I tell Dana.

"Check and see if anything's taped to the underside,"

she says as she rifles through shoe boxes on the top of the closet rack.

I lower myself to the floor and pull out each drawer. There's nothing. I decide this is a worthless excursion before I pat the underside of the desk, beneath the drawers. There's something taped there. Excited, I shine my flashlight at what I think will be evidence against Tamerlane. Instead, there's a piece of copy paper with crayon scribbles from Martin. *Dad, you work too much. Love you. Come hug me whenever you find this. Even if I'm old and have my own kids.*

The tape that holds the paper in place has yellowed. How long ago did he write this? It's so him that I lie on the ground and miss him while I breathe three blue whale breaths.

"Luce!"

I scooch away from the desk and see Dana holding Robert's heavy coat. The one that always hangs on the back of the closet door. There's a small envelope in her hand, which she extends to me. There's no return address. No mail stamps. Only Robert's name and address on a typed label across the front.

Inside is a cut newspaper clipping and a small slip of paper.

The newspaper is the *Paducah Sun*'s coverage of Neil's death.

The paper reads, *One word and you're next.*

Chapter Sixteen

Robert is receiving death threats.

Which category do we put him in now: Villain or victim?

He's the man who saved my mom and pays for her father's home care needs. He's also the man who stayed silent about the company that killed my brother so he could build his hydro plant. Does he deserve to die for that?

"This proves Neil didn't take his own life."

"Not one hundred percent," Dana says. "It's a threat. And in the meantime, making this public will clearly put Robert at great risk. Do you want to chance that?"

I don't answer because we realize her phone is quiet.

The press conference video is no longer playing. "We should get out of here," I say.

Dana puts the note in her pocket and we erase all signs of our presence and slip from the room. "This changes things. Again. Luce, I can't believe I'm saying this, but I don't want you alone with Owl. Not until we find out who sent that note to Robert. Okay?"

"You think it's Owl?"

"I think we're running out of suspects that aren't Owl."

"Okay," I answer and stare longingly at the door to the roof. "I'll meet you in the truck. I need a minute before we leave."

When I lived here, the roof was one of my favorite places to spend time, and since we decided to get a motel rather than stay here, I might not see it again for a long time.

"I'll make us a couple of plates of food," she says before adding, "I'd hurry if you don't want to run into Robert."

I pound up the steps two at a time, knowing the moment I lower my body into the lounger, I'll rocket backward in time to a place I loved. Because of all the places in the house, this is the place I felt the most loved. One last time.

Our rooftop is decadent. There are two tiers to the patio, each with inlayed bamboo. Bamboo on the floors, steps, walls, and end tables. Potted plants are everywhere. The patio is secured with high-end industrial deck rails and taut wires. The loungers up here are worth more than most people's La-Z-Boy recliners.

Hot air hits me the moment I open the door. Galen barks in the distance when one of the women below fires a different-caliber weapon. They'll go at it until sundown. We're into the pinks and purples now. The citronella candles are already lit. I catch a whiff as I lean over the railing toward Grand Hydro.

"Hey, kiddo." The quiet voice comes from the higher-tiered patio.

A tiny scream slips out and I cover my mouth with my hand. "Hey, Owl," I say without turning around.

Chapter Seventeen

"I didn't mean to scare you," he says, his voice deep. Deep like Orson Welles.

"More like startled," I say, holding my breath. "What are you doing up here? I thought you were at the press conference."

I turn and put my back to the railing and look in the direction of his voice. He's sitting on one of the upper loungers, spinning the cylinder of a revolver.

"I'm trying to decide if I've got it in me to kill your stepfather." He slurs the words.

He's drunk.

"Why would you do that?" I ask calmly. If I scream

from here, Dana will hear me, but she can't get to me in time. The ground is thirty feet below.

Owl says, "I read the emails you sent. The files. He let it happen, and then he covered it up. All of this belongs to him. I want to tear him down. I want to put his face under the water and hold it there until a fish eats his eyes out of his skull while I watch. I want to throw him off his precious dam and pray he lands on a boat motor. That's what he deserves. This gun can't make him suffer enough."

I wonder if I can trust this reaction. This anger.

If the anger is real, Owl's not the killer either.

I lower myself to the deck railing and sit, which is a risk. It will be harder to run to the door if I'm wrong, but easier to keep him talking if I'm right.

"Robert's being blackmailed to stay quiet," I say. "I found the note in his office before I came up here. So if you kill him, it's another body to add to the count, and my mom—"

"Will be devastated," he finishes. "I've spent my whole life trying not to devastate your mom, and what did it get me?"

"Me," I say bravely.

Some smiles are audible. His smile can be heard all the way down to the river.

"Owl, is it me?"

"Hmm?"

"Your kid. Am I your kid?"

There. The question is out in the world. He might not

answer, but I asked. Maybe at the wrong time, maybe in the wrong place, maybe to the wrong person. The silence fills up so much time, I decide he won't tell me, and then he whispers, "No, sweetheart," and part of my heart breaks. Part of me had been hoping to have a father again. Then he says the name I never expected. "Astrid."

Everything falls into place at once.

Astrid Clark is Owl's daughter.

"She figured it out," I say.

Owl laughs. "Oh yeah, when she was thirteen. Stole Neil's kayak and paddled all the way down the creek to Topper's Landing and walked the rest of the way to my house." His voice sounds like he's remembering more than telling. "She knocked on my door with authority, and without missing a beat she said, 'I know you're my dad.'"

"And Deuce knew." Her final text messages make sense. They weren't in some weird relationship. They were siblings who shared a secret.

Owl stands, unsteady on his feet, and moves unconsciously down the three steps to the lower-tiered patio with me. I put my hand on his arm and help him maneuver onto the lounger. "Of course he knew. My kids loved each other."

"Owl, did Danny know?"

Owl shakes his head.

"Did she ever tell Neil?"

"Astrid wanted to tell him, but I convinced her not

to. He loved her so much. Neither of us wanted to risk hurting him. So we carried on in our own little version of a secret family." He lifts a flask from the bamboo floor. "No family now. All thanks to Robert."

"You still have me," I say and lean into his chest.

I want to ask Owl about the money. The $250,000. I don't. I stand, kiss the top of his head, and say, "Don't kill Robert," and "I love you."

Love has never been so complicated and so very, very easy.

Chapter Eighteen

The women are no longer shooting target practice. They will be somewhere in the house, and I don't want to see any of them. My face feels like a whiteboard where everyone has written their deepest secrets. I should have asked Owl who else knows about Astrid other than Molly. More specifically, did Danny Clark discover his wife's betrayal?

Danny, the park ranger. Good with a gun. He and his father taught Neil to shoot. And swim. Danny's the one who used to line us up and swim test us before we went camping. Would he have been financially desperate enough to take an off-book job with Tamerlane?

Maybe. And he certainly would have known enough about river dynamics to block the sluice gate. I think of the heroic way he went after Neil during the dam break. And then I remember that before Danny was employed as a ranger in Smithland, he worked for the Army Corps of Engineers. He and Andy Bedford would have worked together over county lines.

And then . . . the video. The language of the attacker. *Underwater, baby.*

Baby is a word lovers use. And also fathers for their baby girls. Even if she wasn't his, she'd been raised like she was. He loved her *and* he called her baby. I hated my next idea, but I'd have to rewatch the social media footage from the day Deuce's and Martin's bodies were discovered. What did Danny do? Did he know his daughter's body wasn't in that blind?

If Danny was Andy's associate, the string of murders and events makes warped sense for a desperate man. The money is the strongest hang-up. Danny never seemed flush with the amount of cash Tamerlane paid for the dam break job.

The Nissan's tailgate is down and two legs dangle over the edge. Dana's lying back, staring at the sky, Galen next to her. The temperature has cooled by ten degrees and there's a wind coming off the river and up the hill. You wouldn't call it nice, but we've moved more toward manageable.

"Sorry," I say.

"I was starting to worry," she admits.

"I've got good news and bad," I say.

We drive to the motel and I tell her everything that happened on the roof.

The hours slip by in a haze of pizza, coffee, and research. By the time the sun rises the next morning, I have watched the video of Martin's and Deuce's bodies being lowered over the duck blind at least forty times.

Astrid's video of her kidnapper another ten.

The reason Neil's frame is in the kidnapper's shape is it is Neil's frame. The one his father gave him. And Danny Clark doesn't look like a man afraid to find his daughter dead; he looks like a man trying to hide behind false shock and exaggerated emotions.

On Facebook, Dana finds an old photo of Danny Clark and Andy Bedford standing on the LaRue Dam with their arms slung around each other's necks. Bedford, a young field officer; Clark in an Eagle Scout uniform. The caption reads: "Boy Scouts and Corps team up to beautify shoreline along Vespers Creek."

Galen curls at my feet, dozing and chewing a bone, and Dana falls asleep sitting up with her computer in her lap. I'm stuck in a social media spiral about Neil. The internet, in all its collective wisdom, has decided the people of Grand Junction can finally sleep at night. For them, justice has come with Neil's death. There is only one voice who doesn't agree.

Seth Yarborough.

I almost laugh. The old podcaster from *Crew Time* is now a staunch supporter of Neil Clark. He has an entire website devoted to Neil's innocence. There in the archives are hundreds of hours of interviews. Remarkably, he has amassed hundreds, maybe thousands of supporters. On the front page, there's a memorial for Neil, and beneath it a headline: "Neil Clark, Murdered?"

I want to devour the entire contents of the site, but my body is screaming for sleep. I can't hold my eyes open for another minute, but in those final waking seconds, I spot a name in the comments section: KaYakittyYak. There's an emoji heart left for Seth.

One click and I scream. It's her.

Dana jerks awake, terrified. "What?" she yells, and her laptop tumbles to the floor. Galen stands and barks.

"I found Astrid. I found Astrid again."

Chapter Nineteen

I'm wide awake.

There are four comments from KaYakittyYak on Seth's website, and the last one was posted hours ago. Astrid is following Seth's commentary, and that means we have a way to get her a message.

Dana helps me film a fifteen-second video. With minimal editing we're able to use The Coasters' "Yakety Yak" song as low background music and put a tiny string of kayak emojis around the border. Hopefully it's enough to send a subtle signal to Astrid without sending her running into the abyss or putting her in danger. I splashed cold water on my face before the shoot, but nothing takes the red out of my eyes or the grief gravel from my voice. I am tired and it will show.

"Hi, Crew Timers. I'm Lucy Michaels from Grand Junction, Kentucky, and Neil Clark was my boyfriend. I wanted to say how much I appreciate your dedication to his memory and innocence. I believe Neil was murdered in prison for what he knew, and I want to prove it. I need to talk to someone from here, and you know who you are. Please reach out. I have evidence that might set you free."

The video ends.

"It's dangerous to send this. If Tamerlane is following sites like this, admitting you have evidence is a bad idea." Dana issues the warning in an obligatory way. The danger can't be understated. So many people are already dead.

"If I don't, Astrid will never come forward." I copy the MP4 link into Seth's "Contact Me" page and ask him to post it.

Within ten minutes, the video is live.

Ten minutes after that, I have a text.

UNKNOWN NUMBER: Meet tomorrow at 4:00 p.m. Old dam site. Come alone. KaYakittyYak

ME: I'll be there. Stay away from campground. Family will be there.

Chapter Twenty

The sleep that comes next isn't the rest of champions. My dreams rage. My brain builds a movie of *The Danny Clark Story*. A cloudy true crime documentary.

There are gaps, as there always are with dreams, but huge chunks are created. Seth Yarborough is there too. This time when he asks, "Who could make a shot like that?" he answers his own question. "The man who taught his son to shoot."

In the dream sequence, Danny Clark tracks Martin through the woods toward the trailhead parking lot. His rifle—the same rifle his son prefers—ready to fire. He's dressed in full camo except for his son's balaclava, which is also green.

LaRue's cold. The frost throws crystals on all the living things. It's hunting season.

He will make the murder look like an accident. Another terrible tragedy in LaRue. Danny can't help but feel like Robert Carlin has this one coming. The man has everything. When he wakes up tomorrow, he'll have significantly less.

One long-range shot takes down Martin at the Hummer. His brain whole one minute and leaking the next. The boy never stood a chance.

Danny gets his first surprise of the day: Deuce emerges from the trail, screaming. The young officer drops to a squat, alert to danger.

Danny checks the scope. Stalls. *This is Deuce*, he thinks. Can he kill Owl's son? He taught the kid to swim. In his moment of consideration, Deuce identifies the direction of the shot and runs straight at Danny's position. Danny is too heavy to escape on foot. He is no longer an athlete.

There will have to be another shot.

There is.

And then another.

It takes two.

Danny picks up the shell casings and walks to where Deuce lies in a heap. He covers the body with leaves and returns to the parking lot to clean up. He will have to move the bodies. There's room for one hunting accident, not two.

At the Hummer, he gets his second surprise of the day: Astrid.

His daughter is bent over the body of Martin, sobbing. The girl runs to her father; he is whistling, as he often does when he's working in the woods. Who knew a wolf could whistle a happy tune?

But Astrid is not stupid.

She sees the sharpness of his teeth and spots the round shell casings in his front pocket. She knows when he walks her to the river and that Orson Welles voice slides from his lips, "Underwater, baby," that her life is over.

Except he cannot devour her whole. This child he has raised and loved. Another man's daughter is his daughter too. He can't trust her and he can't kill her.

So he tells Astrid that now her DNA is at the scene. That she will be blamed. That she has a choice: leave right now or he will swear she killed Martin and Deuce. After all, she's as good of a shot as the rest of the family.

Astrid risks a video and catches only a glimpse and a voice before her camera sinks into Vespers Creek. Danny sends Astrid downstream and she runs.

From there, the dominos fall.

The bodies are moved.

Neil is arrested.

There are weak moments, moments when he longs to confess. But he doesn't. He remains a wolf.

Chapter Twenty-One

I am drenched when Dana shakes me awake midmorning. The dream feels so real. Although the wolf whistle is a teakettle Dana has on the hot plate. She pours the steaming water into a mug and puts it on the bedside table. I close my eyes and open them quickly, not wanting to conjure any part of the nightmare again.

A column of light streams through the center of the hotel curtains. The invasive smells of musty sheets and old cigarettes are like cars driving me from past to present. We are in Grand Junction. Clay's memorial is today. Danny may or may not be a murderer. I can't convict someone because of a dream. Astrid is alive and meeting me. Astrid is Owl's daughter.

"Parson's been calling you."

I scratch the sleep from the corners of my eyes and uncurl my body. The stretching feels good and awful. I clearly tucked into the tightest ball possible to endure sleep. I grunt something inaudible and she adds, "I let you sleep as long as I could."

She's already showered and dressed in typical Dana wear: hiking boots, khaki shorts, and a Brandi Carlile tank she splurged on at a concert in Red Rocks. She's got the JUNK headband with tiny dinosaurs I bought her for Christmas wrapped around her wrist. There's no doubt she'll want that later. It's supposed to be near a hundred today.

Visually, she reminds me of a younger version of my mother. In the split second, a million thoughts register. Maybe I left Grand Junction for Zionsville because I needed to be away from home but not away from Mom. Dana doesn't have the age, but she's rock steady and sneakily maternal. Or maybe it was Galen. Who knows.

"I need something stronger than this," I say, taking a drink of the tea.

"We can get donuts soon," she promises and throws a pillow from her bed at my head.

I throw it back and she dodges. "It's good to see you smile again," she says.

"You too," I say and reach for my phone. "So what did Parson want?"

"To make sure you eat before the memorial. He said

to come over to the lodge around four and he'll feed you."

That's Parson. Always making sure we're fed. "Did you tell him we can't come at four?"

"Yeah. I said it would have to be earlier. Also," she says in a way that makes me bury my face in the duvet, "your video is viral." Dana flips her computer screen toward me. Seth's website is pulled up in one window. The tracker under my video has more than four thousand hits and seven hundred comments.

"That's not terrible," I say.

She clicks a different tab. The CNN website banner has "Hydro Dam Heir Says Neil Clark Is Innocent" in a drop-down menu. Not front page, but there's no doubt the video's making a stir. "You should consider not going today."

"To Clay's memorial?" I ask, with something between mock and genuine horror. "The associate won't have to kill me because my mom will do the job for them."

We both laugh in an ironic way that acknowledges the danger. I tell Dana about my dream and she tells me I moaned off and on all night. The Danny theory feels less like a theory and more like a timeline by the time I expound on the details.

"We can't know for sure," Dana says, followed by, "But if it is Danny, the risk at the memorial goes way down. He wouldn't chance a public scene when he's evaded detection this long."

"Plus we'll have talked to Astrid."

Neither of us says what we fear: that she won't show up.

The memorial is set for later in the day. No one wants to be out in the heat. The cooler it is, the more bulbs we can put in the ground. That's what the group text message says. I am supposed to be prepared to say something, if I want to.

Molly's text reads: Nothing formal, but maybe some happy memories???

Wilma's: Honey, I've got the stories galore.

Owl's: You'll have to be my voice today.

I can do happy memories for all the guys, especially now that my head is convinced of their innocence. For the first time since the trial, I slip the moon, sun, and stars necklace from my purse and clasp it around my neck. Neil's gift no longer feels too heavy to wear.

"What are you going to do?" I ask Dana.

"Get you a donut," she says. And I know she's trying to distract me.

"After that?"

"Scout the area around the dam."

"I thought you were interviewing Andy Bedford," I say.

Dana makes a face. "He canceled. He's doing an interview with CNN instead."

"Because of my video?" I ask.

"Because he's the cause of a dam break," she says. "If

I drop you at the Landing for food with Parson, I'll have an hour or so to make sure things are as safe as possible before you meet Astrid."

Dana turns toward the long mirror on the wall and I notice the slight bulge at the small of her back. Oddly enough, Dana and I never visit the range together. Early in her FBI career she killed someone in the line of duty. She hasn't expressly said, but I think that's why she left the bureau. Shooting is a component of safety. It does not bring her joy. The sight of her weapon is Red Bull in my veins. Part of me wants to tell her she doesn't need to carry, and part of me wants to scream, *You need a bigger gun.* She has a better plan: high-end radios with earpieces. "I'm not relying on cell coverage today," she tells me and shows me how to operate the radios.

I dress and shower and we're out the door and on our way to Parson's in thirty minutes. Robert is standing in the lodge parking lot with his hands in his pockets. Clearly he has been waiting for something. Not until we park do I realize it's me. He marches over to my side of the truck and opens the door with gusto. Galen promptly bares his teeth. "Easy," I say instinctively, and both the dog and the man collapse a little.

I prepare myself for a lecture. Robert's native tongue.

"I know you were in my office and you have the black-mail note too. Cameras," he says after a short pause. "So I need you to listen when I say you're in danger and you're scaring the crap out of me. You already know Tamerlane can and will hurt people. They'll come for you. I don't know who they'll send. I don't know who worked with Andy, but they probably *are* coming for you already. Please, Lucy, I know you don't trust me, but I love you and I'm trying to figure out how to protect you. Please take that video down and issue a statement that you were wrong and grieving before you or someone else gets hurt."

"The video is out there, Robert," Dana says. "She can't simply take it down. You know that."

"Then leave town," he says. "And whoever you're baiting in that video, let it go, unless you want to get them killed. You're in the middle of a trap."

I can't tell if he knows who or not. "I can't leave town before the memorial."

"You can," he says.

His clothes are mismatched. He's sweating profusely from his sideburns. He is more out of control than I have ever seen him.

"Mom will—"

"Lucy, your mom knows everything." The way his voice catches on *everything* tells me that Salome called him after I left.

"You had to tell her, huh?" I say, thinking I forced his hand.

"I told her years ago. About Tamerlane. About nearly drowning and Deuce saving me. That I put money every year in an account for him as a thank-you and to keep my secret. About how Tamerlane's decisions killed her son and then later, mine. She's the one who wouldn't allow me to go after them legally. She didn't want to risk something happening to you or Martin." At the mention of his son, tears well in his eyes.

"If that's true, why isn't she here?"

"She doesn't know that you know," he says, then turns to Dana. "Please reason with her. You are her closest friend, so keep her in this truck and get her out of here." To me he says, "You've held Clay in memorial for years. Come back when the bulbs bloom. I transferred a hundred thousand dollars into your account—"

I am listening, earnestly considering, until he brings up the money. Yet again he's buying the future he wants instead of the present he earned. I'm not Tamerlane. I cannot be blackmailed or bought. "I'm staying for my brother's memorial. The memorial I wouldn't need if you had the guts to stop Tamerlane years ago instead of buying them out. You think money can fix everything, but it'll never fix this. Justice fixes this!"

In the midst of my shouting, Parson approaches Dana's side of the truck unnoticed. "You guys okay?" he asks, hands jammed in his pockets, quirky expression on his face.

I shove my way out of the truck and past my stepfather. "Robert is leaving. Dana?"

She takes a second to answer. "I'm planning to hike."

That means she agrees that we should meet Astrid. She puts on her headband and cranks the engine.

"I'll meet you at the memorial?" I say to Robert, my tone much kinder than it was moments before.

Dana glances at Robert, who is trembling. "Go home," she tells him. "Parson and I have her for now."

"Luce, I'm sorry," Robert says.

"Sorry's not good enough."

He walks away, his shame evident in the curve of his spine. I have never seen such a tall man fold in half.

"What was that about?"

Parson guides me into the lodge's rear door. "Nothing," I say, followed by, "Everything," because what good does it do to lie to Parson?

Moments later, he leads me into the same private dining room where we met after Martin died. This time the raw wood table has a spread of all my favorite foods. "I didn't know what you might want, so we made the entire menu," he says. I'm barely listening because the centerpiece isn't food. It's a rifle. And not just any rifle. Neil's Ruger Precision Rifle. The so-called murder weapon.

My face must be frozen. I know I've stopped moving, maybe even breathing.

Parson explains before I ask. "Every year the police auction off the weapons seized during investigations. Neil's rifle went up for auction, and I don't know . . . I thought you should have the right to decide what happens to it. Shoot it. Bury it. Melt it down. Whatever you want. It's a strange gift, but you're the only one in the world who might understand why I had to get it. I mean, you're a proper marksman and I—"

"Parse." I examine the weapon in a glance. He's cleaned it recently. There's a dab of extra oil on the safety. This is the man who taught me almost everything I know about shooting. He could have kept the weapon himself and he didn't. I'm flabbergasted by the gesture. "How does it shoot?"

"Brilliant." He dumps a few rounds of ammunition on the table. "We can always shoot now if you want. Or, you know, drop it in the river."

"Astrid is still alive." It's the gun that makes me blurt out what I planned to hold in. The way it makes me think that no one else is left in the world who understands what we've been through. "I'm meeting her before the memorial."

Chapter Twenty-Two

Parson backs all the way to the wall behind him and rests his weight against it, his face hidden in his hands. "Luce. That can't be. Someone's messing with you."

"They're not." I explain the KaYakittyYak screen name. "It's her. I'm telling you, it's her. And she's going to be able to tell me everything that happened."

"No." He's emphatic but firm. Parse takes one of the heavy chairs beside me and leans over his knees and boots. He's shaking his head as he sighs, and I feel slightly patronized. "You're starting to sound . . . obsessed. Neil confessed to the crime. This is over."

"Obsessed?" I'm taken aback. "How can you say that?" I'm spitting the words. I'm not sure how Parson has managed to stay emotionally detached all these years. He's stayed here, made his livelihood mere minutes away from the horror of our childhood.

"Easy," he says, and puts his hand on my arm and leaves it there. The warmth is heavy and familiar and I take a breath.

"But Robert and Astrid . . ." I try to explain the threat Dana and I found in Robert's coat pocket. My theory about Danny. All the things that make him the associate hired by Tamerlane.

"It's his alibi. Luce, Robert's going to prison for the dam. That note is his attempt to make sure no one tacks on a murder charge while they're at it. Why would Danny set up his own son? That's asinine."

I fall forward and rest my forehead on his hand. Then he leans too, presses his lips to the side of my head, and whispers directly in my ear, "Today's the day we let this go. Don't meet this crazy person who wants you to think Astrid's still alive. We need to accept that someday we'll have a memorial for her, but today is about our boys. Promise me."

"I can't, Parse. I can't stop until I know."

"Don't say that. I don't want to lose you too." He takes my face in his warm hands and we are eyeball to eyeball, our faces and mouths inches apart. I can't look away and he doesn't either. His eyes are gray and in pain. He is more vulnerable than I have ever seen him. "Please," he says, moving ever so slightly closer.

"I'm sorry," I say. "I can't stop now."

He tips his forehead forward to touch mine and we stay locked together. One breath. Two. A third. "Where are you meeting her?" he asks, resigned.

"Where the old dam was."

"I'm going with you."

"No."

"Then Dana?" he suggests.

"No. Astrid was clear. I have to come alone."

He smacks the table with frustration. "Who else knows about this?"

"Dana. Me. That's it."

"Fine," he relents. "Go out there, meet with this, uh, reporter"—he eyerolls at the notion—"or whoever's trying to get a rise or a story out of you, and then come back to the memorial. After that, we'll wait until someone finds Astrid to talk about this again. You deserve to live."

"Thanks, Parse."

"You know, you're the most talented marksman I've ever worked with." He smiles, knowing that because he doesn't praise me, this praise will mean everything to me. I tilt toward him and kiss him on the cheek. "Thanks, Coach," I say.

"Gold medal. That's the path," he says, eyeing the rifle on the table. "After that, we could always go to Canada and hunt big game."

"I don't think so," I say.

"Yeah," he says, disappointed but not surprised. "Eat all you want, and if you need anything, ask Maria. I'm heading out back to smoke a pig for Auntie. Be careful, please."

Now it's my turn to eye Parson's centerpiece. "Oh, I think you've got me covered there."

I am not stupid. Meeting Astrid is a risk, but I can't imagine walking away from the truth. If she's alive, I need to know how.

I might be obsessed. I might be damaged. But I'm not walking away from the key to every door in my entire life. I'm going out to the site, whether Parson likes it or not, and I'm going to find out the truth. I need someone to blame for Clay's death besides myself.

I'm also going out there armed.

That Weekend

The rain kept falling.

It never slowed.

It wouldn't stop.

I opened my eyes.

The river raged two feet below me. No longer a wave, a being. Like it had always been there, and this tree, and others like it, were little islands.

The trunk swayed like a limb, but held for now. The boys above me screamed and kicked. Andy's voice came again and again: "Keep holding on. Someone will come."

My other shoe was gone. Ripped away by the wave.

I looked left to tell Clay that Mom would find us.

The branch where I put my little brother was gone.

Chapter Twenty-Three

Standing atop a slight berm, I face the Tennessee River. My back is to LaRue. The valley. Duck Pond. A horseshoe of trees where the forest of LaRue begins. The drop-off in front of me is steep. I can't dive from here into the water; there's too much of a slope. But if I were to lie down and roll, I'd hit the surface in maybe ten rotations.

The river is a perfect mirror. Distorted blues and greens of sky and trees. I'm grateful it isn't fall. Those colors on the ground. The crackle of leaves underfoot. They make me nauseous. A crunchy leaf can break my heart into a thousand pieces. Today everything is a shade of lime, the shade of living things, and I'm glad for this.

Robert's company of engineers reshaped the water-ways when they built Grand Hydro. I tried to explain to Martin how the landscape changed on the day he died. How the horizon line was wildly different, and that where we stood, where I'm standing now, didn't exist back then. I'm near where the actual LaRue Dam was. The concrete wall.

I want to take off my shoes and socks, slide down the bank, and stand in the water, but I also don't want to lose my vantage point of the valley or leave Neil's rifle unattended. If Astrid comes, I want to see her. I lift the radio Dana gave me to my lips. "Parson was right. Someone's jerking my chain." They're probably watching from the trees and getting a huge kick out of getting me to turn up. I can feel the comments section of Seth Yarborough's blog laughing in my face.

Far off in the distance, there's a single gunshot. Low caliber. Probably someone shooting squirrels.

"Dana," I say into the radio, feeling both stupid and terrified.

The radio pops and Dana says, "Give her another five minutes." The tension in my chest eases instantly—Dana's fine. She's on the other side of the radio, and she can probably see me from where she's stationed. Still, her answer surprises me. I expect her to advise against being a sitting duck and head to our rendezvous at the lodge.

I spin in every direction. Nothing. The weight of the gun strap digs into my shoulder. I tighten my grip on the stock. There's sweat on the metal and some part of me feels it coming from my palms.

"Astrid!" I scream at the water in frustration, wishing I could manifest her.

Silence.

Above me the clouds shift and the reflection reminds me of flying marshmallows. There's a crack of thunder to the west. We'll get rained on tonight. Another crack tells me the storm will get here before the memorial. I doubt it will stop Wilma, Molly, and Mom from planting bulbs, but I have no intention of staying out here if it rains. Never again.

All my boys will understand.

This I know for sure.

When I turn again to the lake, there's a footfall behind me. I spin, expecting a deer or a rabbit. Not this time.

The figure comes toward me from the edge of the forest. This person is dressed head to toe in black rain gear, the hood pulled completely over their face. He or she isn't hurrying. They're taking very deliberate steps as if walking through a minefield.

"Astrid," I call out, my heart pounding.

Whoever it is doesn't answer.

I'm spellbound, watching, breath caught in my throat.

I whisper into the radio, "Dana. Someone's here. I can't tell who it is, but I'm going to find out."

There's no answer. She's out of range or doesn't want to risk saying something that might scare off the visitor.

I take the safety off and hold the rifle in a loose firing position and begin to advance.

Grasshoppers and gnats scatter as I walk the last twenty feet, angle the gun in the direction of the stranger.

When I reach her, it's not who the person is that scares me. It's not even how sorry she says she is. It's the simple phrase that comes after her apology. "He knows you're out here and he's going to kill you."

Chapter Twenty-Four

The first drop of rain hits my nose. I wipe it away and catch a tinge of red on my knuckle.

A circle of light.

A laser.

A scope.

I react. The instinct faster than the bullet, but not fast enough. *Pop.* I dive at Astrid and burning pain sears my side as I pull her body into mine and roll us down toward the river. I'm disoriented when we hit the water, unsure for a second where the shot came from.

The trees or Duck Pond?

Whoever shot at us has to move positions, across the

open valley and up the berm to get off another shot. We're in the shadow of the land. If we move now, we have a chance. There's blood in the water. My blood.

I will not stop. I will not die.

I drag Astrid to her feet, unsure whose side she's on. "I'm sorry. I'm sorry," she says.

"Run." I point to a place where the forest dips in toward the water. It might be enough covering to hide us.

Astrid's fast and agile. I can't stay on her heels. The pain is too intense. My adrenaline compensates, keeps me upright. I am leaving a trail that anyone can follow. I think of the deer Neil followed into LaRue on the day Martin died. That deer ended up in the bed of a truck.

I will not stop. I will not die.

The rain falls in earnest now. It pelts my face and part of me feels like I did the day of the flood. Back in LaRue. Dying to live. I don't have to outrun the water this time. I have to outrun a bullet. I know which is faster.

My radio is wet. Neil's rifle is strapped against my back. I have two rounds of ammunition, but getting the gun wet might keep it from firing correctly. My best hope is to get far enough away, set up a position, and pray. The shooter will have seen my rifle through his own scope. That might also make him move more cautiously and give us time to gain distance.

Astrid and I make it to the next tree line without being fired on. That feels like a miracle.

"This way," Astrid says, already moving in the direction of the river bend, toward Grand Hydro.

That's the closest road and there are more places to hide there. "Coming," I say and force us higher up the ridge. I'm having trouble catching my breath.

Halfway up, there's an oak the width of a double-sided fridge. "There," I say, and shove us into the rounded base, the hill below us on the other side. The shooter's down there somewhere. The bark tears at my back. I wince when I see the blood on my side. When people in movies say things like, "I think they nicked a rib," I used to laugh and think, *How do they know that?* If I live long enough to watch another movie, I will never laugh again. They know because their bone is screaming.

"I'm sorry. I'm so sorry," Astrid whispers. "He said he would blow the dam if I didn't meet you. There's dynamite at Grand Hydro. The threat. It's how he controls everything. Me. Neil. Everyone."

I scream, "Who?" as lightning cracks the earth a hundred yards away.

Astrid and I scream and immediately realize we've given up our location. This might need to be my Alamo. I check the scope. It's broken. Probably from rolling down the hill. Very carefully, I peer around the tree and down the hill.

There's no movement. And even if there was, the whole world is gray and slick with rain. I lean back into the safety of the tree. If I were hunting us, I would cut diagonally up the hill away from us and work my way back down so I was facing my opponent. I'd take the risk we were doing exactly what we're doing. Hiding.

"Up," I say.

"No," she says, and then I point, not up the ridge but up the tree.

"Up," I say and pat the gun. "As high as you can climb."

"You're coming?"

"No."

I give her a boost to the lowest branch and tell her not to come down unless my mother or me comes for her. I want to tell her Dana is out here, but Dana didn't answer the radio. *Maybe*, I think with horror, *she couldn't.* That lone shot earlier, before Astrid turned up near the berm. Was it before or after the last time I heard her voice through the radio?

Neil was always a faster shot than me. I like to take my time, breathe, make the world stop its orbit for a single breath, and then shoot. I won't have that much time today. I've never shot a target that wasn't paper or cans.

I crouch low and move, not up or down the ridge but across, sprinting from tree to tree. The mud and pain make the going slow.

I've walked LaRue enough to know I'm a long way from anywhere. I rack my brain thinking about who might be behind me. Someone professional hired by Tamerlane?

Danny? I hold the barrel against my chest and pray each time I move positions.

I've darted behind a tree when someone yells, "Lucy! Lucy! Where are you?" I flatten my body against the wet ground and wiggle backward toward a fallen tree. The howl of the wind carries the next words away. Then there's a break in the sound and I hear, "Lucy. Danny's down. You're safe. I've got him."

I leap from the ground, and the moment I do . . . *Pop*. My shoulder explodes with pain and I hit the ground. My blood soaks into the dirt and mixes with the rain.

In the moment I'm falling I think of my dream. The whistle of a wolf.

I register the voice.

Parson.

Chapter Twenty-Five

Here are the things Parson says as he walks in my direction:

"I told you to let this go."

"I never wanted to hurt anyone. Especially not you."

"Luce, you know me."

"I got in a bad spot and the only way out was through."

And then, "I'm a very good shot."

Here are the things I think as he walks in my direction:

I will not stop. I will not die.

I will not stop. I will not die.

I will not stop. I will not die.

And finally, *A hunter never hands their prey a loaded weapon.*

He's counting on me to think I have a shot.

Here are the things I do as he walks in my direction:

I shove Neil's rifle away.

I wiggle through a hole where part of the branch doesn't meet the ground.

I keep going, hidden by the branches of the downed tree.

My hands close around a baseball bat–sized limb.

I wait for my moment.

Chapter Twenty-Six

Once upon a time in a rainstorm, a tree saved me and failed me. I've never forgiven that tree. Now I grip a branch in my hand and thank God for both the seed that grew into this oak and whatever storm knocked this branch to the ground.

Parson's close. I hear his footfalls over the pulse of the rain.

There is no time to think now.

When he steps on the fallen trunk, I move.

His rifle's aimed down. At the place he expected me to take up a position for a shot. He spots the rifle on the ground where I've left it. I have one framed image of his perplexed face before I attack.

I smash the back of his skull with the biggest swing my shoulder can manage. He goes down hard, lands on top of his weapon. I pounce and hit him again in the back of the head.

I keep swinging.

Later I will tell Owl that I hit him three times.

Later, much later, the coroner will tell Owl that he counted twenty-seven strikes.

Chapter Twenty-Seven

There is an after.

A hospital. A surgery. A shower.

I am going to live.

My mother holds my hand when the doctor tells me my professional shooting career is over. The bullet to my shoulder damaged a set of nerves that connect to my hand. I am not surprised, and I'm oddly relieved. I wasn't sure I could stomach firing a weapon again anyway. An injury lets me retire rather than quit. Neil handed me my first air rifle and Parson coached my Olympic career. Shooting is irrevocably tied to both of them. No thank you, extra PTSD. I'll find a new hobby.

Galen takes up more of the hospital bed than I do. Dana says she's never seen him this possessive, not even of her. He lays his chin on my thigh and isn't content unless I pet him. He gets me through all of the police interrogations and then the visitors.

Robert. Owl. Molly and Danny. Wilma. Astrid.

The emotions surrounding the visits are so complicated I could write six books. Mostly we cry. For what we've lost and gained. Because it's over, and also because we're finally at the beginning.

We will all have to start over from here.

Mom says growing up is someone handing you an XXL overcoat when you're four and telling you that you have to wear it for the rest of your life. When you're a child, it doesn't fit; and by the time it fits, it's old and worn. We are never the right size or age for our emotions. I tell her my overcoat came with hundred-pound weights, and she says to me, "Two hundred, baby." I wonder if the things I carry around will always be this heavy, but I don't ask. I'm not sure I want to know.

But there *are* things I want to know.

So many things.

The mystery of Parson. The boy in all our family photos.

Astrid unravels some of the mysteries of how, but none of the whys. Those come later, in the notebooks.

She's going to have her own three-hundred-pound overcoat to lug around. Parson couldn't bring himself to hurt her physically, so he controlled her. Daily threats. *I will blow the dam at Grand Hydro. I will flood the town. I can do it with my phone. The police can't arrest me before I can call that number. I will kill you if I have to, and them. I will kill everyone to cover this up. Keep the secret. Keep your life.* She was seventeen and saw the bullet Parson put through Martin's head and then Deuce's. She was lying in the back of the Hummer with her headphones on.

The kidnapping happened much like I imagined, only it wasn't Danny who tried to drown Astrid. Parson's narrative around his failed attempts to hold Astrid under the water forces us to stop reading and catch our breath. The horror he put her through before he moved her downriver in a kayak, drugged her, and hid her with the one person he could control: Andy Bedford. No one had more reason than Andy to keep his mouth shut. For three weeks Astrid stayed locked in his barn stall. Then Parson cut her hair, got her a fake passport, and sent her to Canada with a hunting friend. For a year, she lived in a cabin north of Toronto with only a violin and a book of short stories. Parson called daily. The quieter she grew, the more freedom she won. Within the year she was allowed to move where she wanted as long as she lived as Ashley Smith, kept her mouth shut, and called Parson every day. "You miss one call and everyone from home will die."

She never missed a call.

We do not judge her.

Even when we want to.

We hold her instead. We hold her like Boy Scouts anchoring their bodies to an oak in a rainstorm.

Ten days after my release from the hospital, Dana, Galen, and I are still in Grand Junction. She's working from the motel; I'm healing the physical bits of me.

Owl calls. "I've got the rest of our whys, kiddo."

That Weekend

"Clayyyyyyyyyyyyyyyyyyyy!"

The rain stopped falling from the sky.

Changing its tactic. Rising from below.

Swelling from my ankles to my knees, up the bare skin of my legs.

Water lapped around the splintery base of Clay's branch. The absence of my brother sent me spiraling. I slapped the surface with my palms. He was there. I put him right there. And now . . . Where was he? My eyes followed the path of the water, hoping I would see him clinging to another tree. He was nowhere in sight.

"Clayyyyyyyyyyyyyyyyyyyy!"

Andy Bedford said, "Higher! We have to climb higher. Boys, up!" The boys, his troop, scraped and scrapped their way higher. Until the branches were too thin to hold them. Thin enough the tree leaned like the top of a Christmas tree with an overlarge angel. They screamed. I supposed they clung to each other. I clung to my branch, the branch that was beside Clay's branch. The branch that held.

"Clayyyyyyyyyyyyyyyyyyy!"

Andy tugged on my shoulder. "You have to climb." I didn't move.

I played it back. The nightmare.

My shoe ripped away . . . gone.

The wave.

"Clayyyyyyyyyyyyyyyyyyy!"

Andy had moved higher, toward his boys. Above me, sneaker treads frowned with mud. Black soles and bare feet and sludge. "We're not safe," Andy called to me. "We have to hang on. Look at me. Look at me. What's your name?"

"Lucy," I answered. "And my brother is Clay. The wave took him."

"I'm sorry, sweetheart," he said. "Lucy, Clay needs you to climb. Clay wants you to be as high as you can so the rescue helicopters will get to us before the water does. Do you understand, Lucy?"

"Where's Clay now?"

"I don't know," Andy said, working his way lower

again. His hand closed around my shoulder, tugging, tugging, the grip painful and urgent. "I do know that you came back for these boys. That you saved them. I almost got them killed, but you, you're a miracle worker, and miracle workers climb."

"I can't without Clay."

I couldn't think of anything except my little brother. He was the person who slept in my bed when it stormed. The person who demanded, "One more story!" after he'd already heard twenty. The person who giggled and giggled and snorted and then farted in my face. And one day he was going to be tall. And I was going to stay short. And I would make sure no matter how tall he grew, I gave the top part of the hug.

Andy's grip on my shoulder tightened, like someone was spinning the wheel of a crescent wrench. "I'm coming lower," he said, and with his other arm, he lowered himself to the branch nearest mine, into the water, where he looked at me eye to eye.

His were blue like my father's and I stopped to breathe. He said, "This is my fault. It will never be your fault, Lucy. It will always be mine. Do you hear me? Now, you're going to climb up my shoulders to the next limb."

Everything was loud, but I heard Andy like we were alone in a church sanctuary. "You have to climb." And then, in a whisper from deep inside, Clay spoke too.

"Climb, Lucy."

I started climbing.

Chapter Twenty-Eight

Dana, Owl, and I sit in Owl's small kitchen. Water for tea boils on the stove; an empty pizza box takes up the counter. Nine notebooks are spread across the table. Parson's journals.

Owl taps the stack and says, "I've never seen anything like this."

Once the evidence was cleared, copied, and logged, one of the guys, out of courtesy, turned these over to Owl. He had a full day with them before he called us and said we might all need a stiff drink after the reading.

Dana's hungry for details. I'm torn. I want to understand, but I'm also afraid of how guilty I'll feel for not understanding Parson better. If I had, maybe I could have stopped him sooner.

I'm not having one of my angry days. I'm glad for that.

The therapist said anger is important. I said it sounds counterproductive, and she said, "The anger will come out no matter what. It can come at him or at someone else or at you, and I think you have been through quite enough already."

"Tell me," I say to Owl, "what this is going to be like."

Owl says, "Parson didn't burn puppies at the stake or get off on violence. He says he hated what he had to do, but once the dam broke, he couldn't think of another way to have a life. Therefore, in some ways, he is very much the coach you've always known." He sighs. "The first two entries are the key to understanding Parson. They're written in an adult's neat script with a pen and were clearly added to the notebook later in his life."

Owl selects a certain journal, a bright green spiral, for Dana and me.

The first chronological entry begins, *I am 6. I live with Auntie Wilma now. I want to be a chef when I grow up.* It's written in blue crayon.

The first added entry reads, *Four: the year I outgrew the crate.*

Dana covers her mouth.

I ask, "Did Wilma know—"

Owl answers, "That his parents kept him in a crate

until he went to kindergarten? No. She had no idea. She knew they were inept, but not . . . not that."

The second added entry reads, *Five: hamburger at school; first meal that wasn't a bowl of Purina.*

The horror I feel for young Parson isn't eclipsed by the horror he created, but nearly. From there, the notebooks touch on other childhood events. At six, his parents divorced and rapidly remarried other partners. After that, he moved in with Wilma and she loved him fiercely.

There's an upswing to his dark side and fears for a long time.

By eight, he was obsessed with food. At ten, Owl taught him to fish. Then the Landing was born in his head. There are recipes and sketches of flies he learned to tie. I remember these books from camping. He always had one on the table, recording the fish he caught. Their sizes. Whether the water temperature mattered to the flavor. Over and over the questions written in the margins showcase his need to bring the Landing to life. To feed other people. To never be hungry again. He wrote, *Money? $100,000 to start? Land in LaRue? Could I do this?*

The bank said no. Auntie said he should go to business school and then come home to build when he was older. He understood, but he was impatient.

The first excerpt that mentions Tamerlane doesn't have many details. *Andy Bedford. Possible money from Tamerlane? Welding job. Enough down payment to approach bank for loan?*

He chronicled taking the job and hiding the work from Deuce. He almost told him. Almost asked him to help. In the end, he decided Deuce would side with his dad and then he would never get to build his restaurant.

When the dam broke and Clay died, Parson ordered a dog crate on Amazon and sentenced himself to sleep in it for weeks. He had no idea what he'd been hired to do or the terrible effect it would have on the people he loved. Pages and pages describe his guilt. He knew he should go to jail, but he couldn't go to jail and he couldn't live in a cage indefinitely. That would make him want to die, and he was more afraid of hell than he was of cages.

He wrote, *I do not want to meet God as me. Maybe I can make a new Parson.*

Parson believed in his own guilt and fear so wholeheartedly that he bounced between extreme service and atheism through several notebooks. He built the Landing with Tamerlane's money and Owl's investment, and we read pages and pages of him trying to do enough good to forgive himself.

He'd nearly done it when Martin started investigating the dam. He wrote, *I have been good. I haven't had to sleep in a cage for years. And now I will have to sleep there again.* That starts an entire journal where he admitted to himself that he found Clay's remains during the initial search parties and was so guilt-ridden he kept the body hidden. He documented how he wrestled over

the years with ways to give my brother back without alert-
ing anyone to how and why he hid the discovery all those
years ago.

"All that time," I say, "he knew where he was." I
don't know how that's supposed to make me feel.

Dana puts her arm around me and says the only
comforting thing there is. "He's home now."

Owl lays his hand over the top of the journal and
interrupts. "When they searched Parson's house, they
found the cage in the basement. It's only forty-eight
inches long."

Parson was six one.

"It gets worse," Owl says.

We arrive at Martin's pages.

The Deuce pages.

There are so, so many. Before the murders. The esca-
lation and fear. The conversation he overheard between
Martin and Astrid at the Landing that led to him planning Martin's murder. He wrote about shooting his best
friend. Framing Neil. He wrote about seeing himself in
Astrid's video at Neil's house and having an out-of-body
experience. And how when he joined my search party that
first night, he was afraid I would hear his heart beating
with terror. He wrote that he practiced what he would do
with his face when the bodies were found, knowing that
if he fooled me, he could fool anyone.

There's a whole notebook dedicated to Astrid in
Canada. She sounds more like his lover than his captive.

He wrote her recipes. He flew there for weeks at a time to cook for her, but he couldn't win her forgiveness. Each time he went back to the threats and forcing her to believe that he had exquisite control over her life.

There are pages about Andy Bedford and the specific, haunting ways Parson kept him silent all these years.

There are pages about me.

He wrote about the two of us and the Olympics. What it was like to be with me in Paris and how much he wished Neil's future had been different. Neil was the fall guy the moment Parson realized Martin would need to be silenced. I wasn't the only one who sat at Parson's bar and bared her soul over mac and cheese. Martin talked to Parson. Neil talked to Parson.

Parson told how he suggested Neil come home the weekend of the regional tournament. He baited Neil into early hunting. Not in an obvious way, where Neil might come back and say Parson told him to come home. He was far subtler. Talk of big game in LaRue. A nineteen-point buck. Hints that Martin was moving into Neil's territory when it came to me and how perhaps he should put together a big gesture to apologize. In hindsight, he played Neil like a fiddle. Then he swiped Neil's rifle from his truck while Neil slept in the cab.

Neil's fight with Martin was double cream in an espresso shot.

Game. Set. Match.

The writing relaxes after Neil's incarceration. Parson

had a safety net. We won bronze and he was able to focus more on the Landing and expand his business. Oddly enough, he wrote about his gratitude to Neil. Like Neil had given him a free cruise rather than gone to prison in his place. Parson sent regular letters and money to the prison. He advised Neil to set me free. "If you love her, let her go, brother. You know she'll wait for you. You can't let her." That's what he told Neil so Neil wouldn't allow me to visit.

There are only a few pages about the end of Neil's life. From them, we piece together Neil's final actions and the deal they struck. A simple arrangement. Astrid got to live and Clay's body would be returned in exchange for Neil's confession and suicide.

Parson was afraid of me.

He didn't want to hurt me and he was worried he would eventually. "Well, he got that right," I say.

"I loved that boy so much," Owl says, like he can't believe the betrayal happened.

"We all did," I say.

The last notebook has only four entries. They follow him from the moment he read the Tamerlane emails I saved to the Dropbox account. The account I shared with him during the Olympics. He had the notifications turned on. So Parson knew the minute I uploaded the video that I was far too close to the truth. Those four entries are panic and pain. They are chaos and murder. They are coercion and suicide. He was sure he wouldn't have to kill me himself because Neil's rifle was rigged. One shot and it would explode in my hands.

"I thought he gave me Neil's weapon so I wouldn't take my own," I say.

Owl nods. "I'm sure that's true, but also so he could make sure it wouldn't fire correctly."

He believed he could live with an accidental misfiring. Although he decided in advance to sleep in the crate for the next year.

Dana says, "He thought you would lean into your strengths."

"I can't tell from this if he planned to hurt Astrid too," I say. "I told him I was meeting her. If I'd kept my mouth shut—"

"He still would have done exactly what he did. Look at the date, Luce. He rigged the gun before you told him you were meeting Astrid. This isn't your fault," Dana says.

"And it's not yours either." I grip her hand and squeeze.

Parson talked to Dana in the woods. He disabled her radio and sent her off in another direction by telling her Galen got out of the truck. By the time she realized the radio wasn't working, she was almost back to the restaurant. Even when she found Galen waiting in the truck, she assumed a stranger helped him rather than Parson lied. That was about the time I was running for my life.

"He outsmarted us at every turn," I say.

"No," Owl says. "He didn't outsmart you, kiddo. Not in the end."

"Speaking of *kiddo*," I reply, "how's Astrid doing?"

"Parson put her through the unthinkable." He bows his head the way only a father can and says, "She needs all the love we can give her."

I twist my water glass in the circle of its sweat. "She's lucky to have you and Molly and Danny."

Owl smiles. "Your stepdad's figuring out a few things about love too."

While I was in surgery, once they were sure I would live, Robert made a full confession about blackmailing Tamerlane to build Grand Hydro. He turned over all his evidence regarding the failure of the LaRue Dam. Even the GoPro footage of Deuce rescuing him. The story made national headlines. The FBI raided Tamerlane and seized documents. No arrests have been made as of yet, but they promise they're coming. Then Robert turned over Grand Hydro to the city of Grand Junction and endowed the profits to do two things: one, award all graduating seniors a significant financial award, and two, pay off the mortgages for everyone who worked for Grand Hydro. It's the first payoff in his life where he received nothing in return.

Mom told me yesterday, after she handed me the deed to PoppaJack's land, that Robert bought her the old farmhouse where Clay and I spent our childhood. The one on the other side of the county. She's going to fix it up. For her, going backward might be the most logical way forward.

For me, the hard work of healing lies ahead.

I think about what will happen if I do the work and what will happen if I don't. I think about my friend who spent the first years of his life in a cage and the rest of his life trying to stay out of one. I think of my brothers, not of their deaths but of their lives and how much I loved them. I think of Neil handing me a box of orange Tic Tacs and how sometimes a small thing is a huge thing.

I think about how I buried bulbs in the ground this morning. Ugly brown knobs of potential. I had to ask my mom when I dropped the first bulb in the dirt which part of the overlarge seed was up. She laughed and showed me the side that would bloom. I tucked it into the dirt and wished it well. One day I'll look across the fields of LaRue and some of its beauty will be mine.

And then I think of Clay's tiny voice. *"Climb, Lucy."*

I will keep climbing.

This Weekend

Cat is out of treats, and I know when I get home he won't let me sleep without them. He's had a long day, and a quick stop at Walmart is the least I can do for him. He trots along at my heels, always the hero among the strangers we meet. They say things like, "What a handsome boy you are!" And "You look like such a good young man."

And he does.

He's a rescue with a ton of shepherd, several smidges of collie, and probably some pit. I never thought I'd find my Galen, but it took a single glance on Petfinder to know Cat was mine. I filed adoption papers and hired Galen's trainer within the hour I brought him home.

Right now he is wagging so hard his entire backside comes off the tiled floor. That's because his favorite treats are tucked under my arm along with two toys he sniffed that I do not have to buy but will. I decide to pick up his next month of heartworm meds since I'm here.

Standing halfway down the aisle is an employee. She's bent over, her hands buried deep in the shelf, restocking the meds.

"Is there another box back there somewhere?" I ask hopefully.

She turns, sees Cat, then me. "Hey," she says kindly and squats to offer her hand to Cat. "What a beautiful dog. And what a handsome red vest you have." He wags and nuzzles her hand. To me, she says, "He's a service dog?"

I smile and feel the deep sense of joy that comes with my job. "Yep. He's search and rescue. We're a search and rescue team."

Acknowledgments

I still can't believe I get to write books. That I get to have readers. That I am spending my life creating. I am so very grateful, not only to the people I will name here but also for the process. Praise the Lord isn't my southern catchphrase; it's my earnest plea and admittance that I do this creative life in partnership with God.

I start this thanks parade with Becky Monds. I have the weirdest process and I am slower than molasses and she not only rolls with it but goes ahead of me and makes the crooked places straight. I love our editorial friendship. Thank you for letting me write mysteries, making them story shaped, and understanding the scope of my librarian life.

I feel incredibly supported by the entire team at Thomas Nelson. Amanda Bostic, your leadership and love for your team is evident. Thank you for the way you support them and how that love spills over into my career. Jodi Hughes and Julie Breihan, the work you do would hurt my brain. I marvel at how you take the details to the next level and push me sentence for sentence to be better. Colleen Lacey, KP, Nekasha Pratt, I have never met a marketing team as authentic and supportive as you. You carry the work I do in my little mud room office into the world. Thank you. I have readers because of you. And KP, I probably have #goatsofinstagram followers because of you.

Kelly Sonnack, ten years! We've spent a decade of our lives shoulder to shoulder, fighting for a safer and more hopeful world. Thank you for sticking with me during the years I wanted to give up and for supporting me now as I toggle between librarian and author. I love you and I am so grateful we make things together.

For the last decade, Ruta Sepetys and David Arnold have been my constant sources of feedback, wisdom, and encouragement. I don't know how to write books without them and I don't want to try. Thank you both for loving and pushing me to be my best. In this season, I also have to tip my hat to Jess Folk. You're a heck of a writer and friend. The editorial thought you put into *Last Girl Breathing* is much appreciated.

Y'all, I have an emotional support dog named Gilbert. He's a handsome young man and a great hugger, thanks to

Canis Major. I kept the name real in *Last Girl Breathing* as a tip of my hat to the company that made my baby dog the best boy ever.

I also have an emotional support team. Mom, thank you for letting me come home to edit and sit in the comfy chair (and making sure I didn't starve). You do far more, but they won't let me write another book in the acknowledgments. Dad (my favorite resident of heaven), I love and miss you every day. Matt and Julie, I love you and I'm glad you finally have a dog ☺. Ms. Ann, you prayed this one into life. I love you so much. There are several groups I absolutely must thank; they function like family and keep me sane. My Gnomies and OTF family, Broadway UMC, my Goonies, and the managers and staff of Warren County Public Library: THANK YOU. I want to name you all. Since I can't, please know, my soul and body are healthier because of how you love and include me. Carla and Christa, if you ever want to build a compound let me know. I'll mow and clean the pool if you'll walk the dogs and grill. I love you best friends.

Ginger, EK, and Chris, if you read all my books, I'll get you a new goat. (Haha. I already did.) You sure do make me feel loved and I sure do love you to the ends of the earth. Thank you for talking in the backseat, telling me facts about hockey, trying to steal my dog, helping me feed all the animals, asking for ice cream, going to Patti's and agreeing to love me for a super long time, and so much more. I know I work too much, but I hope you see my love for you echoed in everything I do.

Finally, to my readers, you will always be my better half.

Discussion Questions

1. Have you ever experienced a natural disaster? If so, how has it impacted your life?
2. Loss is a constant emotional state in Lucy's world. Do you know someone who compartmentalizes their difficult experiences? Does that seem like a healthy approach to tragedy? Why or why not?
3. Lucy uses her athletic life as a way to focus on the present and future instead of lingering on the past. What are other strategies to move forward after difficult times?

4. Grand Junction is a rural town where hunting and outdoorsmanship are part of everyday life. Discuss whether that makes you comfortable or uncomfortable and why.

5. Lucy and Neil are Olympic hopefuls, who have spent years pursuing their dreams. Is there a dream that you're pursuing?

6. In a school assignment, Neil writes about one of his political views. His honesty comes back to bite him. Has there ever been a time you shared a political view and it was taken out of context or used against you?

7. Would you ever want an emotional support animal?

8. Lucy is recognized as a hero by her hometown. They found a public way to honor her willingness to risk her life to save others. Is there anyone in your hometown who you think is a hero? How would you publicly recognize that person?